NEVER AGAIN

A Levi Yoder Thriller

M.A. ROTHMAN

Primordial Press

Paperback ISBN-13: 9781696457927
Hardcover ISBN: 979-8-7774954-8-8

ALSO BY M.A. ROTHMAN

Technothrillers: (Thrillers with science / Hard-Science Fiction)

• Primordial Threat

• Freedom's Last Gasp

• Darwin's Cipher

Levi Yoder Thrillers:

• Perimeter

• The Inside Man

• Never Again

Epic Fantasy / Dystopian:

• Dispocalypse

• Agent of Prophecy

• Heirs of Prophecy

• Tools of Prophecy

• Lords of Prophecy

Special thanks go to:

Dr. John Spears, DO, Orthopedic Spine Surgeon, 18D, Sniper, U.S. Army Special Forces, Director at Forge Tactical – thank you for the help on tactics and weapons. It helped a lot.

Lieutenant John Grimpel, NYPD – thank you for your patient responses to my seemingly never-ending questions on all things police and NYPD procedures.

CONTENTS

"Crises must be prepared for not only politically and economically, but also psychologically. Here propaganda has its place. It [the media] must prepare the way actively and educationally. Its task is to prepare the way for practical actions. It must follow these actions step by step, never losing sight of them. In a manner of speaking, it provides the background music. Such propaganda in the end miraculously makes the unpopular popular, enabling even a government's most difficult decisions to secure the resolute support of the people. A government that uses it properly can do what is necessary without running the risk of losing the masses."

– Joseph Goebbels, Nuremberg, 1934

CHAPTER ONE

"If all you drink is seltzer, how am I supposed to seduce you into seeing reason?"

Levi took another sip of his seltzer and stared across the table at the attractive thirty-something Asian woman. They were sitting in Gerard's, his favorite hole-in-the-wall bar in New York's Little Italy. A few customers chatted amiably at the bar, and the smell of garlic and marinara wafted in from the kitchen.

"Just because you think you're right doesn't mean I'm going to agree," he replied. "I'm not this angel you think I am."

Lucy Chen was nursing a scotch and soda. She leaned forward and shook her head. "I never called you an angel," she said with her slight Russian accent. "I just know you. You're willing to do whatever it takes to get the job done, but you're picky about the kind of jobs you'll take on. Too picky." She motioned discreetly

1

toward two beefy men digging into heaping portions of pasta. "You're loyal to your family, I get that. I admire it. But I want you and I to work together on this. We can do so much good in this crappy world if we cooperate. I need a partner in this."

They'd been having this debate for over a month. Lucy wanted Levi to go into "business" with her, but he had other obligations. Besides, he wasn't sure what to make of her. The smoldering behind those dark brown eyes was… intense. In fact, everything about her was dialed up to eleven. The widow of a Chinese gang leader, she was the epitome of the dragon lady stereotype. And through a strange twist of fate, Levi had managed to get himself entangled with her.

He did trust her. To an extent, anyway. After all, she knew more about him than most. Few outside of his normal mob connections knew he was a member of the Bianchi crime family.

Denny, the owner of the bar, walked over and knelt so that he was eye level with the two of them. "Can I get you guys something to eat? The girls in the kitchen are using Gino's recipes." He hitched his thumb toward the two mob enforcers devouring their food. "It's pretty good stuff, even if I say so myself."

Levi smiled ruefully as he realized how much Gerard's had expanded over the last year. Once a small, some would say cozy, neighborhood bar that only served drinks, it was now a mob hangout complete with a dinner menu. He'd preferred it as a quiet place, because Denny wasn't just a bar owner; the skinny black man born and bred in Brooklyn was Levi's main intelligence contact.

He was a gadget man, a genius with electronics, and had his ear to the ground about nearly everything.

Lucy shook her head. "Levi and I are going out on a date, so it's best we don't ruin our appetite."

Levi worked hard to keep his frown from showing.

The front door's bell jingled as it opened, and with a smile, Denny turned away to greet his newest customer.

Lucy smiled as she stared back at Levi… and he felt as though she could read his mind. She leaned forward and whispered, "You know damn well that anyone who knows I'm staying at your apartment figures we're a couple. And if they know we're not, that can bring up some awkward questions I'd rather not answer."

Levi sat back in his chair and nodded. Of course she was right, which annoyed the hell out of him. She'd been living with him for the last six weeks, ever since the FBI cracked down on the local Chinese gang she'd been affiliated with, and coordinated with the Hong Kong Police Force to take down of one of the major Triads in Hong Kong—the same one that Lucy's deceased husband had headed. He couldn't be sure how much involvement she'd had in orchestrating that revenge, but one thing was certain: she was a marked woman, and he'd offered her whatever protection he could until things calmed down.

Denny walked back over with an odd expression. He leaned down and hitched his thumb toward the door. "Levi, that lady says she's looking for you. But I get the distinct feeling she doesn't really know who you are. Do you want me to send her away?"

Levi turned in his chair. Standing by the door was a woman in her fifties, dressed all in black, wringing her hands and looking very uncomfortable. He waved at her, caught her attention, and motioned her to the empty seat at his table.

Denny shrugged and went back to the bar.

The woman's look of discomfort was obvious as she skirted past tables and patrons, trying not to touch anything. She pulled out the proffered chair, sat, glanced at them both and said, "I was told to come here, and that Mr. Yoder would help me with my problem." She looked at Levi. "Are you him?"

Levi extended his hand. "I'm Levi Yoder. And you are…?"

The woman looked at his outstretched hand and shook her head slightly. "I'm Rivka Cohen."

Lucy extended her hand and said, *"At hassidi?"*

When the woman nodded and shook hands with Lucy, Levi understood. He didn't speak Hebrew or Yiddish, and he was mildly surprised that Lucy knew any, but he knew enough to realize this Cohen woman was very much out of her element. A Hassid was a follower of an ultra-orthodox Jewish movement. Not the type of people Levi often crossed paths with, but there were plenty of them in Crown Heights, only twenty minutes away. And it explained why she wouldn't shake his hand, but would shake Lucy's.

Because he was a guy.

Levi smiled, trying to make this woman, who was clearly a bundle of nerves, more comfortable. "I'm sorry, I would offer you a drink, but I know you won't take it, so how can I help?"

The woman's eyes grew shiny as if she were about to

start crying. "My Uncle Menachem, he's a jeweler at a place on Franklin Avenue. He said that you once bought something from him and left with him a promise. Do you remember that?"

Levi pulled in a deep breath as his mind raced back many years—to when he'd been looking for an engagement ring for his now-deceased wife. "Menachem Shemtov?" he said. "The same Menachem who worked at a jewelry store at Franklin and Park Place?"

The woman nodded.

"My God, that was ages ago. Your uncle did this *goy* a great favor on a purchase. I'm surprised he remembers me. I promised to return the favor someday. What can I do for you?"

Rivka wrung her hands together with a pained expression. "My husband died four months ago. The police say it was a suicide, but I know that he'd never take his own life." She screwed up her courage, even though tears began dripping down her cheeks. "They said he was having an affair, but I know that's impossible too. I have evidence that says so. Can you help me clear his name? It's very important to me, to our kids, to our family. I don't have much money, but I can help pay expenses, I think."

Levi tried to keep what he was thinking from showing on his face. This wasn't what he did. And what she'd described made sense. Religious guy has sex with some random, or maybe some not-so-random person, he feels guilty about it, and he kills himself. This situation had disappointment written all over it.

"What do you mean you have evidence?" Lucy asked.

Rivka looked back and forth between Lucy and Levi.

Lucy waved dismissively at Levi and explained, "Don't worry, we work together."

Levi was about to retort when Rivka turned to him and asked, "Do you mind if I just talk to her? This would be much easier for me."

He opened his mouth, then closed it.

Lucy motioned him toward another table. "Give us girls a little space."

Feeling slightly annoyed, Levi took his glass of seltzer and sat at another table. He sipped at his drink, focusing his better-than-most hearing on what was being said. Unfortunately, there was just enough background noise in the bar, particularly from a rowdy group at a nearby table laughing and having a good time, that he couldn't make out what was being said.

After a minute of whispered conversation between the two women, Lucy clasped hands with Rivka and gave her a sympathetic look. The Jewish woman pulled out an envelope and slid it toward Lucy.

Levi raised his eyebrows as Lucy peeked into the envelope, nodded at the woman, and tucked the envelope inside her jacket pocket.

What the hell is she getting us into?

Rivka then stood, kissed Lucy on both cheeks, and walked out of Gerard's without giving Levi a second look.

Drinking the last of her scotch and soda, Lucy strolled over to him and planted a kiss on his cheek. "It's all taken care of."

Levi stood. "What's taken care of? What did you agree to?"

Lucy dismissed the question with a flippant gesture, then waved at Denny and started toward the door.

Levi followed. "Lucy. Seriously. What did you just agree to?"

She opened the door for him and smiled. "I believe her story, and I told her we'd help."

"We?"

Lucy wrapped her arm around his as they walked out of the bar. "Don't worry about it. We'll talk over dinner."

Having set up a breading station on his kitchen counter, Levi dusted the sliced and peeled eggplant with flour and dipped it in egg, then into the seasoned bread crumbs. He glanced at Lucy as she sliced fresh Roma tomatoes for the salad. He'd promised to keep her safe, but the only safe places were his apartment building and Denny's. So instead of a nice dinner out, it was the Amish fixer and the Chinese dragon lady cooking and eating in a mafia-protected apartment—again.

"So, are you going to tell me what's up with this Cohen woman? Why did you take her money and agree to help her? The story has loser written all over it."

Lucy met his gaze as she laid out the tomatoes on a serving dish and began slicing fresh mozzarella. "Why do you think her case is such a loser?"

Levi shook his head as he carefully laid the breaded eggplant slices in the hot oil. "I don't care if he's a religious guy, when someone's eye wanders, they can succumb just like anyone else. I'm wagering he shacked up with some lady he worked with, probably not even Jewish, and he felt a huge amount of guilt and offed himself. It happens all the time. That's why I don't get why you don't see that. Guys can be like that. I should know."

"Tell me the truth," Lucy said. She'd put the cheese over the tomatoes and was now thinly slicing red onion. "I'll wager you never cheated on anyone in your life."

Levi's mind raced to the few times he'd ever been with a woman that wasn't his wife. He pursed his lips and gave Lucy a sour expression.

"See!" She laughed. "You haven't, have you?"

Levi fished the golden-brown eggplant slices out of the oil and began frying new ones. "No, I've never been accused of cheating on anyone. But if the cops think he was having an affair, there's probably a reason."

"You're right, but it can't be sex."

"Why's that?"

"Rivka and her husband have seven kids, and the only reason they don't have more is because her husband's diabetes caused him to not be able to get it up anymore. Rivka said they'd even tried Viagra, and it didn't work." Lucy scattered the onions onto the tomato and mozzarella. "She says she has the medical reports to prove it."

Levi frowned as he fished the last of the eggplant from the oil and turned off the stovetop burner. "And the cops didn't take that into consideration? What about the person he supposedly had an affair with? Did they get her testimony?"

Lucy shrugged as she sprinkled shredded basil over the food she'd just prepared and grabbed a bottle of aged balsamic vinegar. "Like I said, there's lots of unanswered questions. Rivka has invited us over for dinner tomorrow. She said she'd give us copies of everything she has, let us look over his home office, and field any of our questions."

With a harrumph, Levi picked up the platter of fried eggplant, a pot of freshly made marinara, and headed for the dining room. "Just because it sounds suspicious doesn't mean we can help with any of it. Don't I get a say in any of this?"

Lucy set her plate on the table and began dishing out servings of the caprese salad. "Of course you do. But you just pointed out there's lots of unanswered questions, this is possibly having to do with a murder cover-up, and it sounded like you owed her family a favor. You're not the type to go back on your word, so do I really need to ask you if you're in?"

Levi put two pieces of perfectly fried eggplant on her plate and spooned some marinara on it. As he served himself as well, he glared at her. She was one of the most frustrating people he'd ever met. "It would be nice," he said.

She poured herself a glass of Mondavi white zinfandel and poured him a glass of Perrier. "So? Are you in? Or am I going by myself?"

They clinked glasses. "When are *we* supposed to head over there?" he asked.

Lucy smiled, and for a second he forgot that she was a former mobster who was trying to turn over a new leaf. Instead he saw an attractive woman who was intelligent, assertive, and very idiosyncratic. He was never able to guess what was going to come out of her mouth next, and it was exhausting.

"Before sundown. I guess we should get there at about five-thirty."

Levi took a bite of the salad. It needed a sprinkle of salt.

Lucy nibbled at her own salad and frowned. "I forgot the salt." She pushed back from the table, got the salt shaker from the kitchen, and sprinkled salt on her salad as well as his. "Try it now, it'll be better. Oh, and you'll need to wear your suit."

He shook his head and tried to keep the smile from reaching his face. "Yes, ma'am." He glanced at her tight-fitting white floral dress. It hugged her slender curves and didn't exactly seem appropriate for a dinner event full of religious people. "And what are you going to wear?"

"We'll go shopping in the morning. I know just the outfit. I've been eyeing it at Bergdorf's."

Paulie opened the rear passenger door to the Lincoln Town Car, and Levi and Lucy stepped out.

Levi shook hands with the huge mobster, who was just a couple inches shy of seven feet tall and built like a bodybuilder. Beside him stood Tom, the mobster who'd ridden shotgun.

"It'll probably be a few hours," Levi said. "You guys can go get dinner or something. I'll call you when we're done."

Paulie smiled and shook his head. "Not happening." He pointed at an empty spot on the side of Lincoln Place. "We'll park there and keep watch on things. The don's orders."

"Okay, I understand. I'll call when we're about to finish." Levi knew better than to argue. Vinnie, the head of the Bianchi family, was aware of the Lucy situation and was taking every precaution possible. The last thing Vinnie wanted was some unnamed character from a foreign gang rubbing out someone he'd agreed to put under protection.

Levi looked over at Lucy and for the first time took in the details of her outfit. She'd said it was a Kay Unger mikado gown, which meant nothing to him, but the long form-fitting dress had an Asian look to his eyes. It was a dark, shimmering affair with colored sequin embroidery that reminded him of her dragon tattoo. It had a long slit up the side, revealing hints of her athletic build.

"You're going to make some of the rabbis faint with that outfit of yours," he said.

"If they are truly godly men, they won't be looking. And besides, I've been eyeing this thing forever, and it finally went on sale. I'm glad you like it." Lucy wrapped her arm around his and winked. "Let's go. I'd like to help Rivka with the setup for dinner if she'll let me."

With Paulie and Tom watching, they walked up the steps to the townhome.

Levi pressed the doorbell, and soon he heard the

sound of footsteps. The door opened and an older man with a full white beard greeted them with a curious expression. "*Oy vey*, Mr. Yoder, you haven't aged a day in what must be twenty years. God has truly blessed you. Do you remember—"

Levi smiled as he spotted the younger man in the old man in front of him. "Menachem, please call me Levi. Of course I remember you."

They hugged and then kissed on both cheeks. Levi motioned to Lucy. "This is my business partner, Lucy."

Menachem smiled at Lucy and bowed his head while stepping aside for them to enter. "It's a pleasure to meet you."

"Lucy! Mr. Yoder!" Rivka's voice echoed in the hallway as she rushed toward the door, a smile on her face. "*Gut Shabbes* to you both. It's so good that you came, and just in time."

Within moments, Rivka had taken Lucy with her to the kitchen, and Menachem had led Levi to the living room where nearly a dozen men had gathered ahead of dinner.

Menachem cleared his throat and addressed the men. "This is Levi Yoder. He's the guest I spoke about earlier."

The men introduced themselves, and Levi took a seat on one of the wooden chairs.

The men were dressed in traditional black Jewish garb, fringes of their prayer shawls peeking out from under their formal jackets. All wore a head covering, which Levi knew was called a *kippah*.

Levi patted the top of his head and asked, "Should I be wearing a *kippah*?"

Most of the men's eyes widened, but the oldest of the group chuckled and said, "If you wouldn't mind wearing a *yarmulke*, I think that would be very nice." He fished from his pocket a hand-sized circular head covering with Hebrew letters sewn into it and handed it to Levi.

"I might be a *goy*, but I've lived in New York long enough to know there are some traditions I should respect." Levi put the prayer cap on, and the mood lightened as the men began talking about their day.

Suddenly, what seemed to be an endless stream of kids raced through the room with an older child chasing after them and yelling, "Get cleaned up for Shabbat, we only have fifteen minutes!"

Menachem pulled his chair up alongside Levi's, patted him on the back, and whispered, "We'll talk more after dinner."

The main dining room wasn't big enough for everyone to be seated, so the tables spanned past the dining room, into the kitchen, and into the next room as well. Zalman, the eldest of the Cohen family, and the one who'd handed him his kippah, sat at its head, and Levi had been seated beside him. Lucy was at the far end of the table—still in the dining room—smiling as she interacted with the other women, many of whom were helping with the nearly two dozen kids gathered.

Zalman stood, and all three rooms quickly quieted.

"We have guests today who might otherwise be confused by the significance of this day, so it is a *mitzvah*, a blessing, for us all to help them at least understand why we do what we do.

"Tonight is the beginning of Shabbat, the seventh day of the week. The prayers that follow will recount how the Almighty rested on the seventh day and sanctified it. We will then have a blessing over the wine and a blessing thanking the Almighty for giving us this day of rest."

Zalman lifted a cup of nearly overflowing wine and focused on the sabbath candles flickering on the table. They'd been lit by Rivka earlier. In a deep voice he began some prayers.

"Yom Ha-shi-shi. Va-y'chu-lu Ha-sha-ma-yim v'ha-a-retz, v'chawl^ts'va-am.

"Va-y'chal e-lo-him ba-yom ha-sh'vi-i, m'lach-to a-sher a-sa

"Va-yish-bot ba-yom ha-sh'vi-i, mi-kawl^m'lach-to a-sher a-sa.

"Va-y'va-rech e-lo-him et yom ha-sh'vi-i, va-y'ka-deish o-to ki vo sha-vat mi-kawl^m'lach-to a-sher ba-ra e-lo-him la-a-sot."

The man next to Levi showed him a prayer book written in English, and pointed to the translation of what Zalman was saying.

The sixth day. And the heavens and the earth and all their hosts were completed. And God finished by the Seventh Day His work which He had done, and He rested on the Seventh Day from all His work which He had done. And God blessed the Seventh Day and made it holy, for on it He rested from all His work which God created to function.

As Zalman's prayer rang through the home, Levi

14

looked at everyone around the table. They were all mouthing the same words, their heads slightly bowed.

They then prayed over the wine, and finally over the bread. And then it was time to eat.

He glanced at Lucy, and their eyes met. She smiled and gave him a wink.

There was a wholesome feel to this gathering. It reminded him of his Amish upbringing in some ways. Even though he'd left his Amish community when he was eighteen and had never really looked back, he'd also never outright rejected formal religion as a groundwork for beliefs. These people believed in what they practiced, as did his family, and that was something he could relate to, even if he didn't share in the day-to-day practices of either of them.

Menachem handed him a piece of the braided egg bread that was traditional for the Sabbath. "I wonder," he said, "do you like gefilte fish?"

Levi shrugged. "I don't know what a gefilte is, but I like fish. I'll try anything that you put in front of me."

Zalman leaned over with an amused expression. "It's okay if you don't like it. I'm not a fan either."

And that started a heated debate over gefilte fish that led to other amusing discussions that occupied the better part of two hours.

After dinner, Rivka led Levi, Lucy, and Menachem up the narrow stairs to a closed door. She pulled a key from a hidden pocket in her dress and unlocked the door. "This is

Mendel's office. It hasn't been touched since the break-in. Please, have a seat."

Lights automatically turned on as they entered the room. Levi had learned during his visit that this was a feature in some Orthodox Jewish households.

Levi followed Menachem and Lucy into a cramped study filled with a large desk. It was a working office, that was obvious. Two of the walls had built-in shelves crammed with books. Nothing fancy, just lots of books on random topics, including an Encyclopedia Britannica from 1969 that occupied one entire shelf. Many of the books had Hebrew letters on their binders.

Levi turned to Rivka. "Can you start from the beginning? What exactly did your husband do?"

She closed the door to the office. "He was a consumer reporter. It was his passion." She smiled, looking much calmer than she had at the bar. "It was how we met many years ago."

"What kind of things did he report on? And where? Was it for TV stations, the newspaper…?"

"Mostly newspaper, but sometimes he'd be interviewed on television. When he started, he had a column in the local papers." She blushed and pursed her lips. "You'll probably think it's silly, but back then he would investigate kosher restaurants and report any violations or questionable behaviors so that others would be warned. That eventually led to him reporting on international food imports and exports, and that's when the *Intelligencer* picked him up."

The *Intelligencer* was a huge newspaper with millions

of daily readers. "Is that where he worked most recently?" Levi asked.

"Yes. And he became agitated about things at work, and I suppose that's what you want to know about. He told me about some of it. Over the last couple years, he'd noticed how some of his work was being edited to remove names, or it was not being run at all, even though the local editor had given his approval."

"Isn't that pretty normal?" Lucy asked. "From what I understand, there's usually more stories than there's space to print, isn't there?"

Rivka nodded. "True, but Mendel's been doing this for over twenty years… I mean… he *had* been doing it for that long." She sighed. "And even though it was his job to warn people about problems, he always gave the targets of his stories the benefit of the doubt. It would ruin him professionally if he wrote anything that was inaccurate or misleading.

"But he confided something to me that he wasn't yet prepared to put into print. In fact, he wasn't sure if he ever would be. He was almost convinced that the company he was working for was purposefully trying to deceive its readers. To shape the narrative, if you will."

Levi frowned. "I don't understand. Isn't that a newspaper's job? I see outlandish stuff in the papers all the time."

"That's the editorial sections. My husband worked in what people in the trade like to call *hard news*. It should involve no opinions, just the facts. But Mendel was convinced that the management at the paper wasn't interested in telling their millions of readers the truth."

"Okay," Levi said. "I understand why that would upset your husband. But do you really think that would be cause for him to be murdered?"

Menachem cleared his throat. "My brother-in-law was a very righteous man. He felt it was his calling to bring the truth to the people. You need to realize that to him, what the paper was doing was a sin. I also heard plenty from him in the last year about this issue. He made it clear that even though the newspaper never lied, by ensuring certain things were never said in print, they molded the public narrative. It was a sin of omission."

Lucy nodded in understanding. "I suppose it would be like talking about how a police officer shot a teenager on the streets, and leaving out the fact that the teenager was aiming a gun at him."

"Exactly," Rivka said. "Anyway, in the days just before Mendel died, he was particularly upset. He wouldn't talk about it, even to me. And then... and then he was dead."

"And you think he was murdered because...?"

Rivka picked up a manila folder from the desk and handed it to Levi. "That includes the medical examiner's report. They said he was poisoned, though they initially labeled the manner of death as undetermined." She took in a deep, shuddering breath. "But later, the manner was changed to suicide based on the testimony of someone who had to be lying."

Levi recalled what Lucy had told him about the claim of an affair. He wasn't going to push that for the moment. He flipped through the folder. In addition to the ME report, it also contained a police report, with some names redacted.

"You mentioned a break-in," he said. "Tell me about that."

Rivka hid her face and began sobbing. Menachem patted her shoulder, and Lucy moved closer to her and handed her a tissue from a nearby dispenser.

Her uncle responded for her. "It happened during Mendel's funeral. Someone broke in and tossed this office, and touched nothing else in the house. Whoever did it had to know we were all gone for the funeral."

Levi thought of the ornate silver menorah and all the other valuable items he'd seen downstairs. "What was in the office worth taking while ignoring the rest of the house?"

"We don't know." Rivka wiped her face, looking both distraught and embarrassed. "They took all the books off the shelves and emptied his drawers, but the only thing I know of that was missing was his work notebook."

"They stole his laptop?"

"No, a spiral notebook. Mendel preferred writing things longhand. I know it was on his desk, where he always had it. But it was gone."

Levi surveyed the office. There was something definitely not right about this. What could possibly be so important in a reporter's notes that someone would break in to steal them?

Levi stepped over to the mahogany desk and pulled open one of the drawers. It was full of empty file folders. The notebook had been lying in plain sight on top of the desk, yet the intruder had gone to the trouble of ransacking the drawers and shelves as well.

"Do you know what he kept in these drawers?" he asked.

"Not specifically," Rivka said. "When we cleaned up, we just put things back where it felt like they belonged."

He exchanged a glance with Lucy. They were both almost certainly thinking the same thing. Not just a note-book was missing.

On top of the desk was a book with Hebrew writing. Levi thumbed through its pages of unintelligible script and stopped when he discovered a yellow sticky note. There were seven names written on the paper, with an arrow pointing to some of the Hebrew print in the book.

He turned the book toward Menachem and Rivka. "What does it say in the section the arrow is pointing to?"

Menachem leaned forward and squinted through his thick glasses. "Ah, this chapter of the Bible would be what you call Proverbs. This section says, 'A false witness shall not be unpunished, and he that speaks lies shall not escape.'"

Rivka smiled. "That would be just like Mendel. He'd find a passage with layers of meaning to him."

Levi drummed his fingers on the desk. He wasn't sure what to make of all this. But the least he could do was track down whoever had given the testimonial and learn about the truth of the affair.

He removed the sticky note from the book and noticed that it had more writing on the back, in Hebrew. He showed it to Rivka. "What does this say?"

She leaned forward, and her face grew pale. "It says, 'It's the Nazis.'"

CHAPTER TWO

Levi leaned forward in the rear of the Town Car as Paulie pulled away from the Cohens' residence. He tapped the back of the front seat and said, "Sorry it took that long. Anything unusual happen out here while you guys were waiting?"

Tom, who was one of the Bianchi family's second-story guys, said, "It was pretty dead, except the coppers sure patrol that street a lot."

Levi turned to the thin, jockey-sized man. "By a lot, you mean...?"

"I counted fourteen times in the three hours you guys were in there. And the cop riding shotgun gave Paulie and me the stink eye each and every time they passed by. But the driver, he was a mean-looking son of a bitch, he had his eyes on that Cohen place. It was like he was casing the joint."

"You guys didn't by chance—"

"What kind of *mamelukes* you think we are?" Paulie took a slip of paper out from inside his suit coat, handed it back to Levi, and then turned right on Rogers Avenue. "It didn't seem right, so I jotted down the plate number."

"Always thinking, that's great." Levi glanced at the identification scrawled on the paper and patted Paulie on the shoulder. "Hey, I know it's late, but instead of home, let's head over to Little Italy. I got something to do over at Gerard's."

"Oh, that'll be good," Tom said. "I'm starving."

"While you two eat, Lucy and I are going to have a sit-down with Denny about some stuff."

"You got it." Paulie merged onto Bedford Avenue.

Levi leaned back against the padded rear seat, and Lucy scooted closer, lifted his left arm, and snuggled up against him while wrapping it around her slender waist. She played the role of mob girlfriend convincingly, always touching him or cuddling up to him in public, and especially when there were Bianchi associates around. But there wasn't anything going on between them when they were alone. Well, she'd purposefully kissed him full on the lips a few times, but that was more her way of getting his attention than anything sexual. The woman had her own agenda and her own rules, and that both intrigued and frustrated Levi.

"What did you think about Rivka's story?" Lucy whispered, her head leaning against the crook of his neck.

Levi breathed in the scent of her jasmine body wash and gave her a light squeeze. He turned his attention to the front of the car and addressed the two mobsters. "Hey, imagine there's a reporter who offed himself, and when

23

the family's off at the funeral, someone breaks in and tosses his office, but doesn't take anything but some of the files. Why might someone do something like that?"

Tom twisted in his seat. "They just took the guy's files? No jewels, watches, or anything else?"

"Just the guy's work notes."

Paulie turned right on Flatbush Avenue and said, "If he's a reporter, maybe he's doing a story on someone who doesn't want the story to ever come out."

Tom nodded. "Makes sense to me. Either that, or it's his boss. Whoever he works for wants to finish the story he started."

"No way," Paulie said. "Some newspaper or TV station isn't going to commit a felony just to get some of his old work. They'd probably just ask his old lady if they can collect his work papers. Why would she deny them?"

Levi glanced down at Lucy. "Paulie's got a point. We should ask Rivka what the paper said to her."

Pursing her lips, she gave him a slight nod. "I've got her phone number. She won't answer her phone during the sabbath, but I'll call her tomorrow night or on Sunday."

Levi was about to say something more when Lucy clasped his right hand and gave it a soft kiss. For someone who didn't like people touching her, she'd sure been doing a lot of it. It was pleasant, and he had to remind himself that she was merely playing for an audience. Though for her to do it now, for an audience that wasn't even looking, made him wonder what was going on in that head of hers.

"Levi, we've got a tail," Paulie announced.

Glancing over his shoulder, Levi spotted more than a dozen cars in the heavy traffic behind them, but his gaze immediately zeroed in the NYPD cruiser three cars back and one lane over. It had the same license plate number as the one Paulie had jotted down. "Let me call some of the boys in."

Levi dialed a number and put the phone to his ear.

"Hey, Levi. What's up?"

Levi put the phone on speaker. "Lou, we've got a cop car on our tail. We're doing a slow roll on Flatbush Avenue heading north. We just passed Johnson Street and we're heading toward Midtown. Can you help us out with a blocker?"

"Sure thing. Let me see who we've got in that area. Paulie's got you in the bronze Town Car, right?"

"Yup, that's the one I took," Paulie said.

Lou talked to someone on another line in the background for a few seconds before he spoke again. *"You're in luck. Right behind you is Three-Chin Romano. He's in the black Cadillac, says he's two cars behind you and just ahead of the cop car. He says, 'I got this, don't worry.'"*

Twisting to his right, Levi saw the Cadillac turn on its hazard lights and veer sharply right, directly in front of the NYPD's finest, effectively blocking his forward progress.

Paulie gunned the engine, and the Town Car launched itself through the next intersection and took an immediate right on Bridge Street. With a few more turns they were out sight of the cop car and heading toward Midtown.

"Lou, that worked like a charm. Thanks a bunch."

"You got it. Let me know if you need anything else."

Levi tucked the phone back inside his suit jacket.

Lucy sat up and looked out the rear window. "Is Gino going to get arrested for that?"

"Nah," Tom declared with confidence. "We all have a little switch in the car that will kill the engine. What's the cop going to do? Poor Gino's car was having trouble and he was trying to get over when the engine just stopped." The man gave her a devilish grin. "It's just bad luck how that sometimes happens."

Lucy tilted her head toward the two mobsters in the front as she whispered to Levi, "Was that cop car following them or us?"

"I'm not sure. Let's see if we can get some answers when we talk to Denny."

"Denny? How would he know—"

Levi put a finger to her lips. "You'll see."

It was almost ten p.m. when they arrived at Gerard's. The place was packed with folks from the neighborhood and at least a handful of Bianchi family associates.

Levi caught Denny's attention and motioned toward the back. The bar owner nodded and whispered something to Rosie, a pretty but grumpy Puerto Rican woman who was tending the bar. Rosie flashed Levi a glare, like she always did when he took Denny away from what she felt was his primary work. He returned her glare with what he hoped was a winning smile. She began wiping even harder at the bar with a dishrag, almost certainly cursing at him under her breath.

As Paulie and Tom took a seat at one of the only empty tables, Levi escorted Lucy toward the back. They walked past the bathrooms and turned left into a poorly lit hall that led to a small office. The right-hand side of the hallway was tiled with a gaudy mural of a beach scene.

Denny joined them in the hall and pressed his finger against a spot on the tiled wall. Something clicked, and with a whoosh of air the outline of a door became evident in the tile. Denny pushed it, and it swung silently open into his secret back room—the real purpose behind Gerard's.

Levi handed Denny the copy of the redacted police report he'd gotten from the Cohen widow. "Do you think you can pull up a version of this without the blacked-out names?"

Denny sat at his desk and glanced over the photocopied report. "I don't think that'll be a problem." He set aside the report and logged into his computer. His fingers became a blur as the computer genius did what Levi had seen him do countless times.

"Okay, this isn't what I expected," Lucy said as she panned her gaze across the warehouse-like collection of shelves chock-full of electronic surveillance equipment, oscilloscopes, bits of dissected state-of-the-art security systems, and just about every other gadget imaginable.

Levi smiled at her dumbfounded expression. His eyes followed the curves of her body as she sat on a hard-backed chair. Seeing her in that form-fitting dress, he couldn't help but admire what he saw. "What exactly *did* you expect?"

She reached over and briefly touched Denny's shoulder. "No offense intended, but when Levi said you're a gadget guy, I kind of pictured you with a soldering iron making, oh I don't know, maybe listening devices or other little trinkets." She pointed at the expanse of equipment and devices. "I didn't expect all of this."

Without looking up from the computer, Denny pointed to his left and said, "Over there by the wall you'll find a solder station. I make tiny gadgets as well. Ah, I'm in."

Levi pulled up a chair as an unredacted copy of the police report appeared on Denny's screen.

"Did you want me to make a printout of this?" Denny asked.

"Nah." Levi shook his head. "Just scroll through it so I can read all the names that the cops didn't want to share."

As Denny slowly scrolled down the report, he looked over at Lucy. "This guy has the memory of an elephant. Did *you* want a copy?"

She smiled. "No, but thanks for asking."

When Denny reached the end of the report, Levi nodded. "Mindy Cross is the woman the cops talked with about the affair. Do we have any info on her? An address, who she works for, what she looks like?"

"One second." Within moments, Denny had brought up everything the NYPD had collected on her. "She's a reporter at the *Intelligencer*. Thirty-three years old, a journalism degree from Cornell. And she has an Instagram account." With a few more keystrokes, a series of pictures popped up of a blonde with a narrow waist, big bust, and a pretty face.

Levi whistled with appreciation. "This Cohen guy knew how to pick them."

"She's a hottie," Lucy remarked. "She's dressed professionally, but it would be hard to hide those curves even if she wore a burlap sack."

Denny tapped on the bottom of the screen. "Her profile says she's single and works as a domestic affairs reporter."

"Domestic affairs?" Levi shook his head and grinned sardonically. "I'd say that about sums it up."

Lucy flashed him a disapproving look. "Remember, this guy couldn't do much with her even if he wanted to."

"Speaking of which." Levi pointed at the monitor. "Can you pull up whatever you can about a guy named Mendel Cohen?"

Within moments, Denny had the man's life laid bare. "Okay, the guy's credit rating was over eight hundred, so he was paying his bills on time. Based on his bank balances, it looks like they weren't exactly rich, but they're doing okay. And no debts to speak of. It looks like he owned a property on Lincoln Place, and from what I can see, the loan on it was paid off almost seven years ago."

Levi nodded. "Yup, that's the place his widow and kids are living at."

Lucy leaned forward, her eyes darting back and forth across the monitor. "Does he have any outstanding warrants or trouble with the law?"

With a few keystrokes, the screen changed. "Well, what do we have here?"

Denny clicked on the citation, and Lucy frowned at a scanned copy of a signed ticket. "What does it mean that he created a safety hazard by unsafely crossing a roadway?"

"That, my dear, is called jaywalking," Levi said. "I didn't think they actually gave tickets for that."

Denny looked at Levi. "Try being a black dude crossing the street where you're not supposed to at three a.m. Trust me, they'll hit you up with a write-up pretty darn quick."

Levi tilted his chair back and frowned. "Okay, so we have a guy who is living clean and has no real history with the law. There's no reason why the cops would want to screw him over."

"But they did," Lucy insisted. "We don't have a reason to disbelieve the medical records—"

"And we don't have a reason to disbelieve the alleged mistress's testimony, either."

Denny ignored the exchange. "You need anything else?"

Levi snapped his fingers. "Actually, yeah. We had an NYPD car casing the place we were at. Can you find out who checked that vehicle out?"

"Did you get the plate?"

Levi rattled off the four-digit number, and Denny pulled it up in seconds. "I've got two plates running with that number. Did you catch the small number on the plate? That'll be the car's model year."

Paulie hadn't written down the smaller number on the

plate, but Levi closed his eyes and recalled the scene on Flatbush Avenue. The cops following them had been a few car lengths behind, but that was close enough. "Nineteen."

Denny nodded. "That car was assigned to the seventeenth precinct. I'll have to make a couple calls to tell who it was rolling with."

"Where is the seventeenth precinct?" Lucy asked.

Levi drummed his fingers on his leg. "They cover the east side of Midtown, Murray Hill, Kips Bay, and most of where the UN is located. Nowhere near Crown Heights, if that's what you're asking."

"Is that normal?" Lucy asked. "I mean, do cops normally patrol out of their area?"

"I don't think so." Levi turned back to Denny. "I need those names as soon as you can get them. Oh—and one more thing." He rattled off the list of names he'd found on the note in Mendel's office, and Denny scribbled them down. "We got those names from Mendel's notes. Can you run those through your computer and see what you can tell me? Like how these people are connected to each other, if at all?"

"Roger that," Denny said.

Levi stood and pulled out his phone. "I'll be right back." As he dialed, he walked to the far side of the warehouse-like space. Behind him he heard Lucy asking Denny to pull up something else.

A voice answered on the first ring. *"Yeah?"*

"Frankie, do we have any friends at the *Intelligencer*?"

"The newspaper?"

"Yes."

"Ya, we've got someone. A guy named Dominic Maroni. He's an editor over there. Why? You trying to put in an ad or something?"

Levi smiled. "No, nothing like that. We'll talk about it later. Can you arrange a sit-down for me and him?"

"How quick do you need it? Tonight?"

"How about a lunch thing tomorrow?"

"I'll make sure he's there."

"Thanks, Frankie."

"Hey, since I got you on the phone. Vinnie and I want to talk with you about this arrangement you've got with your girlfriend. There's a change in her status, and we need to talk."

A chill raced up Levi's back. "Sounds serious. Should we talk tonight?"

"I'll go ring up Vinnie to make sure, but ya. I think sooner is better."

As Levi hung up, he turned his gaze to Lucy and felt a tightness building in his gut. Vinnie, the head of the Bianchi crime family, thought it was important to talk about the woman hiding out in Levi's apartment. That could not be a good thing.

He walked back across the room and put a hand on Denny's shoulder. "We have to get going. Give me a call as soon as you learn more."

"Will do." Denny stood and bumped fists with Levi.

Lucy wrapped her arm around Levi's. "It was good seeing this side of you, Denny. I'm impressed. You're a man of many unexpected talents."

Denny smiled and led them back to the front of Gerard's.

As soon as they emerged from the back, Paulie waved to Levi and motioned to the front door questioningly. When Levi nodded, Paulie quickly wiped his mouth, pushed back from the table, and he and Tom wordlessly led Levi and Lucy out of Gerard's.

Lucy looked up at Levi and gave his arm a little squeeze. "Is everything okay?"

Levi didn't like how he was feeling. The tone of Frankie's voice had set him on edge. He quickened his pace as they walked toward the car. "Everything's fine. When we get to the apartment, you go on up. I'll be going to the top floor for a bit."

She already knew that the top floor was where Vinnie lived, and knew enough not to ask questions.

Tom opened the rear passenger door, and Levi slid in right after Lucy.

As Paulie pulled away from the curb, Lucy patted Levi's thigh and gave him a look. It was a look that anyone could have read.

She knew something was wrong.

CHAPTER THREE

"They've upped the price on her contract," Frankie explained as Levi and the don sat in front of the fireplace in Vinnie's parlor. Frankie sipped at his scotch and soda and continued. "It's up to six figures, and for that price, lots of people are going to come out of the woodwork."

"Levi." Vinnie's gravelly voice was quiet, almost a whisper. "Someone must have made her out on the streets. They wouldn't have upped the price unless they thought the fish was in the pond." He swirled the amber liquid in his crystal tumbler and took a sip of the amaretto. He leaned forward, a curious expression on his face. "You knew that keeping her here was a risk, but the stakes are higher now. What's the story with you two? I mean, really, she's all lovey-dovey to you in front of the guys, but I don't see it. It doesn't sit right with me."

Levi smiled at his long-time friend and shrugged.

"She helped me out with some stuff, and I yanked her out of a nasty situation…"

"Stop bullshitting me, Levi. Do you have a thing for this chick or what? I need to know how serious you are about sticking your neck out for her. No offense, but if she's just some piece of ass you're banging, I'd tell you to cut her out of your life." Vinnie dragged a finger across his neck.

Sipping at his seltzer, Levi thought hard about how he was going to answer. Even though Vinnie was his friend, probably his best friend, Vinnie had a business to run, and Levi knew Lucy posed a possible security risk.

"Our relationship is complicated," he began, then hesitated. He knew so much about her, yet what she thought and what motivated her were still mostly a mystery to him. "Sometimes I think I know what's she's about, and we're totally on the same page, and then other times… I just can't read her."

"He's sweet on her," Frankie said with a grin. "Can't exactly blame him. She's a looker, for an Asian girl."

Vinnie merely looked at Levi and waited.

Feeling the pressure of the mob boss's stare, Levi shrugged again. "Vinnie, I don't know. Am I getting hitched tomorrow? No. Do I like her? Yes."

Vinnie sat back in his chair and looked at Frankie. "Go look into the contract. Let's see what we can learn about who's funding it." Then he turned to Levi and said with a serious tone, "If my senses are right, and they usually are, someone's spotted her on the streets and probably followed her here. If they're looking to whack her, I don't want my guys involved. This is her business and her trouble. If you want her to stay under our protection, for the time being, she needs to stay put. No more going out of the apartment building. You got me?"

"I got you. She's grounded."

Vinnie glanced at his watch, then stood and finished off his amaretto. "It's after midnight—you guys see yourselves out. I promised Phyllis and the kids I'd take them to the beach in the morning."

Frankie and Levi both stood as the don left the parlor. Frankie threw an arm over Levi's shoulders and they headed for the double doors together.

"Momo, open the damned door," Frankie bellowed.

The doors swung open, and two beefy mobsters nodded at them as they passed.

At the elevators, Levi pressed the down arrow and waited.

"I sent you an email a little while ago," Frankie said. "You're all set with the *Intelligencer* guy for tomorrow at noon. What's with your interest in that newspaper?"

"I'm just following up something that caught my eye. If it's a good business opportunity, I'll let you know."

Frankie smiled. "You have a knack for finding interesting things that turn into profit for us. And if it turns a profit, you've got my blessing, whatever it is."

With a ding, the elevator doors slid open. Levi and Frankie stepped in and pressed the buttons for their respective floors, and the doors slid closed again.

As the elevator went down, Levi recalled what Vinnie had said about Lucy being grounded. Levi wasn't eager to find out how she'd take the news. Telling her to do anything she didn't want to was like bathing a cat: all claws and bad temper.

Levi had showered, dressed for his meeting with the editor, and was brushing his hair in the mirror when Lucy walked into his bedroom. With a smile, she swiped her hands along his shoulders, brushing away imaginary pieces of lint.

"Are you ready for your date?" she said coyly.

He turned to face her, and the pleased expression on her face reminded him of the Cheshire Cat. It was also eerie, since Lucy wasn't much into smiling—or showing many emotions at all, for that matter.

"First of all," he said, "it's not a date. I'm meeting with some guy who probably owes the family a favor, and if I'm lucky, maybe I'll get to ask this Mindy chick about how she knows Mendel Cohen."

Lucy tilted Levi's head up as she adjusted his tie. "We don't know how she'll take questions about someone who just died. She might have been in love, or maybe she was working a scam. Or who knows, maybe this Cohen guy was her knight in shining armor. I guess my point is, don't be blunt like you always are. Finesse her a bit. I'm sure you've done that kind of stuff before. You're a pretty boy—use your charms."

Levi frowned as her smile grew more pronounced. "You're up to something. Just remember, until we figure out what's going on with that contract, you can't leave. If you need anything, just call downstairs and they'll get it for you. Okay?"

She kissed her finger and pressed it to his lips. "Don't worry. I'll be waiting right here to hear all about your *date*." Lucy motioned toward the door. "You'd better get going. With midday traffic it'll take a while to get anywhere in the city. You don't want to be late."

Levi walked to the door, turned to her, and once again felt uneasy at the sight of that eerie smile. What was she really up to?

He was about to say something when she pushed past him, opened the door, and said, "Go." Her Russian accent becoming more pronounced. "I swear I'll be okay just watching TV and waiting to hear how it went."

Levi forced himself to walk out the door and catch the car that was waiting for him downstairs.

In all the years he'd lived in New York City, Levi had never been to the Trump Tower. As he waited for the editor from the *Intelligencer* to arrive, he panned his gaze past the entrance to the Trump Grill and focused on the infamous escalator that Donald Trump had descended before announcing his unlikely candidacy for president. Politics didn't serve a purpose in Levi's life, but he wasn't oblivious to it.

An Asian tourist walked into the tower, made a beeline for the escalator, and began taking photos. Yes, that escalator was famous all right. And Trump was a man who held many fans and enemies alike.

Levi checked his watch again. He didn't like having to wait.

Suddenly, a large black-haired man came rushing in through the street entrance. The worried look on his flushed face said it all.

This was the guy.

The editor raced past Levi to the hostess's stand. "I'm Dominic Maroni. I have a reservation for two, the corner seat. Oh, and do you know if someone—"

"Oh, yes sir." The young lady at the stand motioned to Levi. "Mr. Yoder is here. He didn't want to be seated without you."

Dominic turned, and the beefy Italian's face grew pale as he realized Levi was standing only five feet away. He clasped his hands together. "*Marone a mi.* I'm so sorry for being late. The damned cabbies in this town…"

Levi smiled and shook hands with the distraught editor. "You're only five minutes late. There are worse things."

With a look of relief, Dominic nodded. "If it's okay with you, we'll sit and talk." He glanced at the woman, "The table's ready?"

"Yes, sir. Follow me."

They were seated in a corner of the cozy restaurant, and within minutes their orders had been taken. Levi appreciated the warmth of the wooden accents and the overall tidy look of the place. It felt comfortable, not nearly as ostentatious as he'd expected for a place associated with the name Trump. And though the dining room was nearly full, all the tables immediately adjacent to theirs were empty—giving them some privacy.

"So," Dominic said. "Mr. Minnelli told me you have questions about the *Intelligencer*. He was a bit vague about what you needed to know, but I've been working there for twenty years, so if I don't have the answers you need, I probably know who does."

Levi drummed his fingers on the white linen-covered table as he thought about how best to approach the subject. He allowed the uncomfortable silence to hang between them—he knew Dominic wouldn't break it. Though Levi had barely met the man, he already recognized his type. Dominic Maroni was a mafia asset, and as such, the man knew that the head of security for one of the most prominent mafia families in the city would not have called him unless it was important to the don. And if it was important to Don Bianchi, then this guy would practically kill himself if that's what it took to earn favor with the family.

"Dominic, let me cut to the chase. There's a reporter that used to work for your newspaper who is now dead. I want to talk to people he knew and get a feel for what he was into."

Dominic's eyebrows furrowed. "May I ask who it was?" He pulled out his cell phone and unlocked it. "We have over three thousand employees, but I can look him up on our directory app and see what beat he was covering, his editor, pretty much anything."

"The name is Mendel Cohen."

Dominic's eyes widened and he lowered his phone. "Mendel? I don't need to look him up— I was one of his editors. He worked a couple different beats over the years, so he got around. What would you like to know?"

"Let's start with what he was like."

Dominic wiped his forehead with a cloth napkin and began fidgeting with the beads of water on the outside of his drinking glass. "Oh, he was nice enough—"

"Listen to me." Levi jabbed a finger at Dominic. "I don't know this guy from Adam. I just want to hear the facts. No BS. You got me? No sugarcoating things."

"Uh-uh, ya. I got you. Okay, the truth is, he was a bit standoffish. Not a bad guy, just typically kept to his own kind, if you know what I mean."

"You mean he stuck to other Jews."

"Well, ya. I guess so. Honestly, he did his work, turned in stories on time, and never gave me a reason to complain about anything. He was reliable, just not much in the conversation department, if you know what I mean."

Levi nodded. "When I talked to his wife, she claimed that he'd been annoyed lately about the edits on his work. Claimed that the edits were taking out names or even sometimes not being published. Any thoughts on that?"

Dominic almost choked on the water he was drinking and coughed for a full ten seconds before he got himself under control. "I never cut any of his stuff—that kind of stuff happens above me—managing editors, executive editors. I just make sure that everything is properly sourced and it reads well. But you're right, he did complain about that. About the only thing he ever complained about. He took that kind of stuff personally."

"What kind of stuff was Mendel writing?"

"Mostly local stuff—New York laws and such. But sometimes he'd work a piece that had something to do with Israel or the Palestinian conflict. It was all good stuff, and I let it through because I thought it was interesting, but when the higher-ups see certain political stuff, they get a bit twitchy."

Levi focused on Dominic, looking for any signs of deception. Raised eyebrows, avoiding eye contact, a nervous smile, even the slightest fluctuation in speech patterns. But he saw no indications of lying. "Mendel's wife claimed he thought the paper was trying to shape the news to a narrative that he believed didn't represent the truth."

Dominic sighed and nodded almost imperceptibly. "I don't do that myself—that is, try to conform to a preconceived narrative—but it's an understood thing in the business that the news isn't always what people think it is. I've been around long enough to know that, and so had Mendel." He leaned in closer and lowered his voice. "We've got an audience to cater to, and my management is all about selling more copies and getting more clicks. They know that if it's stuff people want to hear, the revenue will be higher. Same goes with TV. Ratings are gold, and the one with all the gold wins."

Levi kept his expression neutral, even though he didn't like what he was hearing. "Don't you think people want to hear the truth?"

Dominic's eyes widened and his voice took on a tone of mild indignation. "We always tell the truth. We just don't always tell *all* of the truth."

Levi pressed his lips together as he recalled the words Menachem had said when he and Lucy were in Mendel's office. *"He made it clear that even though the newspaper never lied, by ensuring certain things were never said in print, they molded the public narrative. It was a sin of omission."*

Their waiter arrived with a serving tray and set a plate in front of Levi. "Sir, for you we have the blackened fish tacos made of skate wing, with purple cabbage slaw and cilantro-lime sour cream, all wrapped in a corn tortilla with an avocado, tomato, and roasted corn salad."

He set another plate in front of Dominic. "And for you, sir, a caprese salad made with fresh buffalo mozzarella, Campari tomatoes, wild baby arugula, aged balsamic vinegar, and extra virgin olive oil, with the added gulf shrimp."

As he refilled the water glasses, he asked, "Is there anything else I can get you?"

Dominic looked to Levi, who shook his head. "No, this is great," Dominic said. "Thanks."

The waiter left as quickly as he came, and Levi motioned for Dominic to start eating.

"What do you know about Mendel's death?" Levi asked.

"Practically nothing." Dominic speared a piece of tomato and mozzarella with his fork, popped it into his mouth, and chewed quickly." I heard he offed himself, but I have no idea how or why." Dominic held a pensive expression as he tapped his finger on the side of his glass. "Well, that's not exactly true. After he died, I did hear rumors in the hallways about him having some kind of affair or something. But I'm not sure how much of that I believe. Mendel had a picture of his family on his desk, he had like a whole bunch of kids and a pretty decent-looking lady. And he didn't seem the type to run around like that."

"Okay," Levi said, "a slight change of subject. I'm looking for more information on someone else who works at the paper. Mindy Cross. Do you know her?"

With his mouth full of tomato and mozzarella, Dominic swallowed hard and nodded. "Oh, her. Ya, she's on our floor. What do you want to know?"

"What's her story? What's she like?"

"Oh, man. Where do I start?"

Levi's eyebrows rose a fraction of an inch.

"Well, you always know when she's around, because the woman has this scent of flowers about her that is just unmistakable. You know the type. You can walk into an elevator and know that she was in there not too long ago. Usually it's the hags that think perfume will attract attention, but this chick doesn't need it. She's a real looker, but as to her personality, that I don't really know. I know half of the floor wants to get a piece of that action, but as far as I know, nobody's gotten anywhere with her."

Levi took a bite of his fish taco. It was excellent. "Keep this between you and me, you got me?"

Dominic nodded.

"What would you say if I told you that the cops claim Mendel had an affair with her?"

Dominic burst out laughing. Then he stopped suddenly, realizing that Levi wasn't joking. "No fucking way. Excuse my French, but I'd have known. I'd have heard rumors or something." He shook his head. "I mean, since every unmarried horndog on the floor is trying to get with her, along with a few of the married ones, you can guarantee that if *any* of those guys had seen those two as much as talking in private, I'd have heard about it. Mendel barely talked to anyone, period, and I'm pretty sure that I've never seen him say as much as 'hello' to a chick. Not even the receptionist. I mean, he's super religious, you know. Or he was." He shook his head again. "Mindy? Really?"

"Really," Levi said. "Do you think you can arrange for me to have a meet-up with her? I'd like to ask her a few questions."

"Let's see what I can do." Dominic grabbed his phone from the table and began texting. A moment later, he nodded. "How about right after lunch?"

"That'll work."

After a few more pokes at his phone, he set it back on the table. "Okay, it's all set. She'll be at her desk." Dominic looked Levi up and down with an approving smile. "You know, you're a good-looking guy. If she doesn't like *you*, she probably doesn't like anyone."

Dominic led Levi through the fifth floor of the *Intelligencer*'s headquarters. There were cubicles as far as the eye could see, most of them filled with workers typing, on the phone, or doing both at once.

Before they even got to Mindy's desk, Levi detected a floral scent in the air. Sure enough, Dominic soon stopped at one of the cubicles and tapped lightly on the cubicle wall. "Mindy?"

The woman who looked up from her monitor was the

same woman Levi had seen pictures of at Denny's place. And she was just as good-looking in person, which was really saying something. Her hair reached the back of her shoulders, a waterfall of honey-blonde that shimmered brightly even in the dull office lighting. With matching eyebrows and skin coloration, this Mindy Cross may have been one of the few people he'd ever met who had naturally blonde hair.

"Hey guys," she said. She looked from Dominic to Levi. "Are you Levi?"

"I am," Levi said, shaking her hand. She had a surprisingly firm grip.

Dominic stepped back. "I'll leave you two to talk." To Levi he added, "If you need me, just have the receptionist page me. She'll know where I am."

As he wandered off into the sea of cubicles, Mindy stood. "Dominic texted me about you, but he was vague about what this is about. He said you're an investigator, but not what or whom you're investigating."

Levi motioned toward the elevators. "I saw a café downstairs. If you can spare a moment, it'll be my treat. I'll explain on the way."

The reporter tilted her head and stared at Levi for a couple seconds before nodding. "Okay. I don't see the harm in that."

Soon they were seated in a comfortably appointed café on the ground floor of the *Intelligencer* building. Levi resisted asking who made the scent she was wearing. It was unusually strong, but for some reason, it didn't bother him—in fact he liked it. His sense of smell, like his other senses, was particularly sensitive, and he could tell from walking behind her that the scent wasn't coming from only one particular part of the attractive woman's body. It was almost like a vapor trail that followed her from head to toe. Likely a body wash of some type.

Mindy waved at the waitress, an older Asian woman, but was unsuccessful in catching her attention. The waitress was laughing and talking in Mandarin to an elderly Asian couple who'd already been served.

Levi turned toward the waitress, and in well-practiced Mandarin, said, "Excuse me, can we get a menu or get help ordering?"

The waitress's eyes widened at the sight of a non-Asian speaking Mandarin. She hustled over to their table, pulling a notepad from her waistband.

Before she could say a word, Levi spoke—again in the woman's dialect. "Do you have black tea?"

The waitress smiled and nodded. "We have some Dien Hong tea," she said in Mandarin, enthusiastically. "It comes from my home province of Yunnan. A very smooth tea with fruit-like flavors. It's excellent."

"I'll take that." Levi turned to Mindy, who was staring at him with surprise. "What would you like?"

"Tea and a scone?" Mindy said.

The waitress replied in English, with a strong New York accent. "Okay, dear, do you have a type of tea you'd prefer, or I can get you the standard orange pekoe."

Mindy shrugged. "Standard is fine, I guess."

The waitress jotted something on her notepad and scurried away.

Mindy stared at Levi. "How in the world did you learn to speak Chinese like that?" She leaned forward, and Levi couldn't help but notice her bust bulging slightly from the top of her form-fitting dress.

Levi met her unwavering blue-eyed gaze. "I've picked up a thing or two over the years."

"I'll say. Well, what thing or two would you like to pick up now? On the elevator you said you were hired to investigate 'personnel issues.' Care to elaborate?"

Levi knew he had to tread carefully. But he'd gotten her attention, which was good. "I can't be too specific, but I'd like to get your view on the people you work with."

The waitress returned with two ceramic teapots and Mindy's scone. She set them on the table, along with a bowl containing a large dollop of strawberry jelly. She poured the tea silently and then disappeared.

"I'm not sure I understand," Mindy said. "Did someone file a complaint against someone?"

Levi shook his head. "I can't really say. How about you start with telling me about your position?"

"Well, I'm on the city desk—you know, local stories. And to be honest, other than our daily work meetings with the editor, I really don't interact much with many of the other reporters."

"Really?" Levi raised an eyebrow and smiled. "I'd have figured there'd be lots of fellow reporters who would want to collaborate with you. I don't mean to be rude, but you're an attractive woman, and you're not wearing a wedding band…"

"Mr. Yoder." She gave Levi a stare that was so frosty, he could almost feel the chill. "I'd rather work on my own than have to fend off these drooling morons who pretend to know what a man is like."

Levi noted that he'd gone from "Levi" to "Mr. Yoder" in an instant. Not good.

"I'm sorry. I didn't mean to offend you. I'm just doing my job."

Her cheeks flushed. "No. I'm sorry." She reached across the table and put her hand on his. "I didn't mean to bark at you like that. And I shouldn't have called anyone a moron. It's just…"

She blinked rapidly, and her chin quivered. It was just for a fraction of a second, but it was enough for Levi to notice. Something was clearly bothering her.

Levi gave the tips of her fingers a light squeeze. He leaned forward and whispered, "What's wrong?"

Mindy swallowed hard and shook her head. "Nothing. It's silly. I'm just tired of the office politics. And I'm really sorry for snapping at you. You didn't deserve that."

"Tell me about the politics."

She dabbed at her eyes with a napkin and gave him a genuine smile. "You probably know what I'm talking about. You're an attractive man. You seem smart, and you dress well. You probably have girls throwing themselves at you all the time."

Levi wasn't sure how the conversation had suddenly become about him. He needed to turn it back around. "You'd be surprised. But what's that have to do with the office?"

"Can I tell you something in confidence, and it won't go any further?"

Levi sat back and studied Mindy's expression. Some

people wore their emotions on their sleeves, whereas others held their emotions inside until it was too much to bear and it forced its way out. It was obvious from her stiff posture, pursed lips, and serious expression, that she was one of the latter. She was trying hard to bottle up whatever was threatening to come out.

"It'll be just between us," he said. "Nobody else."

Mindy's eyes bored into him, unblinking. "I'm gay," she said in a low voice. "I've known it since I was twelve, and I am *not* totally out of the closet. That's why what you said bugged me so much. These guys keep throwing themselves at me, and then when I don't respond to their advances, I'm 'the ice bitch.' And then I get stiffed over for assignments because they think I'm not a team player. I'm just so tired of it all. I can't really be myself around these people."

Levi sat back in his chair as his mind raced with what she'd just said. She was clearly sincere. She'd just unveiled a deeply held secret, and he believed every word. But if she was a lesbian...

"I'm sorry that things are difficult for you, Mindy. I really am. If it's not too bold of me to ask... is there an option to come out of the closet? Or do you think the folks at the paper won't understand?"

"Whether they understand or not isn't the point. It's up to me what I do or don't choose to share about my wife, or my personal life. And frankly, I don't feel inclined to share my business with these dipshits."

"I totally understand. And I noticed you don't have any photos on your desk. Is that why?"

"Pretty much. My wife, Karen, is the center of my life

—along with Fuzzy, our dog. But I don't need photos on my desk. My life is my business."

Levi pulled out his wallet and showed Mindy a picture of twelve kids. *His* kids. "These girls are my pride and joy."

Mindy held the picture and smiled warmly. "They're gorgeous. But they can't all be yours... can they? I mean, they're all so close in age. Is your wife Asian?"

"Well, that's complicated. Let's just say we adopted."

The truth was, Levi had rescued these kids from the streets and had given them a new life. They were being raised by his mother in Pennsylvania, and he visited as often as possible.

"I'd love to see pictures of Karen, and especially Fuzzy, if you have any."

"Really?" Mindy hesitated, then smiled and opened her purse. After a moment of digging around, she pulled out her phone, unlocked it, swiped through a few photos, and showed him an image. "That was taken last weekend at home. Me and Karen, just hanging out with Fuzzy. It's those moments that I like the most."

Levi studied the photo—two women giving each other a kiss while holding up champagne glasses in a toast—and a feeling of wrongness fell over him. "You make a beautiful couple," he said, his mind reeling with the conflicting information he'd just been presented. "And you're right. Screw those guys at the paper. You don't owe them anything."

As she returned her phone to her purse, Levi considered how to get this conversation back on track without revealing too much. He recalled the names on the cubicles he'd passed on the way to hers, and decided to make use of them.

"Listen, since you don't interact with a lot of folks, how about I just give you a few names, and if you don't know anything, that's fine. If you do, you tell me what you can. Should be quick and painless. Sound good?"

Mindy took a long pull at her tea. "Sounds good."

"Do you know Josh Hayes?"

"I've heard the name, but I don't think I even know what he looks like."

"What about John Crawford?"

Mindy sighed. "Honestly?"

Levi nodded.

"He's an asshole. He's the national desk editor, and he's married with two kids, but he's one of the horndogs that offered to show me the ropes when I first started—*if* I was willing to give him a neck massage at his desk. I told him off, of course, and he's given me the stink eye ever since."

Levi felt the heat of anger rising up into his neck. "Okay, Crawford's a grade-A asshole. Got it. Anything else on him?"

"No. We've barely spoken since that incident."

Focusing on the woman's every motion, he asked, "How about Mendel Cohen?"

"I might have heard the name, but no clue who he is."

Levi's heart thudded heavily in his chest as he observed her response. She kept her eyes on his, and her body language showed no sign of deception. No fidgeting, no shrugging of her shoulders, nor any of the playing with her hair that he'd expect to see when someone was lying. She really didn't know the man.

He rattled off a few more names to make it look like he was doing his job, then concluded the interview by saying, "Well, I think I've got everything I need. I really appreciate your patience with me, and I'm sorry I upset you."

She again put her hand on his and gave it a squeeze. "Thank you for listening. And for being open-minded. I can't tell you how rare that is."

"Hey, Mindy!" The shout came from across the café. A man in his twenties, wearing a grimy Cornell sweatshirt and jeans, an *Intelligencer* badge clipped to his belt, walked up to their table, was staring intently at their clasped hands.

Levi began to pull his hand back, but Mindy held on to it, completely ignoring the guy who'd called her name. She leaned across the table and whispered, "Can you play along with me?"

"Sure."

The man was still staring at their table, holding a cup of coffee. Something about him made Levi want to walk over and slap the hell out of him.

Mindy took a final sip of her tea, wrapped her scone in a paper napkin, and stood. "Thanks for the break, honey." She said it loud enough for the *Intelligencer* guy to hear. Then she leaned over, gave him a quick peck on the lips, and walked toward the elevators.

Levi understood what she was doing, and he barely gave it a thought. His mind was on the police report, the sworn affidavit, and the examiner who'd interviewed Mindy Cross about the "affair" she'd had with Mendel.

There is no way.

The young man from the *Intelligencer* walked over, pulled out Mindy's chair, and sat in it with a smile. He held out his hand. "Hi, I'm Greg Puckett. And you are…"

Levi stared daggers at the kid. "I'm the guy who is going to introduce you to your dead relatives if you ever talk to me or Mindy again."

CHAPTER FOUR

"Hey, Denny, do you have anything yet on the... guys who were following us?"

As Levi held the phone to his ear, he glanced at his Uber driver, who was weaving his way through New York City's Midtown traffic. This wasn't one of the family's connected guys, so Levi needed to be really careful about what could be overheard.

"Yeah, man," Denny said over the line. *"I've got some info on your cops. The guys who checked that squad car out are Sergeant Felix Mendoza and Officer Doug Jenkins. Mendoza has eight years in the NYPD. Jenkins is a rookie with just one year on the streets. Mostly traffic duty, nothing unusual. Except... those guys were off duty when you said they were tailing you.*

"So I did a little further digging, and something popped up. They each recently got a deposit of five thousand dollars wired into their accounts from a bank in the

Caymans. That's a small enough amount that it wouldn't attract any attention from the feds, but, come on—both guys, same amount, same day? There's no goddamned way that's a coincidence."

"Do you know who sent the payment?"

"Yeah, I tracked it, but so far it's a dead end. Though the account is in the Caymans, the owner of the account is just a shell company with a PO Box out of Los Angeles. I'll keep digging, though."

Levi frowned as his Uber pulled up to his apartment. "Okay, Denny. The guy who interviewed the looker in the report, can you figure out if there's anything unusual about him? I've got some data I need to follow up on with her, but I'm starting to doubt just about everything in that report. I'll be over tonight to follow up."

"Roger that. I'll see what I can find out."

Levi hung up, leaned forward, and flipped a twenty-dollar bill as a tip onto the front seat. "Thanks, Mohammad. I'll call for your car again. It was a good ride."

"Thank you, sir."

Levi hopped out and breathed in the air from the Upper East Side as he walked toward his stately old building. Marble columns flanked the entrance, and the words "The Helmsley Arms" were emblazoned in gold leaf above the ten-foot-tall opaque glass doors.

As he stepped into the immaculate lobby, one of the elevators opened on the far side of the space, and out strode Tony Montelaro. Tony was a big guy—two hundred fifty pounds at least, and a full four inches taller than Levi's six feet. And like all the made men in the Bianchi family, the mobster was well dressed.

"Hey, Levi. Just wanted to let you know that your lady friend had a few things delivered to your place."

"Oh? Like what?"

"A couple big packages from Saks Fifth Avenue."

Levi felt a cold sense of dread. "You checked the contents before letting it up, right?"

"What do I look like, some kind of *stunad*? Ya, we scanned the box before letting it go up. It was just some kind of luggage."

Levi pressed the button to call the elevator. "Luggage? You sure that's it?"

"Ya, that's it. Mr. Minnelli was really clear about not letting anything up without it getting a once-over with that scanning device your friend Denny gave us. Works like a charm."

The elevator doors opened, and Levi stepped inside. "Thank, Tony. I appreciate you keeping your eyes peeled."

As the elevator climbed to the fourth floor, Levi's mind drifted back to what Denny had said about the cops being on the take. He wondered what they were being paid to do. Was it to watch the Cohen household? Or had they been paid to follow Lucy? Either way, things were getting more complicated than he'd anticipated.

Levi swiped his finger on the biometric scanner, and the locking device whirred. He walked into his apartment... and stopped.

The remnants of a shopping spree were scattered

across his living room floor, including a half dozen empty monogrammed cloth bags, some eye-popping Louis Vuitton price tags, and a few large shipping boxes from Saks. Lucy was lounging on the leather chaise, a silk robe wrapped around her, talking on the phone in Cantonese. "So we're going to put an end to this as soon as you get here," she was saying.

She nodded idly in Levi's direction, acknowledging his arrival, before returning her full attention to her conversation.

Levi had a knack for languages, and he'd picked up a few over the years, including the most common dialect of Chinese. Lucy knew this. But what she didn't know was that recently, thanks to audio lessons from the New York Public Library, he'd begun adding Cantonese to his repertoire. Cantonese was the dialect native to Hong Kong, where Lucy had spent much of her adult life. So he was able to get the gist of her side of the conversation. The details were unclear, but one thing was: Lucy was definitely planning something.

Levi sat in the leather chair facing her, waiting for her to get off the phone.

She shifted her gaze to him and smiled. "Ting, you'll really like Charlie." Lucy then said something he didn't understand, but the sentence ended with, "... and he's very pretty."

When she hung up, Levi said, "What was that about?"

Lucy ignored the question. Adjusting herself into a sitting position, she said, "How was your date?"

The amused look on her face told him that she already knew.

"It went well. I even got a kiss out of the deal."

"Really?" Lucy cocked an eyebrow and grinned. "I'm sure her wife, who happens to be a district attorney, wouldn't be too thrilled to hear about that."

"Okay, how the hell did you know about that?"

Lucy hopped off the chaise lounge, walked over to him, and sat in his lap.

"What are you doing?" Levi asked.

She leaned into him, snaking her left arm around his neck. "Was it a real disappointment when you learned she had a wife?"

Levi didn't take the bait. Their faces were only inches from each other, and they were breathing each other's air. "Why would I—never mind. You knew about this before I even went out. You were acting weird this morning. How'd you know?"

Lucy adjusted her position slightly. "Last night, when we were at Denny's place and you were on the phone talking to Frankie, I asked him if this Mindy Cross had any other social media accounts. He did some poking around using a facial recognition app, and he found a Facebook page listed under a different last name. Evidently Mindy Cross is also Mindy Weber. Married to Karen Weber, the local district attorney."

Levi tried to ignore the fact that she was sitting in his lap. His gaze shifted to the stuff on the floor. "What's with the delivery?"

She leaned closer, gave him a nip on his earlobe, flicked it with her tongue, and purred, "You really need to focus your attention on straight girls."

He froze at those words and tried to control his body's reaction to what she was doing. "Is that an offer?"

Lucy laughed and sat back. "Of course not."

Feeling an urge to shove her off his lap, Levi said in a louder voice than he'd intended, "Listen, I'm kind of sick of you playing around with me. I get it in public—you're playing an act, and it's a pretty good act. But it's confusing the hell out of me when you do it while we're alone. This kind of stuff... how do you expect me to react? I know you have this thing about not being touched, so what do you want? If you want to be more than what we are, let's talk. But this... I don't even know what to call it... this is not cool."

Lucy cupped his chin with one hand, and for a split second he thought he saw a hint of emotion on her face. "I'm sorry. I don't mean to tease you."

Levi was pretty good at reading what people were thinking, but this woman was a complete cipher to him—and it drove him crazy. Even now, when only inches separated them, he couldn't read what was behind that placid exterior.

"I don't have plans for us to ever be a couple, if that's your concern," Lucy said. "It would make things too awkward." She trailed a finger along Levi's jaw line and gave him an awkward, almost shy smile. "I just like to touch you on occasion, see how you react. I don't mean anything by it. If it really bothers you, I'll stop."

With a deep sigh, Levi shook his head. "I guess it doesn't bother me. I just like to know what's going on." He tilted his head toward the cell phone she'd placed on the coffee table. "Who was that on the phone?"

Lucy hopped up from his lap, pulled him up into a standing position, gave him a quick hard kiss on the lips, and turned him toward his bedroom. "Go take a cold shower. I know you need it." She gave him a light push toward his bedroom.

Levi wanted to continue pressing her about the phone conversation, but she'd already turned away from him to gather the stuff up from the floor, and as she reached across the coffee table to grab one of the empty boxes, her silk robe rose higher up the back of her thighs.

Levi quickly entered his bedroom. That was enough of that.

As he began getting undressed for a shower, he heard Lucy speaking to someone, in English this time. *"Let's close this deal."*

Levi walked over to his bedroom door, which was just barely ajar.

"I'll agree to the purchase price on one condition—"

Lucy's voice was cut off as he heard her bedroom door close.

He shut his own bedroom door and wondered aloud, "What the hell is she up to?"

The smell of garlic and fresh basil wafted from the kitchen as Gerard's prepared for the evening clientele. It was a quiet evening, still a bit early for the usual neighborhood crowd, but several regulars were at the bar, and Rosie, the bartender, was chatting them up like she always did.

Levi nursed his seltzer at his table in the back of his long-time hangout, waiting on Denny. Denny was acting squirrely, which meant his research on the Cohen police report hadn't gone as expected.

The bell above the entrance jingled, and two people walked in. The first was a tall, good-looking white man in his forties, wearing khakis and a brown sports jacket. The other was a woman, maybe late twenties or early thirties, in a black pantsuit with a form-fitting jacket that had a plunging neckline. And she had the darkest skin Levi had ever seen on anyone, including people from the tribal areas of Africa and Australia.

"I'll be right with you," Rosie called from the bar.

The two new arrivals scanned the room, and Levi felt their gaze land on him before they approached.

As Levi looked up from his seltzer, the woman elbowed her partner. "You owe me five bucks."

The man shrugged and faced Levi. In a very posh Londoner accent, he said, "Mr. Yoder, a mutual friend has sent us to talk with you." He motioned toward the two empty chairs at Levi's table. "May we?"

Levi gave a slight nod. He was sure he'd never seen these two people before, even in passing. His mind had a way with pattern-matching that even he didn't under-stand. "How'd you know where to find me?"

The man took the seat directly opposite Levi. "That's thanks to our mutual acquaintance."

"And who is this mystery person?"

The woman smiled, and Levi was struck by the stark contrast between her dark skin and pearly whites. It was almost like a living cartoon sat beside him.

"I think you know him as Doug Mason," she said.

"Oh, him." Levi somehow wasn't shocked to hear that man's name again. Doug Mason had been partially— no, wholly responsible for Levi having met Lucy in the first place. He was also responsible for their current situation. "I thought my business with him was complete."

"It is," the Brit responded. His voice had a warm tone that was no doubt intended to be reassuring, but which instead gave Levi a very bad feeling. "But we have some information for you and your… friend."

"What friend would that be?" The hairs on the back of Levi's neck stood on end.

The woman jabbed her partner in the ribs with her elbow. "He's so delicious. Protecting her, even though she doesn't need it. At least not from us."

Levi narrowed his eyes. "You have me at a disadvantage. You know my name, but I don't know yours."

"You can call me Winston." The man sat up a bit straighter, shook hands with Levi and his eyes flicked to the side. "And this is—"

"You can call me Annie, or anything else you like." The woman licked her lips. "And any *time* you like."

Winston frowned at her. "Stop flirting with the man. We've got other things to get done tonight."

"Jealous?" Annie said coyly.

At that moment, Denny approached. The look of confusion on his face was apparent as he looked over the two newcomers.

Winston stood. "Mr. Brown, I presume?" He held out his hand.

Denny shook it. "Do I know you?"

"Not yet," Winston said. "But we were briefed on you, and on this location, by our superiors." He looked around. More people were starting to fill the restaurant. "Perhaps it would be best if we continue this conversation in the back?"

Denny gave Levi a wide-eyed look that bordered on panic. These guys couldn't possibly know about Denny's operation in the back of the bar—could they?

Levi cleared his throat and stood. In a tone that brooked no argument, he said, "I'm sorry, but this isn't going to happen, guys. It's neither the time nor the place."

Chairs scraped across the room as two beefy mafiosos from the Bianchi family rose to their feet, their food unfinished. Both were skilled mob enforcers whose job was to crack skulls. They looked to Levi, just waiting for a signal to do just that.

Winston noticed the two and smiled. He pulled his phone from his pocket, dialed, and put it to his ear. "Yes, we're here. He's here, but she's not." He looked at Levi. "Do you mind if Director Mason calls you directly?"

Levi put a hand on Denny's shoulder and gave his friend what he hoped was a reassuring nod. Then he nodded to the Brit. "Go ahead."

Seconds later, Levi's phone rang. He put it to his ear without a word.

"Levi, I know what you're thinking. You're thinking we were all done, and we are. I know that Lucy is staying with you—but unfortunately, so do some of her former Triad gang members. So I sent a team over with some information that we can't act on, for reasons that will be apparent, but that someone in your position might be able

to use. Also, my head of technology wants to talk with both you and Mr. Brown, and I expect you'll want that to happen in a secure environment."

"Listen, Denny is not part of our—"

"Oh, but he is. He's been working with us for a very long time. He just didn't know it. Can you put him on the phone?"

With his heart thudding a bit faster than normal, Levi handed the phone to his friend. "It's for you."

Looking puzzled, Denny took the phone. "Hello?"

A few seconds passed, and even though Denny was black, Levi swore the color drained from his face.

"Okay, Marty, that's something we can talk about later... no shit." Denny glanced at the two strangers. "You sure they're okay? ... Fine. I'll dial you up in a few." He hung up, handed the phone back to Levi, then called to Rosie, "Rosie, I'll be in the back for a bit."

The woman glared at Levi, as she always did when he took Denny away, leaving her to run the place by herself. Levi wanted to tell her that it wasn't his fault this time, but instead he merely motioned to the two waiting mobsters, giving them the sign that things were okay.

"Okay, everyone," Denny said. "Follow me."

As the two newcomers followed Denny, with Levi trailing, Levi wondered what information Winston and Annie had that pertained to Lucy. Did it have anything to do with the contract out on her? And why couldn't Mason's group act on it?

Levi still didn't even know what group that was. He had first met Doug Mason at CIA headquarters in Langley, but it was clear the man worked for an even more secretive organization than that—one that didn't even have a name, or at least a name that Mason would admit to. An organization that knew things and did things that, to Levi, had seemed impossible.

All Levi knew was that things were about to take an unexpected turn, and that made him particularly nervous.

CHAPTER FIVE

"Madam Chen, we just landed in San Francisco. We'll be through customs in about half an hour, and then arriving in New York tomorrow morning."

"Good. You didn't check any bags, right?"

"No, just like you asked. We left everything behind. We're starting over, yes?"

"Exactly. I've arranged for a car to be waiting for you at LaGuardia. It'll take you to our new place. I'll see you tomorrow."

Lucy hung up and panned her gaze across her room. All of her clothes were neatly packed, and she was ready to start phase two of freeing herself from the Chinese gangsters who'd been a part of her life for almost as long as she'd been alive.

She looked past her bedroom door and into the living room. She wasn't sure when Levi was going to be back, but when he did, the conversation was going to be tense. She'd been holding back a lot of information from him, and tonight was the night it was all going to come out.

Levi, Winston, and Annie sat on metal folding chairs arrayed around Denny's desk in the back room of Gerard's, but Denny remained standing as he put his desk phone on speaker.

A nasally voice came over the line. *"Is everyone there?"*

"We're all here, Marty." Denny said.

"Okay, I'm putting you on speaker on my end. It'll be just me and my boss."

Levi heard the hollow background noise typical of most speakerphones.

"Okay, now that we've got everyone together—"

"Let me stop you right there," Levi interrupted. "I'm sick of this cloak-and-dagger nonsense. We all know you're about to drop some crap in my lap and try to guilt me into helping you. And that's not going to happen unless you tell me what part of the government is yanking my chain this time. It's not the CIA. So what is it?"

Mason chuckled. *"Levi, I've always liked your straightforward approach. But the answer to that question is kind of complicated."*

"I'm all ears."

"Okay. I'll try to be as complete and forthright as I can. Why don't I start with introductions. The British

gentleman with you is Winston Bennett. He's one of our field agents, specializing in espionage, and he's fluent in nine languages. He's really good, and probably the closest thing we have to James Bond.

"The lovely lady accompanying him is Anastasia Brown—"

Annie cleared her throat loudly.

"Sorry, she prefers to be called Annie. She's what we call a wet ops person. She has... her own special talents that come in handy with that line of work."

Levi knew the term "wet ops." A similar term was used by the KGB—*mokroye delo*, which translated to "wet affairs." Meaning the operation would involve the spilling of blood. Typically involving an assassination.

Levi looked at Annie appraisingly. "Really?"

She smiled back at him in what could only be described as a predatory fashion.

Levi had seen plenty of women who were very willing to kill. And while Annie looked harmless enough, that expression... Yes, she looked quite capable of luring her prey in close, then dispatching them when the time was right.

"Marty Brice is in the conference room with me. He's our chief technologist, and is often acting as a quarter-master of sorts for our field operations. And Levi, you know me already, but for the sake of Mr. Brown, I'll intro-duce myself as well. I'm Doug Mason, the director of a special operations group within the Outfit. I focus on enlisting and working with select members of organized crime units."

"The Outfit?" Levi said. "Are you serious? Is that really the name of your organization?"

"Yes, I'm serious. And I'm extending a large amount of trust in exposing even that name to you both. This organization is entirely off the books. We're outside the IC, but we have our fingers deep within it."

Denny looked questioningly at Levi, who mouthed the words *intelligence community.*

"Levi, I'm hoping to enlist both you and Mr. Brown in an official capacity. And before you decline out of hand, let me tell you that the job does come with a few perks."

"Perks?" Levi said.

He glanced at the two newcomers. They were both looking at him. The Brit's expression was unreadable, but Annie's was appraising. Uncomfortably so. Like she was looking at a side of beef.

The woman was disturbing.

"Yes. But we'll get to that later. First, let me get to the heart of the matter that brings us all together. I look after my own, and even though Lucy has cut herself off from me, I still feel responsible for her. I'm sure you can appreciate that. I'm also sure that with your mob contacts, you are aware of the contract on her life. I'd hoped to erase that contract by eliminating the common threat to both our nation's security and to Miss Chen, but... we ran into a snag. The Outfit has certain lines that we won't cross, even for one of our own. One of those lines is fratricide."

"Fratricide?" Levi asked. "Are you saying one of your own is responsible for the contract?"

Mason's chuckle came across the speakerphone. *"No. You'll understand better in a moment. Annie, would you hand the photos to Mr. Yoder? I think he and his people will be able to make good use of them."*

Annie pulled an envelope from a pocket in her suit jacket and handed it to Levi. "It isn't my best work," she said, "but it'll do."

Levi opened the envelope and slid nearly a dozen photos onto Denny's desk. They featured Annie in what, for most people, would be considered compromising positions. In about half of the pictures she was with a young man in his twenties; in the other half, with a slightly older man, perhaps late thirties. Levi didn't recognize either of them.

Levi looked up at Annie. "What the hell do you want me to do with these?"

Denny shuffled through the photos, nodding. "Hey, these are the cops who were following you." He tapped on the younger guy. "This is Jenkins, the rookie." Then he tapped on the older man. "And this is Sergeant Mendoza."

"Levi, like I said, I take care of my own. I've been watching, and you obviously have been as well. So I sent Annie and Winston to gather some info for us."

Understanding washed over Levi. He looked at Denny, who was still studying the photos with a smile. "Hey, buddy, stop ogling the pictures of the pretty half-naked lady."

Denny looked up, embarrassed. "What? I was just… looking." His eyes darted nervously at Annie, who tore her gaze away from Levi just long enough to give him her own predatory smile.

"Denny, are these cops married?"

Denny nodded. "Yup. Mendoza has been married for like fifteen years. He has three kids. Jenkins is married for only a year or two. He has a newborn."

"Perfect." Levi nodded approvingly and turned his gaze to Annie. "You got blackmail shots because you learned these cops were keeping tabs on Lucy. Yes?"

Annie smiled and rested her chin on the palm of her hand. "You really think I'm pretty?"

Winston cleared his throat and handed Levi a folded sheaf of papers. "We also have some banking records indicating both men were recently paid five thousand dollars apiece by a member of a Chinese organized crime syndicate."

The papers documented account numbers, names, and transferred amounts. He showed them to Denny, who nodded.

"That matches the stuff I found," Denny said. He leaned closer to the phone. "Marty, was that you who resolved the shell company out of LA?"

"Yup." Marty Brice's voice was slightly nasal. *"I had a slight advantage since I'm tapped into the Utah data center. I could trace back not only the history of the shell company, but even got the image of the guy who opened the bank account. I pattern-matched his face to a known ex-associate of Miss Chen's deceased husband."*

As he listened to Denny and Brice talk, Levi's Spidey-senses kicked into gear. "Hang on. Denny? Do you two know each other?"

Denny's eyes briefly avoided his, a sure sign of deception or embarrassment, and Levi could almost see Denny screw up his resolve to finally meet Levi's stare.

"Ya, Marty and I go back a long ways. He and I were classmates at MIT, and he's been a contact of mine forever. But all I knew was that he worked in the government and he was able to dig up some things I didn't have direct access to."

"And now, I'd like for us to start working as a team," Mason said.

"Mason, you know my loyalties are elsewhere," Levi replied firmly. "I'm not about to break any confidences for you—or for anyone."

"I'm not asking you to. Levi, the people I deal with at the Outfit are folks very similar to you and Mr. Brown. We talked about this before: you guys bring something that we can't teach. We can help each other for mutual benefit, and as in any friendship, we wouldn't impose on you in a way that would violate your current oaths.

"Let's look at our current situation. We have two officers that are helping, maybe unknowingly, the remnants of one of the Chinese Triads. The only option the Outfit has is to out them, and sure, that'll take them off the street and out of commission, but it won't get us any closer to discovering who their contacts are. Whereas I think you and your family contacts might have other options—including ways to gain leverage on these dirty cops. Am I right?"

Levi chuckled as he imagined talking to Frankie about two cops they could put the squeeze on. With the pictures and the evidence of bribery, Mendoza and Jenkins were clearly compromised, and the Bianchi family had all sorts of ways to take advantage of people in precarious situations like the one these two officers found themselves in.

"I see where you're going with this. And I appreciate the evidence and the info, but—"

"Levi, let me make this really simple. I'm not asking anything of you other than to keep our confidence when members of our organization communicate with you. And we'll do the same."

"I have no problem with that. But if you're this super-secret organization, how do I even know who is a member and who isn't?"

"Well, that's the rub, isn't it? When last we met, I told you that we don't carry IDs. But that's not exactly true. Winston, I think it's time. Go ahead and hand them out."

Winston pulled two small lacquered boxes from the inside pocket of his sports jacket. He handed one to Levi and the other to Denny.

Levi turned the black box over in his hand. He couldn't tell what it was made of. Wood, maybe, but it felt heavy for its size.

"What's this?" he asked.

"Marty, tell them about the coins. I think that'll help fill out the picture for him."

Marty cleared his throat. *"What Winston handed you is not just a black box. Each of those boxes has a lacquer coating that is actually an arrayed microheater fabricated on a silicon substrate. The electric resistance of each heater element will measure temperature differences between what is in contact and not in contact between each of the ridges of your finger."*

Levi turned to Denny. "Translate?"

Denny grinned. "All he's saying is that these boxes are big fingerprint readers. But much more accurate than most."

"Exactly. Anyway, those boxes are waiting to be programmed, as are their contents. I'd like to ask both Denny and Mr. Yoder to lay their boxes on a flat surface, press your right thumb down on your respective box, and keep it there for ten seconds."

They both placed their mysterious containers on Denny's desk and touched their thumbs to the lacquered surface.

"You might notice a puff of smoke—that's to be expected. I've got the circuitry embedded within the box to take the fingerprint data along with galvanic informa-tion and a few other proprietary pieces of biometric data. With that information, they'll program the coin inside to your body's signature."

Levi did indeed see a wisp of smoke rise from the box as a line burned across its perimeter. He counted down from ten, then said, "Okay, it's been ten seconds. Now what?"

"Has the box unsealed itself?"

"If you mean did it burn through whatever lacquer you had painted on it? Yes."

"Roger that," said Denny, "mine looks unsealed as well."

"Okay, lift your thumbs up and open your boxes."

Levi held the box in one hand and slowly wiggled the top off. Inside, on top of a velvet-lined bed, lay a silver coin emblazoned with a pyramid with an eye in it, surrounded by some Latin. Levi picked up the coin and turned it over. On its reverse side, the familiar image of a wolf stared back at him.

He chuckled as he noticed the halo hovering above the wolf. "Okay, now I get it. Mason, is this where you got the angel in wolf's clothing phrase?"

"Come again?" Mason said.

"You'd called me an angel in wolf's clothing before. Oh, never mind. It doesn't matter."

"Let me explain a bit," Mason said. *"On one side is what is called the Eye of Providence. Our organization goes back hundreds of years, in fact all the way to the founding of our great republic. When the Outfit was created, this was the logo the founders felt embodied who and what we are. 'Novus Ordo Seclorum' means 'New Order of the Ages,' and 'Annuit Coeptis' means 'Providence Favors Our Undertaking.'*

"You probably would recognize the pyramid logo.

After it was adopted by the Outfit, the same logo was eventually used for the Great Seal of our good ole US of A. You'll see it everywhere in DC if you pay attention. It's even on our dollar bills.

"On the reverse is what identifies you to others in our organization. There are several variations on this image, symbolizing the role you hold in the Outfit. Levi, I know you better than you think, and that predatory veneer of yours most certainly hides a person always looking to do the right thing. Mr. Brown, I've read Marty's briefing on you, and you fall into the same category."

Levi flipped the coin in the air and caught it. "So what's the point of these?"

"Like I said, they act as an ID of sorts. One that can't be spoofed, but also doesn't identify you as anything but the holder of an odd coin. If someone approached you and claimed they were a member of the Outfit, you'd be fully within your right to ask for proof. This coin is that proof."

Levi turned the coin over and studied it with a frown. "Stuff like this can be faked easily enough."

"Not exactly, Mr. Yoder. When two members of the Outfit grab hold of an identification coin, it quickly becomes obvious whether they're a member or not. Go ahead and try it."

Annie fished a coin from her pocket and extended it to Levi. He reached out and grasped one side of it. For a moment, he noticed nothing. But then, after a second or two, the coin grew warmer, and the eye in the pyramid began glowing.

"Son of a bitch. That's cool as hell."

"I take it you're seeing the Eye of Providence glow. That wouldn't happen on a fake. Nor will it glow if one person holding it is a member and the other is not. It requires two to make the connection."

Winston glanced at his watch. "It's late, and Annie and I have an early flight to catch."

"Winston, as always, check in with Marty on arrival. He'll forward you the location of the supply depot. Levi, I know this is a bit much for you to absorb all at once. Did you or Mr. Brown have any questions?"

Levi glanced at Denny, who shook his head. "I think we're good for now. I'll put your data to good use."

"Of that I have no doubt."

The call ended, Winston and Annie left, and within minutes Levi was back at his table in Gerard's, nursing a fresh seltzer and listening to the cacophony of bar noises that surrounded him. He was flipping the odd coin from one knuckle to the next, when suddenly he remembered why he'd come here in the first place.

He waved for Denny, who finished pouring a customer his drink before walking over, wiping his hands on a towel, and taking a seat.

"What's up?"

"With all that just happened I almost forgot why I came. What's the story with the transcript for the Mindy Cross interview? I'd like to see the details of the actual interview where she supposedly confesses about the affair, not just the summary."

Denny grimaced. "Listen, man, I tried getting access to it, but the file is missing."

"Aren't there supposed to be copies of everything taken as statements, with signatures and stuff?"

"Yes, but I'm not finding squat. Hell, even the police report that I printed out for you is gone. I looked tonight and I can't find any record of it. It's like it vanished. Good thing I kept a copy. All I know is that there's a Detective Carter who interviewed her, and he's out of the seventy-seventh precinct."

Levi leaned back in his chair. "Curiouser and curiouser."

"Where have I heard that before?"

"*Alice in Wonderland*." Levi pursed his lips as he thought about his next steps. "This case I'm working on, it feels like I've tumbled down a rabbit hole. I'm seeing things that don't make a lot of sense." He paused. "You make any headway on those seven names I gave you from the dead guy's office?"

"Not yet. Still working on that."

Levi nodded. "Let me know as soon as you get anything."

They bumped fists, and Denny went back to the bar to help out Rosie and her sister, Carmen.

Levi knew he had to talk with Frankie soon about those two dirty cops—and that after he did, those cops were going to get a little visit that might just change the dynamic of things. He finished the rest of his seltzer, then stood. On the way to the door, he patted the shoulder of one of the Bianchi family associates.

It was too late to talk with Frankie tonight, but not too late to talk with Lucy. It was only fair to let her know about what he'd learned. And he had to admit, he was curious to see how she reacted to learning that Mason hadn't forgotten about her.

Besides, she'd been acting squirrely, and leaving her alone didn't sit well with him. He couldn't let her jeopardize his safety, or the safety of the family, by doing something crazy. He knew she was up to something—he just had no idea what it was.

CHAPTER SIX

"You didn't seriously expect me to sit here like a damsel in distress, letting you protect me from what's out there, did you?" Lucy said with a frown as she finished packing her last suitcase.

Levi leaned against the guest room doorway, feeling somewhat at a loss. "No, of course not. But I thought we were on the same page. I want to help you, but if you don't share what's going on in your head, I can't—"

"Protect me?" Turning from the Louis Vuitton suitcase on her bed, Lucy put hands on her hips and glared at him.

"No, damn it. I was going to say I can't *help*." Levi's frustration was giving an edge to his voice. She was pissing him off. "I mean, I get what you're saying. And I'll admit that I agreed to have you here because I was worried what was going to happen to you with all the chaos that was going on out there. We knew both the feds and the gang were going to be looking for you. And even after we learned that Mason cleaned up the FBI mess and they weren't looking for you anymore, we still had the gang to deal with. We still do. But this place is safe. So... I don't get why you'd be leaving."

Lucy took a step closer, and her frown lines softened a bit. "Levi, this is my problem to deal with, not yours."

"Friends do things because they want to, not because they're obligated. I'm helping because I want to. Hell, the way you're treating me, holding all this back, and probably lots more... well, maybe I'm wrong. I was looking at us as a team. We were working together. But..."

Lucy smiled and pressed a finger to his lips. "Did you just pull the 'Friends do because they want to do?' line on me?"

"Huh?"

"I may have been born on a farm in Guangzhou, but even I've seen the *Rocky* movies. You just quoted Rocky."

"I don't know what you're talking about."

Lucy's smile grew wider, and she gently pulled him by his tie toward the living room. "I was planning on getting a few hours of sleep before tomorrow, but I guess I need to let you know about the ladies I've got coming into town." She led him to one of the leather armchairs and sat him down.

"Ladies?"

"I have three friends who just recently landed in the US. All widows of gang members, somewhat like me."

She sat opposite him on the other armchair. "I've also bought some property in the city. Actually, an entire floor of a high-rise that's not even officially open for occupation yet. That's where the four of us are going to be. A headquarters of sorts."

"What about the contract on you? And I told you there's some cops on the take. We don't know if we've identified all of them or not."

"You don't have to worry so much about me." Lucy folded one of her legs under her and shifted into a somewhat reclining position. "Levi, did I ever tell you what my role was when my husband was alive?"

"You said you advised him and... I don't know, kept your finger on the pulse of everything?"

She nodded. "True, but maybe I failed to mention that I was trained from the beginning to be his personal bodyguard. I'm very capable of handling myself, and so are all three of the women who are joining me. We all have the same goal."

Levi wasn't in the least bit surprised that she was a bodyguard. He'd seen the conditioning of her body. She moved like a cat, like a fighter, and she'd always been absolutely fearless in front of him.

"And what's the goal that you all share?" he asked.

"Wipe the last of my husband's organization off the face of this earth."

Levi leaned forward in his chair and gazed intently at the proud woman sitting opposite him. She was strong-willed and very certain of herself. *Too* certain, for his tastes. "I'll be honest with you," he said. "I'm worried that you might be going into this without enough planning. Why make yourself a target so soon? Give me a few days to see if we can get any more information out of these cops. I can talk to the don and see about maybe getting you and the other women one of the empty apartments in here or something."

"You're really sweet, but no." Her tone brooked no argument. She'd made up her mind. "I want this over with, and I have a few ideas about where to go to get at the folks who are looking for me. If you really want to help, do you know someone I can talk to locally about getting some equipment?"

"What kind of equipment?"

"Guns, explosives, things I might need to deal with a handful of human targets. I need a reliable weapons dealer who is well connected, doesn't ask too many questions, and likes cash. The people I used to go to were rounded up during the FBI's raid."

Levi sat back in his chair. "I have someone I can introduce you to in the morning. But first we'll need to stop at a bakery."

When Levi knocked on Frankie's apartment door, he heard the muffled sound of someone grumbling, followed by, *"Carlita, where the hell's the can of coffee?"*

Then the door opened and there stood Frankie, still in pajamas, his hair disheveled. He motioned for Levi to come in.

Levi followed Frankie into his kitchen and sat at the table while Carlita, Frankie's wife, yelled back from somewhere in the apartment.

"We don't have none of the regular coffee no more! We've got those new Keurig pods!"

"What the hell communist bullshit is that?" Frankie shouted as he scanned the contents of the cupboards above their coffee maker. "I just want some damned coffee and you're telling me shit I don't understand!"

Levi watched with amusement as the domestic drama unfolded.

Carlita walked into the kitchen with a thick terry-cloth robe wrapped around her. She saw Levi and harrumphed. "Look at you, Mister. You're about to split in half laughing at my idiot husband. I'll bet you know what a goddamned Keurig is and how to use it."

Levi smiled and shrugged. He did, but he wasn't about to get between these two ahead of their morning coffee. "Good morning, Carlita."

"Good morning, yourself. The kids better still be asleep when I check on them or… or I'll be pissed." She pushed Frankie aside, opened the cabinet under their Keurig, pulled out a coffee pod, stuck it in the machine, slapped the top down, and pressed the start button. Within a few seconds, steaming coffee was coming out of the machine.

Frankie nodded approvingly. "That's pretty damned quick. Thanks, honey." He leaned over and gave her a quick kiss on the lips.

Carlita sniffed loudly and stomped away.

"You want a coffee, Levi?" Frankie asked.

"Nah, I'm fine."

Frankie poured a bit of cream and sugar into his mug, stirred, then took a seat at the kitchen table. "Okay, what's this important stuff you wanted to talk about that couldn't wait until a more civilized hour?"

Levi leaned forward and spoke in a hushed tone. "I've got a development on the Lucy thing."

"Oh?" Frankie scooted his chair closer. "Like what?"

Levi pulled out the photos and other evidence he'd received from the Outfit's crew, and pushed it across the table. "It seems we have a couple of cops that were getting paid by some Asian gangsters to keep tabs on her."

Frankie began smiling as he scanned the printouts detailing the suspicious banking transactions. "This is good stuff." He looked up at Levi. "I assume you want to be in on squeezing them?"

"Of course. Lucy thinks she can weed out the gangsters herself," he tapped his finger on the nearest printout, "but since we've got some solid stuff here, I want to make sure these Triad assholes are taken care of."

Frankie nodded. "I like it. I'll get some of our guys to figure out where these two *momos* are living, and we'll arrange a sit-down with our new friends. I'm sure we can come up with a mutually beneficial arrangement." He picked up one of the photos. "This is a real good touch. If these guys are married, you'd be surprised what kind of leverage stuff like this can get. We just have to advise them how photos like this can find their way into the hands of their in-laws... or maybe to the wife's divorce lawyer. Ya, this'll be good. Give me a day or two to work out the logistics and I'll let you know."

"That works for me." Levi bumped fists with the Bianchi family's head of security. "I appreciate it. The sooner I can get leads on these Triad guys, the better. Oh, and I figured you should know… Lucy's got it in her head that she's done being held prisoner by the contract she's got on her head, so she's moving out."

"Oh, shit, man. I'm sorry to hear that—"

"No, it's not bad." Levi waved dismissively. "She's always been headstrong and she thinks she knows what she's doing. I gotta give her some credit for having the moxie to stand up to them on her own."

Frankie snorted. "Ya, but knowing you, you're not going to let that dame do her own thing. You're going to be tailing her ass the entire time."

Levi shrugged. "I can't say you're wrong about that." He stood and patted Frankie on the shoulder. "Well, I've got to get back before she starts getting stir crazy. Lord knows what she'll do. Besides, I told her I'd hook her up with a few folks I know."

"You going over to Rosen's?"

"Yup, how'd you guess?"

Frankie chuckled. "I figured your lady friend ain't going to take down those mob friends of hers with her bare hands. And if that Rosen lady doesn't have it, they don't make it." He walked Levi to the door and patted his cheek. "I'll call you."

"Thanks again, Frankie."

As Levi walked out of the apartment, he wondered what Lucy had in mind that called for dealing with one of the biggest black-market weapons dealers on the East Coast.

~

Levi opened the door to Rosen's Sporting Goods, on the outskirts of the city's Little Italy, and motioned for Lucy to enter ahead of him. A pimply-faced teen was scanning a woman's purchases at the counter, while a handful of other people were browsing the racks of newly arrived summer sports equipment.

Lucy looked doubtful. "Are you sure this is the place?"

"It is," Levi said.

The cashier looked up and recognized Levi. "My grandmother is in the back," he said. "I'll buzz her for you."

"Thanks, Moishe."

"I'm Ira," the cashier corrected him for what had to be nearly the hundredth time.

Levi and Lucy headed toward the rear of the store, skirting past the racks of soccer balls, field hockey equipment, and all variety of shoes and clothing. As they arrived at the back, a door opened and a large heavyset woman stepped out, her gray hair arranged in a bun.

"*Bubbaleh*!" she said to Levi. "I wasn't expecting you today." She wrapped him up in one of her rose-scented bear hugs, then held him at arm's length and shook her head. "You're such a good-looking boy, but you need to put more meat on your bones."

Levi returned her smile, but before he could even

respond, Lucy said, "But you have to admit, he's got a nice *tuches*."

The owner of the store turned Levi to the side, glanced at his rear, nodded approvingly, and gave Lucy a wink.

Levi motioned toward Lucy. "This is Lucy, a friend I can vouch for. She's got need of your special services, Esther." He handed over a bag from Nonna's Bakery. "And I have some of Nonna's special cookies as an apology for not calling ahead of time."

"Don't be silly. You're *mishpokhe*, just like my own family—but usually you're giving me less headaches than them." Esther peeked in the bag, sniffed deeply, and let out a low moan. "I can smell butter, almond paste, and sugar… the key ingredients needed for a happy life, and I absolutely adore them all. But I need this like a hole in the head, you wicked, wicked man."

She smiled at Levi and motioned toward the back door. "Go ahead, you know the way. Lucy and I will follow." She leaned closer to Lucy and said in a stage whisper, "We can both stare at his *tuches* as he leads the way."

Esther and Lucy were seated on leather armchairs, facing each other, and Levi sat to one side, watching with amusement as the grandmotherly proprietor of an unassuming sporting goods store demonstrated how she'd become one of the largest weapons and armament dealers on the East Coast.

The older woman leaned toward Lucy. "Are you sure you want a compressed-air gun? I don't think that would be the best choice. I promise you, you'll be *kvetching* at me how unsatisfied you are with it. How about this, let's start from the beginning. What do you *really* need this stuff for?" She hitched her thumb at Levi. "I've seen it all, especially with this *meshugana* and the stuff he comes up with."

"Hey," Levi protested good-naturedly. "I'm not crazy, I just have special needs at times."

"Special needs is right." Esther snorted and waved his comment away. "Anyway, there's nothing you can say that'll surprise me. I want my customers satisfied, and I don't think a glorified BB gun is going to satisfy anybody."

Lucy looked over at Levi, who nodded reassuringly. "She's the best," he said. "Just tell her what your goals are and let her come up with some ideas. Esther's never steered me wrong."

"Okay." Lucy leaned forward and lowered her voice to just above a whisper. "I need something that's conceal-able, will be lethal at upwards of one hundred feet, and won't draw the attention of any nearby pedestrians."

"Oy, and that's why you're thinking of an air gun? To avoid the noise?"

"Well, yes, and if it's in the evening, also the muzzle flash."

Esther shook her head. "Okay, so here's what I can tell you from some former Army Special Forces members whose job it was to eliminate targets in urban settings. The army's tested various compressed-air weapon kits, and even the ones that throw .45 slugs are fairly pathetic. Inaccurate, and the lethality is dubious. Also, a double or triple-tap with those things is often impossible, or at the least very unpredictable because the gas inlets can super-cool and sometimes even freeze up. Last thing you want is a jam, right?"

Lucy nodded with concern.

"Also, you'll want to be assured you have enough compressed air for double the shots you think you need, if not more. That means a fairly sizable tank—rated for three thousand PSI or better. That's bulky and heavy. And as far as transporting the rig…"

"Okay, okay, you've convinced me." Lucy shook her head and sighed. "It was a stupid idea. I get that—"

"No, *bubbaleh*, it's not a stupid idea." Esther reached forward and patted Lucy on the knee.

Levi saw Lucy wince, but she did a good job of not jumping out of her skin like she sometimes did when people touched her. It was one of the woman's oddities. For some reason she couldn't stand being touched—though she clearly had no problem *initiating* contact, as she'd proven time and time again with him. Levi didn't know why she was like that. At first he'd thought there must be some hidden trauma buried in her past, but she'd said that she didn't like being touched even when she was a child.

Esther sat back and made a clicking noise with her tongue. "A stupid idea would have been to not come to someone like me, who can help you make a good decision for your particular situation."

Lucy nodded. "So what would you suggest, Esther? I

need lethality at a short distance, no muzzle flash, and it needs to be reasonably quiet. Oh, and maybe three to four targets."

Levi sat up straighter. "Are you serious? At once?"

"Yes," Lucy responded without even looking at him.

Levi didn't like the sound of that.

"Oy, how concealed does it need to be? Regular street clothes, or can you have a windbreaker or the equivalent?"

"I'll be able to conceal almost anything but a full-length rifle," Lucy said confidently.

"It's warm outside," Levi said. "A jacket will—"

"I've got this, Levi," Lucy said, sounding exasperated. She gave him a dirty look.

Levi sat back and tried to stay out it. Lucy not only had a short fuse, she also had that weird Asian saving-face thing in spades. And questioning her in front of Esther had clearly triggered it.

Esther tapped her chin and scanned the shelves of the back room. Levi knew that most of the boxes contained ordinary sporting goods, but of course Esther knew which boxes contained the good stuff. She stood, walked among the shelves, and returned with a box that had a stylized red dragon logo on the side.

Levi recognized the symbol and nodded approvingly.

The shopkeeper opened the box, laid two plastic carrying cases on the table, and flipped open the latches. "I'd recommend carrying two pistols. You want reliability, and the Ruger Mark IV is an excellent choice. It's concealable, and as you can see, I can attach a suppressor to it."

"What's it fire?" Lucy asked.

"A .22 caliber round. And it has a ten-round maga-zine." Lucy was about to say something more when Esther held up a finger. "I know what you're going to say. Stopping power. Yes, a .22 won't compare in ballistics to a .357, 9mm, .45 ACP or any of the other larger rounds, but no matter what kind of suppression you use, if you're shooting that on the city street, someone's going to notice it."

She picked up a long metal cylinder and screwed it onto the end of the pistol. "I used to recommend some custom 5.56 cans, which are hands down the most silent pairing for this type of gun, but the manufacturer recently came out with their own silencer, and I have to say it's a quality build. The rear cap is made of 7075-T5 aluminum with a titanium housing, and both the front cap and baffles are made of 1704 heat-treated stainless steel. And it works. Why don't I show you?"

Levi watched with interest as Esther loaded the Ruger's magazine with ammunition. He'd never seen the old woman actually use one of her weapons before.

The heavyset woman stood once more and pointed to the far end of the storage room, which was about fifty feet away. A beige-colored gel torso sat on a table up against the wall, and several bullet traps lay behind and beside the dummy. Esther rammed the magazine into its well, released the slide, aimed, and squeezed off three shots in quick succession.

A grin spread across Lucy's face as she looked back and forth between Esther and the target.

It was only then that Levi realized that none of them

had been wearing ear protection, and yet all he'd heard was the cycling sound of the gun's action. On a city street, with cars and other normal street noises, nobody would hear even that much.

Esther pressed a button, and the magazine fell into her hand. The grandmotherly woman racked the slide, popping out the chambered bullet, and caught it with a deft hand. She set the pieces back onto the table, then motioned for Lucy to follow her to see what she'd done to the target. Levi joined them.

Esther examined the dummy, placed her finger on an entry wound, and nodded. "See here?"

Within the gel torso, which was not completely opaque, was a replica of a human skeleton.

Lucy stuck her finger into one of the entry wounds as well. "It broke a rib. Impressive."

Using needle-nose pliers, Esther extracted a bullet that had penetrated so far it almost went out the dummy's other side. "For a quiet killer, you won't find anything better." She looked to Lucy. "Are you able to shoot with either hand?"

"I think I could manage. More than likely, I'll be up close."

"Good." Esther patted the shoulder of the jiggling torso. "It might take a bit of practice, but you should be able to take out a handful of people, especially at close quarters, and if they don't see it coming." Her voice took on a warning tone. "But let's be honest. If they're wearing vests or body armor, your target placement will be key." She pointed at various spots on the dummy. "You'll want to turn their lights off instantly. That means shots at the base of the skull, either from the back or the front. A shot in the eyes will also do it, but that's harder to land. If they don't have vests, lethal shots can be had in the chest, though the .22 pistol round will have trouble getting through the sternum," she tapped the center of the dummy's chest, "so you'd need an oblique angle to get to the heart."

Lucy looked at the dummy's head and smiled. "I think this'll work," she said.

When Levi saw what had caught Lucy's attention, he laughed. "Damn, Esther. I didn't know you were such a good shot."

One of Esther's shots had drilled through a rib, another had sailed almost straight through the dummy's non-existent heart without hitting a bone, and the third entered the dummy's left eye socket. That one would have caused an instant lights-out as it sprayed shards of bone through the brain.

The older woman frowned at Levi. "You think I've always just been a merchant?" She winked. "I've done things in my life. And some things you learn when you're younger, you never unlearn them."

Lucy put her hand on Esther's arm. "I need four pairs of these, with silencers, and a few boxes of ammunition for each."

"Eight guns and silencers in total." Esther glanced at the shelves and nodded. "I think I have two more of each, but let me make a call, and I can probably get the rest by the end of the day. But if you're able to wait, I can maybe get it all put together for a better price."

95

Levi's phone buzzed, and he pulled it out and glanced at the screen. It was from Denny.

I finally got info on your seven names. It took some crazy measures for me to hunt them down, and there's no doubt someone didn't want these people to be looked up. It kind of worries me. Come by and I'll show you what I got.

A chill raced up Levi's back. Denny never worried about anything. What the hell had that Cohen guy stumbled into that could give the computer whiz even a bit of concern?

"I'd like it as soon as possible," Lucy said. She pulled a thick envelope from her purse and handed it to Esther. "I'll also need a few more things. The best sniper rifle you can find, and—"

"Ladies, are you okay if I step out for a little bit? I have an errand to run. I'll be back in half an hour." The ladies were going to be a while, and as long as he was in the neighborhood, it only made sense to make some progress on other stuff if he could.

Deep in the midst of their transaction, both women waved him away without a glance.

He exited the store and dialed Denny's number. The bar owner answered almost immediately. *"Hey, Levi. I'm guessing you got my text."*

"You bet I did. Are you at the bar?"

"Yup, I was about to head home."

"I know it's late for you, but I'm a few blocks away, mind if I drop in?"

"No, go ahead. But let me tell you something, man. Someone knew what they were doing when they tried to erase these names you gave me. It's kind of spooky how complete their erasure was. What the hell did you get yourself involved in?"

Levi shrugged and quickened his pace. "I don't know, Denny. That's what I'm trying to figure out."

CHAPTER SEVEN

Levi sat in the back room of Gerard's while Denny brought up his results on the computer.

"When you handed me those seven names and asked me to figure out what they might have to do with each other," Denny said, "I had no idea it was going to be as rough as it was. Normally a quick computer search would do most of the work for me. The first thing I did was try to see if I could create a profile for each of these guys, limited the search to a twenty-mile radius of here, and then widened the search pattern. Luckily, some of the names weren't particularly common. I mean, how many people are actually named Redbone? I'll tell you: there's like thirty in the whole country. Most of them in Louisiana.

"Anyway, the problem was, I wasn't finding anything that made any sense. A few children, some people who were in their nineties, a lesser-known author of cozy mysteries. These people literally had nothing to do with each other, no matter how I looked at it. So. Then I asked Marty—"

"The guy from the Outfit?" Levi kept his tone neutral even though he was a bit anxious about using that mysterious group as a resource.

Denny nodded. "Yup. I asked him to help with the scan and see if he got anything different. Those guys have access to a huge NSA database that takes snapshots of basically the entire word's data traffic. For all I know it has a complete archive of everything that's ever been uploaded anywhere."

Levi shifted in his chair, trying hard to squelch the uneasy feeling he had about the Outfit. "Did he find anything?"

"Actually, he found a bunch of stuff. There was a Cyrus Redbone working for the *Intelligencer* about a decade ago. He lived in the city, yet there's absolutely no electronic record of him ever having existed." Denny scrolled through the data on his screen. "In fact, almost all of the names you gave me belong to people who worked for the media in some capacity. The only exception was a DC lobbyist. Redbone and one other guy worked for the *Intelligencer*, two of the names were investigative reporters for the major networks, and the other two were very popular news bloggers that one day just… vanished."

"What do you mean, vanished?"

Denny met Levi's gaze. "I mean vanished. It's actually freaking me out a bit. All seven of the names you gave me are either dead or missing."

The hairs at the base of Levi's neck stood on end. "Dead how?"

"None of them were by natural causes, if that's what you're wondering. It seems like the folks on your list had a nasty habit of committing suicide or having car accidents. And then they were scrubbed from the official records. I'm telling you, it's just like with that Mendel Cohen guy when his police report just up and vanished. Someone's trying *really* hard to hide something." Denny shook his head. "You handed me a list of ghosts, Levi. As far as anyone's concerned, these guys never existed."

Levi sighed and sat back in his chair. "This case was just supposed to be about some guy screwing around and offing himself because he felt guilty." His mind raced. There was something very wrong with all of this.

"I don't know what to tell you, Levi. I've never seen anything like it. Whoever did this cleanup knew what the hell they were doing."

Levi raked his fingers through his hair as he replayed the facts in his mind. What had Mendel Cohen uncovered that had led him to meet the same fate as those seven names? And who was behind all this?

"I hate having more questions than answers," he said, shifting his gaze back to Denny. "Okay, so I assume you now have a profile for all of these guys, right? Anything notable about them?"

Denny turned back to the computer. "Marty gave me a dump of everything he had, and I've worked it through my pattern matcher." His fingers were a blur on the keyboard, and the screen updated with new information. "There were a few angles I followed. Since your guy was a religious Jew, I looked into these people's religions first. They were kind of across the board. Three Jews, two Muslims, two Christians. Then I began cross-checking against their work. Like I said, other than the DC guy, they were all in the news business in one way or another, but I wanted to see what their particular interests were. Fortunately, Marty was able to give me all the stories they'd reported on. And they all had one thing in common: an interest in Israel, especially the Palestinian-Israeli conflict. Even the lobbyist was focused on influencing congressmen and senators against the BDS movement."

"Damn it to hell, I hate politics." Levi frowned. "What's the BDS movement?"

"I had to look it up. It's an anti-Israel movement that's supported by a fringe group in Congress and is gaining some traction in the press. It's about boycotting, divesting, and sanctioning Israel. Evidently, these people think Israel is the boogieman and Jews are—"

"At the root of all things that have ever been wrong in the world," Levi said sourly.

Denny nodded.

"What a bunch of crap. People have been saying that about minorities since the dawn of time." He shook his head. "Do they have anything else in common? How about the places they worked? Is there any relationship between the reporters and whoever was funding the lobbyist?"

"No, I looked into that. The *Intelligencer* has been around since the fifties and is privately owned. The two networks had different parent organizations, and the lobbyist was getting his funding from some DC think tank that supposedly gets its funding from public donations. No connections between any of the organizations. I'll email you a summary."

Levi got up and pulled out his phone.

Denny looked up from his screen. "Hey, before you make that call, Mr. Wu dropped off a few of your suit jackets, and I managed to modify one of them so far. If you've got time, I'd like you to try it out. Make sure it's all working as expected."

Levi glanced at his watch. "Okay. I have a few minutes."

"Good. The email dump is in your inbox. I'll go get your suit." He rose and disappeared behind the shelves.

With a quick swipe of his finger, Levi dialed a number. It rang twice before being picked up.

"Hello?"

"Dominic, this is Levi Yoder."

"Oh, yes, sir." The newspaper editor sounded nervous. *"I mean, yes, Mr. Yoder. What can I do for you?"*

"First of all, it's Levi, not Mr. Yoder. Anyway, I wanted to have another sit-down. I have some questions for you about the newspaper business and some former co-workers of yours. When can you meet?"

"I'm actually in Newark right now, but I can be back in the city in a couple hours."

"Don't worry about it. How about tomorrow morning at nine? Let's meet at that café on the bottom floor of the *Intelligencer* building."

"You sure you want to meet there? I mean I can—"

"There's no need for you to make a special trip. I'll be there."

"Oh, it's not a problem..." Dominic hesitated for a long second, then: *"Okay, I'll see you downstairs at nine."*

"See you then."

As Levi hung up, Denny was wheeling over a mannequin wearing one of Levi's suit jackets. He handed Levi what looked like a thick, rubberized belt.

"Okay, Levi, this is the power pack. It's a new design, should be quite comfortable. Just cinch it snugly around your chest and click the leads together. That'll complete the loop, which will create a magnetic field for the resonant circuits to operate."

Levi shrugged out of his suit jacket, laid it carefully on the back of his chair, and looped the strap around his chest.

Denny tilted his head as he watched Levi adjust the length of the power pack. "It looks like the vest you're wearing under that shirt doesn't have any plates, but just in case you wear any that do, I made the strap for the battery pack adjustable to accommodate."

"Nah, I don't do plates. Too bulky. And besides, they're only good if you're hit on the plate. Knowing my luck, I'd get shot between them." Levi tightened the strap and twisted left and right to make sure it wasn't moving. "Esther's made me some custom mesh stuff that works just as well as type-four body armor, plus the suit's fabric—"

"I know, that's why that stupid jacket of yours is so heavy. That Mr. Wu of yours gave me a bunch of shit about not messing with the suit's protective liner. Let me guess, it's some kind of STF material? That new liquid body armor the army's been experimenting with?"

Levi nodded. "Actually, I think Mr. Wu somehow layered it into the suit, and Esther provided the material. She told me it's some kind of nano-particle silica nonsense that stiffens on impact. It actually saved my ass a while back." He pointed to the jacket draped on the mannequin. "Do I just put that on?"

"First, let me go over briefly what we've got here."

Levi glanced at his watch again. "Just make it the short version. I don't have time for a physics lesson just now."

"Fine," Denny said with a bit of a huff. He gestured to the suit jacket. "You complained that the hat I made for you was sometimes too conspicuous to use on the streets, especially if you're normally dressed in a suit. So I worked with Mr. Wu to embed the infrared emitters along the suit's pinstripes." He ran his hand over the material. "Here—feel the little bumps where the emitters are. But anyone just looking at it would never even suspect there's anything odd."

Levi studied the suit at arm's length for a full ten seconds, but didn't see any hints of the hidden infrared light-emitting devices he knew had to be there. He lightly dragged his fingers across the material, and even then he just barely felt the tiny bumps along the dark-gray pinstripes.

He smiled. "Denny, you're the man. This looks great."

"Well, try it on."

Levi lifted the suit off of the mannequin and shrugged into it. He'd gotten used to the heavy weight of the somewhat-bulletproof and stab-proof suit, so this one felt natural to him. He was about to ask how to connect the power supply to the light emitters when he felt a tapping sensation coming from the strap around his chest.

"Are you feeling it?" Denny asked.

Levi focused on the tap-tap-tap. He realized it was isolated to one spot under the power pack. "Yes. What is that?"

Denny walked slowly around Levi, all the while keeping his gaze locked onto him. The tap-tap-tap moved with him, following him in a complete circle.

Levi was speechless. The core technology wasn't new for Denny—the electronics whiz had created a hat that would flash bursts of infrared light, something humans couldn't see, and detect any light reflections that came back, so that if anyone was watching Levi, even behind his back, the transceiver would notice the reflection from the observer's eyes and alert him to their presence. But this suit… it was way more complicated than that. Way more elegant, too.

"How is it working already?" he asked. "We didn't even plug it into the battery pack yet."

Denny grinned. "Oh, that's old technology. These emitters are running off of a resonant circuit matched to something I've built into the power supply. It's called resonant inductive coupling. They do the same kind of thing nowadays for wireless charging of phones and stuff like that. Oh, and I've upgraded other things a bit, too.

We'll have to test it more, but it should be able to handle more than one possible direction at a time."

"So if I've got two people paying attention to me, I'll get taps from both at the same time?"

Denny nodded. "If you're up for it, that suit and battery pack are ready to roll right now. Why don't you field test it for me and let me know how it works? I'm working on a second power supply, but the one you're wearing should be good for twelve hours. And you can use the same charger for this as you use for the other stuff I gave you."

Levi motioned to the jacket he'd been wearing. "Can that one be retrofitted with this?"

"I don't see why not, but that's something Mr. Wu will have to take care of. I'll talk to him."

Levi looked at his watch again, and winced. "I really have to get going." Lucy had dropped a hint that she had some people to meet after finishing with Esther, and he wanted to weasel his way into that meeting. That woman was up to something, and he wanted to know what.

Though Levi couldn't see Lucy as he entered the sporting goods store, he heard her slight Russian accent over the din of shoppers. He headed in that direction and spotted her near a display of tennis rackets. She smiled and quickened her pace toward him.

"Did you get what you need?" Levi asked.

Lucy wrapped an arm around his and steered him back toward the street. "Of course." A dark SUV pulled in front of the store, and Lucy waved. "The Uber's right on time. You up to meeting the girls?"

"I suppose, if you don't mind me tagging along."

The girls. Whoever these mysterious gang widows were, Lucy had brought them into the country for a reason.

The driver hopped out of the idling car and opened the rear passenger door. Lucy and Levi climbed into the back of the luxurious Escalade, and within minutes they were on the FDR, heading toward the East Side.

Lucy wrapped Levi's arm around her shoulders and settled her head in the crook of his arm. "What took you so long?" she asked in Mandarin.

Levi glanced at the driver, a red-headed man in his thirties. He almost certainly didn't speak Chinese, but Levi nonetheless weighed his words carefully before responding in Mandarin. "Denny had some information for me."

"What information?"

"Well, the seven names from the prayer book. There were some oddities there." He lowered his hand and pointed at the driver. "Let's talk about that later."

"You're really careful. I like that." Lucy smiled and rubbed his thigh. "You know, since it took you so long, I got a chance to talk with Esther quite a bit. She's an amazing person. Did you know she almost made it onto the American women's shooting team for the 1984 Olympics?"

"Really?" Levi chuckled. He had trouble imagining the grandmotherly woman as a competitive sharpshooter.

"Well, that explains those shots she took on the dummy. Damn."

"Yup. She gave me some shooting pointers. And I think she's had some real-world experience in close-quarters situations."

"You think she was a hitter?" Levi blinked as he tried to imagine Esther as an assassin.

"I don't know for sure, but she was warning me about clothing choice and blood splatter. I can't imagine she learned that in any class."

"Probably not." He looked through the windshield and saw they'd gotten off on East 61st Street. "We're pretty close to home."

Lucy nodded. "My place is at Lenox Hill."

"Is it that new place being built on Third Avenue?"

She smiled and patted his leg. "You'll see."

Shortly after passing Bloomingdale's, the car slowed in front of the construction site for a residential building.

The driver turned. "Is this where you wanted to be dropped off?"

"This is perfect," Lucy said. "Thanks." As she and Levi got out, she swiped on her phone to tip the driver.

Before Levi could ask why they were at a place that wasn't ready for occupation, a beefy man in a yellow hard hat approached and gave Lucy an awkward bow. "Miss Chen, I'm the site foreman. I can escort you through the construction safely and get you to your apartment. Everything is ready, and your guests are already settled in."

Lucy nodded, and she and Levi followed the large man into a lobby that promised, when complete, to be breathtaking. There was already marble throughout, and the exposed metal shone brightly with a gold sheen that was reminiscent of the Trump Tower's ostentatious style. They weaved past pallets of unlaid marble tiles, five-gallon buckets of paint, and industrial-sized spindles of blue wire, eventually arriving at a golden elevator. The foreman inserted a key, then pressed the button for the eighteenth floor.

Levi asked in Mandarin, "How did you get permission to occupy before the city issued their occupation certificate?"

Lucy looked up at him with an amused expression. "Truth?"

Levi frowned.

Lucy smiled and tapped his lips with the tip of her index finger. "I made arrangements with the builder. Officially, I'm not yet occupying it. I'm listed as a contractor, and I'm doing quality control."

The elevator dinged and the doors opened. The foreman stepped through first and pointed at the uneven flooring. "Follow me, but please be careful—the floor's not done. Even the tiles that have been laid aren't cemented in yet."

About half of the floor had rose-colored marble tiles laid in an undulating pattern. Large stacks of tiles in a variety of other colors were waiting to be set, and the floor had already been marked by color, showing what ultimately would be a snake-like pattern along the hallway.

They stopped at a high door, where the foreman handed Lucy a keycard and gave her another bow. "If you need an escort to the street, just dial the asterisk on your phone. It'll ring me or whoever is on duty at the time." He removed his hard hat, wiped a few beads of sweat from his forehead, and put the hat back on. "Is there anything else I can do for you?"

Lucy shook her head. "Thank you."

Before the foreman could depart, Levi slipped him a twenty-dollar bill. The man stared at the money with surprise. Levi gave the man a wink and patted him on the shoulder. Finally the foreman smiled and gave a nod of appreciation.

Lucy swiped the keycard over the reader, and a green LED lit up. As she turned the knob, she said, "Are you coming?"

"Yes," Levi said. "I'd love to see this new place of yours."

CHAPTER EIGHT

As Levi stepped into the foyer, he had to pause to take it all in. There was marble as far as the eye could see, silk tapestries adorned the walls, and that unmistakable smell of newness permeated the air. But before he could say a word, three women rushed in from another room, huge smiles on their faces. Lucy and the women hugged and began chattering away in Cantonese.

It was almost a minute before Lucy waved for Levi to join them. Shifting to Mandarin, she said, "This is the man I was talking to you about."

The three women looked like they were in their thirties, and all were quite attractive in their own ways. "Hello, ladies," he said in Mandarin.

All three gasped and looked at each other with shock. One of them asked in Mandarin, "You speak Chinese?"

"I do." Levi smiled at their dumbstruck reaction as he held his hand out to the woman who had spoken. She was taller than the others, and had a thicker, more muscular body than most Asian women he'd met. Her hair was in a long, braided ponytail. "My name's Levi. And yours is…?"

"I'm Feng Min." She shook his hand, blushing furiously.

"I'm Liu Ruxia," said another. She seemed more confident than the first as she stepped forward to shake Levi's hand. "But please, call me Ruth."

"And I'm Ye Ting," said the third, also giving him a firm handshake.

"Let's show our guest the new headquarters," Lucy said.

"Headquarters?" Levi asked.

Lucy wrapped her arm around his and led him forward. "Of course. I told you we're starting a new business. It'll be something special."

She ignored the look he sent her way as she led him through a great room with a huge U-shaped sofa that could easily seat ten. The smell of fine leather permeated the air. The decor was very reminiscent of Lucy's previous apartment—a unique combination of Asian and European flair. Not exactly minimalist, but focused on practicality, comfort, and style.

It took a full five minutes to make the complete circuit through all of the sitting rooms, the gourmet kitchen, the five bedrooms, a room with gym equipment and a large open space for yoga, and finally the balcony with a view of Central Park.

"This place is beautiful," Levi said. "You have the entire floor to yourself?"

"Thank you, and yes. The entire floor, all sixty-five hundred square feet."

As they returned to the great room, the four ladies sat on the couch and began talking rapidly in Cantonese. Levi could still only pick out only about sixty percent of what they were saying, but he could tell that Lucy was filling the others in on some gang members who'd escaped the FBI roundup.

He pulled out his phone, motioned to Lucy, and mouthed, "I'll be right back."

She nodded, and he walked to the foyer, dialing a number on his quick-dial list.

"Rosenberg and Rosenberg, this is Melanie. How can I help you?"

"Hey, Melanie, it's Levi Yoder."

"Oh, hey, Levi. When are you going to finally say yes to my offer of dinner and the movies?"

Levi laughed. Melanie was Saul Rosenberg's sister, six times divorced and about twenty years older than him. She'd been flirting with him since he was in his twenties.

"Melanie, you know that if I ever said yes I wouldn't be able to control myself, and I need to keep Saul in mind when it comes to such things. He wouldn't like me messing around with his sister."

A heavy sigh came across the connection. *"I am kind of irresistible—the curse of being me, I suppose. I'm guessing you want to talk to Saul?"*

"Please."

"He just finished with another client. One moment."

The phone was silent for a few seconds before Saul

Rosenberg's nasal voice came through. *"Levi! What can I do you for?"*

"I need help from a big-shot attorney. What else is new?"

Saul laughed his hyena-like laugh. *"Well, I just looked around and I don't see any big-shot attorneys in the office, so you'll just have to make do with me. What's up?"*

Levi glanced at the women, who were all still speaking in hushed tones, ignoring him. Occasionally one glanced up at him before turning just as quickly away.

"A friend of mine got a redacted police report that left off a couple key names, like the detective's name who was in charge of the investigation. But I happen to have acquired an unredacted copy of that report, and I want to follow up with that detective. So I need—"

"This is an NYPD report?"

"Yes."

"I don't want to know how you got an unredacted report. The only reason a name would be redacted on a police report was if he was working undercover."

"That's what I figured. Which is why I have to come up with a legit excuse to go to the precinct and talk to the detective. I was hoping you might have an idea."

"Oh, sure, make me the heavy." The line went silent for a second or two, then Saul said, *"Why don't we try this: I can issue a subpoena for the police report, and you can serve it yourself. If the guy you're looking for is undercover, then it won't help, but they at least have to give you what they have, and someone's going to have to*

talk to you about the case if you're a named party to the report."

"Well, that's just it. I'm not mentioned in the report. A friend of mine is. And she asked for a favor."

"Unfortunately, for me to issue a subpoena, I'll need to be the attorney of record for an involved party—so we'll need to make that happen first. I can electronically send you the paperwork. If your friend can just sign it, I can get it filed the same day."

"That'll work. I think I can get that turned around to you pretty quickly."

"Actually... you've got a PI license that's active, right?"

"I do, you're the one who helped me get it, remember?"

"Okay, good. That's the hook we'll use. I still need you to get the paperwork signed so I'm the attorney on record, and I'll have you, since you're an officially licensed private investigator, act as my hired agent. As a PI, you can legitimately investigate most things without the cops hassling you. Make sense?"

"Sure." Levi nodded.

"Hold on a second." The line went silent for a full minute before the Bianchi family attorney came back on. *"I've got a client that just did something... well, let's just say I need to switch over to him. Get me the signed documents right away, and I'll have a courier file them so I can issue the subpoena."*

"Perfect. I'll probably be in your office this afternoon."

"Okay, see you then."

"Thanks, Saul, you're a lifesaver."

As Levi hung up, he caught two of the women staring at him. He started walking back toward the great room, and they both quickly averted their gaze.

Min said in Cantonese, "He's very pretty, don't you think?"

The other ladies tittered.

Ruth asked Lucy, in Mandarin, "Is Charlie staying with us?"

"Charlie?" Levi said.

Lucy covered her mouth as she laughed. She explained in English, "They keep calling you Charlie because *Charlie's Angels* was very popular on TV back in Hong Kong, and they think you're mysterious and handsome like Charlie."

The other women clearly didn't understand English, because none of them reacted to this; they just looked at Lucy and Levi curiously.

Levi frowned. "Wait a minute, I've seen the movie version of the show, and I don't think you ever saw Charlie—"

Lucy sat up straight, her eyes widening with surprise, and said in Mandarin, "There's a movie?"

Levi seamlessly switched to Mandarin as well. "Well, there's the Charlie's Angels with Farrah Fawcett—"

"Yes, that's the one we saw in Hong Kong."

"That's the old one," Levi said. He tried to hide his smile as all four women looked surprised. "And the movie version, which I believe has the same premise as the old TV show, has one of the angels looking a lot like you."

"Really?" Lucy's eyes threatened to pop out of her head.

Levi nodded. "Sure." He pointed at the plasma screen mounted above the fireplace. "I'm sure you can find it if you search the on-demand catalog. Anyway, I have to get going. I'm going to go follow up on one of the threads for the Cohen case."

Lucy hopped up from the sofa, put her hand on his upper arm, and gave it a slight squeeze. "I'm hoping you'll be a part of this." She was speaking in English once again.

"A part of what?" Levi glanced at the other women, who were all staring at him. Although they couldn't understand what was being said, he lowered his voice anyway. "I told you that I'd help however I can with your contract issue. I don't like it when women are the targets of—"

"You're so American." Lucy touched his cheek and shook her head. "I sometimes forget that. We don't need help taking care of that. And I'm not talking about the Cohen case either. I want you to join my new business."

Levi stared into Lucy's dark eyes. For a moment, he thought he could see vulnerability there. He got the distinct impression that her offer was more than what it seemed.

"One of the spare bedrooms can be yours if you want it," she added. "It'll be easier to make plans that way."

"Lucy... what is it you're really asking? You don't think I'd leave the family, do you? Because I'll tell you right now, that won't happen."

Lucy glanced at the women, who were still staring. "I

know you won't do that, but that doesn't mean you couldn't join us."

"I don't even know what this 'us' is about. What are you girls planning?" He glanced at his watch. "Listen, we'll have to talk later—I have to get going. Are you sure you're safe here?"

Lucy smiled. "Esther is having a small arsenal delivered in the next couple hours. We'll be fine."

Levi pulled his SIG Sauer P229 from the back of his waistband and held it out. "Take this, just in case. It's a nine-millimeter with a round in the chamber, fifteen in the mag, and it's got a very light trigger."

Lucy's mouth dropped open. She looked at the gun and then at him. "But you can't—"

He patted at the other gun he always carried in a shoulder harness. "I've got backup."

"Okay." Lucy took the gun and walked with him to the door. "I'm sorry that I've been so... so... I don't know how to say it." She took a deep breath and seemed to stand a bit taller. "I'm sorry for delaying you."

"It's fine. I'll call you tomorrow."

Levi forced himself to turn away.

As he waited for the elevator to arrive, he couldn't help but worry about those women. Lucy had said that Esther was having a "small arsenal" delivered. That sounded like much more than a few pistols and a rifle. What were those women going to do? And would they do it tonight?

The elevator doors opened, and a chilling thought entered Levi's head.

What if this was the last time I'd see Lucy alive?

"Corner of Utica Avenue and Bergen Street," Levi said as he hopped into the cab.

"Utica and Bergen?" The cabbie was an older guy with a thick New York accent. He began plugging the address in, then paused. "Oh, I know where that is. Seventy-seventh precinct's police headquarters, up near Crown Heights."

"You got it."

After leaving Lucy and the other ladies to whatever mischief they were inevitably going to perpetrate, Levi had taken most of the remainder of the day hunting down Rivka Cohen's signature for Saul's paperwork and then fighting commuter traffic to get back to the lawyer's office. Now, with subpoena in hand, he was going back to Rivka's neighborhood to see if he could flush out a lead on the Cohen case.

His phone buzzed with a text from Doug Mason.

Levi, your name is getting some buzz on a couple networks. You've caught someone's attention, and I wanted you to know. We're trying to trace the queries, but so far, no luck. Watch your six.

After a moment of silent thought, Levi pressed a speed-dial number and put the phone to his ear.

"Hey, Levi, what's up?"

Lowering his voice, he whispered, "Do me a favor. I

might be kicking a hornet's nest at the seventy-seventh precinct when I confront a Detective Carter about the Cohen case. That'll be in about twenty minutes. Do you think you'd have a way to monitor what outgoing communications happen from that precinct while I'm there, and just afterwards?"

"Shit, man, I don't have any way to do that with such short notice. I can reach out to Marty and see if something can be done, but I can't guarantee anything."

"That's fine. I'm not necessarily expecting much to happen, but I figure if it's possible, more eyes on the situation can't hurt."

"I'll do what I can."

"Thanks, buddy. I'll talk to you later." Levi hung up and settled back into the seat, and as the late afternoon traffic built, he closed his eyes.

He had no idea what the detective's reaction would be to the subpoena. This whole thing could backfire in Levi's face. But he had to try.

∽

"Mr. Yoder, how can I help you?"

Levi was taken aback by how young Detective Carter was. He looked like he was barely old enough to order a drink, much less run a murder investigation.

He took two copies of the subpoena out of a manila envelope. "Detective Carter, I'm here to serve a subpoena for records. This is the original copy of the subpoena, and your copy." He handed the detective the duplicate and returned the original to the envelope.

Carter accepted the copy and looked it over. "This says Saul Rosenberg, Esquire, is requesting a copy of a police report on behalf of Mrs. Rivka Cohen. I don't understand. Mrs. Cohen already received a copy of the police report."

Levi smiled. "Oh, so you're familiar with the case?"

The detective's expression suddenly turned dark. "Excuse me, but that's not exactly your business."

Levi handed him a copy of his PI license along with a notarized letter. "Actually, Mrs. Cohen has hired me to look into a few irregularities regarding the police report, and her attorney, Mr. Rosenberg, has requested I act as the courier for the aforementioned police report he's requesting."

The officer's eyes darted back and forth across the paperwork. After a moment, he shrugged. "Wait here a second, let me see what I can do."

The precinct house was surprisingly empty of civilian traffic. Levi drummed his fingers on the counter as he waited, glancing now and then at the large digital clock hanging on the wall.

It took a full ten minutes before the detective returned, looking somewhat apologetic. "Mr. Yoder, I'm afraid I'm not going to be able to give you what you'd like right now. Normally I'd have printed you an official copy, but there's some kind of technical glitch in the computer system. I called downtown where the physical records are kept and asked for copies to be made and forwarded to Mr. Rosenberg's office. Hopefully they'll get there in the next couple days."

Levi made a show of looking disappointed, even

though he'd fully expected this. After all, Denny wasn't able to retrieve the records either. "Do you mind if I ask you some questions about some of the witness testimony referred to in Mrs. Cohen's copy of the police report?"

The lieutenant shook his head. "Not at all, but to be honest, I work on lots of cases and I may be fuzzy on some of the details."

Levi pulled out the redacted copy of the police report and pointed to the accusation of infidelity. "Here it says that Mrs. Cohen's husband had an affair with someone whose name is blacked out. I'd like to investigate the witness further and possibly ask her some questions."

The officer smiled and shook his head once again. "Frankly, I'm surprised anyone is following up on this. I thought this was an open and shut case of a guy having an affair and regretting it badly enough he killed himself. Why are you asking about this now?"

Raising an eyebrow, Levi leaned forward a bit. "Is there a reason why you're not giving me the witness name?"

"No, not at all. I don't remember the name." The detective replied smugly.

"So why was the witness's name blacked out in the report Mrs. Cohen received?"

"I was trying to do the right thing, Mr. Yoder." The lieutenant sighed. "Frankly, I think you're barking up the wrong tree. This is really simple. The witness learned that I was following up on Mr. Cohen's passing and stopped me on the street. She was very distraught over Mr. Cohen's suicide, and she told me everything.

"But at the end, she asked that her name not be part of

the record. She didn't want trouble with Mr. Cohen's family, which is understandable. I think she felt guilty. Of course, I couldn't give her total anonymity, and if Mr. Rosenberg wants to get it through the courts, he'll probably succeed. I purposefully excluded the witness's name from Mrs. Cohen's copy of the report and again, I don't remember her name."

Levi frowned. "Very well. Thanks for your time." He turned away and left through the front doors. As he'd arranged, the cab was coming back from having circled the block, probably countless times by now.

As he hopped into the back of the cab, he handed the cabbie the other half of a hundred-dollar bill. "Park Avenue, Upper East Side."

"You got it, sir."

Levi dialed Lucy's number. It rang five times before the automatic answering service picked up. Levi didn't leave a message.

He let out a deep breath and resolved not to focus on what she might be doing. She was more than capable of handling herself without his interference.

Instead he focused on the detective's words. *She was very distraught over Mr. Cohen's suicide.*

He replayed the interview he'd had with Mindy Cross. When he mentioned Mendel Cohen and she said she didn't know him, her gaze didn't falter, and she showed no outward sign of deception. He'd been watching carefully.

Uncertainty welled up inside Levi as he called Denny. *"Hey, man, what's up?"*

"Remember that Mindy Cross chick from the report?"

"The good-looking blonde? What about her?"

"Can you get me her home address? I want to check something out."

"Hold on a second." Levi heard Denny talking to someone about manning the front, and a minute later he got back on the line. *"I got it here. You want me to text it over?"*

"If you can, yes. I think it's about time I visit her and verify her story." Levi was beginning to have doubts.

"Okay, man. It's on its way."

Levi's phone buzzed with the incoming text message. "Thanks."

He hung up and groaned as he realized this was going to be an even longer day. "Change of plans," he said to the cabbie. "I need to get dropped off over in Queens."

The cabbie nodded. "Okay, you got it. This'll be my last stop for the shift. Where in Queens?"

"It's a place over in Bayside—Bell Avenue and 46th. Any idea how long it'll take to get there?"

The cabbie pulled a hard right onto Eastern Parkway. "With traffic it'll be about half an hour."

"That'll work."

Levi closed his eyes and relaxed as he tried to remember if he'd ever been in that neighborhood. He didn't think so. They'd get there right around when people would begin getting off work.

He'd be waiting for Mindy when she got home.

CHAPTER NINE

Levi felt a bit conspicuous wearing his regular outfit—a dark-gray pin-striped suit with Italian loafers—in this neighborhood. It wasn't what he normally would have chosen for a stakeout. But it would have to do.

The neighborhood was colorful, a mix of all types. Juan, a local Puerto Rican kid was running a three-card monte operation, and he demonstrated a deft hand with the cards as he flipped them over on the large cardboard box that served as his playing table. He'd show the faces of the cards, turn them over, and then quickly rearrange them. One of his buddies pretending to play, but really he was trying to lure in suckers by purposefully not guessing the right card when the dealer was done moving them on the game table. And sure enough, eventually a sucker would step up and bet, and then the dealer's movement became much faster, almost impossible to follow.

Together they were doing a pretty good job of earning a buck or two.

He tried to sucker Levi, but Levi had been on the city streets before Juan was even born, and he managed to turn the tables on him. Then Levi offered a deal: keep the game on the current street corner, and he'd pay the kid fifty bucks. He figured that was a deal that a sixteen-year-old wouldn't ignore, and he was right. And Levi wanted to be surrounded by a crowd. Because here at the corner, he was within sight of a barber shop, a nail salon, and most importantly, the two-story walkup apartments above the storefronts. He'd already checked out Mindy's apartment, but nobody was home.

So he waited.

It wasn't until eight in the evening when a car pulled into one of the parking spots reserved for the residents of the apartments. By now the three-card monte game had broken up, and Levi was standing in the shadows of a broken streetlight.

A woman stepped out of a late-model Subaru, but she wasn't the shapely blonde he'd interviewed. The Subaru beeped once as she unlocked the clear door to the stairs, and a minute later he saw a light come on in Mindy Cross's apartment. A roommate, then.

Levi had no idea what hours a reporter worked. Maybe they worked shifts. He groaned as he realized it might be until after midnight before she got home.

Still he waited.

And at an hour past midnight, he'd had enough.

Stepping out of the shadows, he approached the building. The light in the apartment was still on.

He pressed the button for Apartment 2B.

A voice came through the call panel. *"Mindy?"*

"No, I'm Levi Yoder. I'm a private investigator, and I'm very sorry for coming this late. I'm investigating a case where Miss Cross was a named witness. Do you know where I can find her?"

Sobbing sounded through the speaker, followed by a few seconds of silence. *"No. She's been gone for a day. I have no idea where she is."*

A chill raced up Levi's spine. "Can we maybe talk somewhere for a short bit? I'd like to ask you some questions."

A second passed, and then a buzz announced that the door had been unlocked. *"Come upstairs, but be warned, I have a gun, and I'll use it if you give me reason to."*

Levi took the stairs two at a time. The haggard face of a woman who'd been crying greeted him at the door to Mindy's apartment.

"Mindy always calls me when she's leaving work. She did that the day before yesterday, and as far as I know, she never made it home." The woman's shoulders shook, and she hugged herself as tears streamed down her face. "I just know something's happened."

Despite the woman's flushed face, tear-streaked makeup, and puffy eyes, Levi recognized her. This was the woman in the photo Mindy had shown him.

"You're Karen, aren't you? Mindy's wife?"

The woman rubbed her tears away with the heels of her hands. "How'd you know?"

Levi was now more certain than ever. Mindy Cross, the reporter at the *Intelligencer* who'd denied ever knowing Mendel Cohen, she wasn't the person who was lying.

～

An alert flashed in the security room of the *Intelligencer* building, and an agent glanced at the camera feed. "Antonio, the facial recognition software just tagged an incoming."

A man in a suit had walked through the turnstile entrance and was making for the ground-floor café. The computer had superimposed the name *Levi Yoder* over the well-dressed man.

Antonio rolled his chair over to the bank of monitors to take a look. "Oh, shit, Carl, I remember that guy. He was here a couple days ago talking to that hot chick up on the fifth floor." He zoomed in and turned on the sound.

Yoder was now standing with one of the company's employees, a heavyset man. The computer superimposed the name *Dominic Maroni*.

"Hey," said Maroni. *"I grabbed a table for us to talk."*

As the two men sat, Carl tapped on the screen. "I recognize him. He's an editor over on the fifth."

"Dominic, when's the last time you saw Mindy Cross?"

"I'm not sure. I walked by her cubicle to get to the elevators, and she wasn't there." Maroni frowned. *"Now that I think about it, you know that perfume she wears, it sort of lingers. I haven't noticed it in a while. I guess,*

maybe the last time I saw her was when I introduced the two of you."

Levi suddenly turned and looked over his shoulder, straight into the camera.

Antonio brought his head closer to the monitor. "What the hell is Yoder looking at?"

Levi's gaze was unwavering, and his annoyance was obvious.

"I don't know," said Carl, "but it sure as hell looks like he's staring right at us."

Levi stood. *"Let's go somewhere else. We need to talk in private."*

Antonio nudged Carl. "Contact Mr. M. He gave specific orders about this guy."

Levi groaned as the phone rang on his nightstand. It was just past noon, and he'd only gotten into bed an hour ago.

Without opening his eyes, he reached over and clumsily picked up. "What?"

"Hey, sorry, Levi. I know you had a late night, but there's some Asian lady here who I can't understand a thing she's saying. But I think she's here to see you."

"Tony, I'm not…" Levi sighed and tossed off the covers. "Can you just put her on the phone?"

"Sure. Here she is."

A woman's voice came on the line. *"Charlie? It's Min. Can we talk?"*

It took Levi a moment to kickstart his mind into translating the Mandarin. He really was exhausted. "I guess.

Hand the phone back to Tony. He'll tell you how to find my apartment."

"No, that wouldn't be appropriate. Can you come out so we can walk and talk at the same time?"

Levi groaned again. "Are you serious?"

"Yes. I think you should know something about Lucy."

Levi took a deep breath and tried to psyche himself into getting up. "I'll be down in ten minutes. I need to get dressed."

"I'll wait for you downstairs."

Levi heard a fumbling noise, then Tony's gruff voice returned. *"Should I send her up?"*

"No, she'll wait in the lobby. Just... oh, I don't know. Keep her entertained."

"How the hell am I supposed to do that? She don't speak English."

"Not my problem." Levi hung up, groaned and tried shaking off his mental cobwebs. His only solace was imagining the beefy mafioso trying to entertain the Asian lady with no way of communicating with her.

As he slipped on a clean t-shirt, he grabbed his vest and wondered what Min could possibly have to say that was so important about Lucy.

Levi shook his head and smiled when he stepped off the elevator and took in the bizarre scene. Tony had gotten a card table from the security room and had set up two chairs. He and Min were playing chess, and by the look of the board, the lady was kicking Tony's ass.

Min returned Levi's smile. "He's really terrible. I could have won twice already."

Tony looked from Min to Levi. "What'd she say?"

"She said you're pretty good."

Tony's chest puffed out a bit.

Min stood and shook hands with the mobster. "Thank you," she said in heavily-accented English.

"You're welcome."

Levi motioned to the front door. "You said you wanted to go for a walk?"

Min nodded, and they walked out onto the sidewalk. A black SUV was idling right in front of the building, with an Asian man behind the wheel, his gaze focused on Min.

"Is this yours?" Levi asked.

"Yes. He's waiting for me to be done."

Levi shrugged. "Okay, let's take a lap around the block."

She grabbed his hand, and they walked together along Park Avenue.

Levi looked curiously at their clasped hands. "I didn't think it was customary in Asia for men and women to hold hands like this unless they were a couple. Am I mistaken?"

Min laughed and nudged him with her hip. "Girls who are friends hold hands all the time. I'm just treating you like one of the girls."

"Gee, thanks."

Levi felt the tiny taps from the belt around his chest—

coming from his left. He glanced to the side to see a kid looking in his direction while his mom was talking to another adult.

Denny's new gadget was working well, but of course it didn't know how to distinguish a threat from a staring kid.

As Levi and Min turned the corner, she began. "I've known Lucy for almost fifteen years. She's a very private person, and she would never tell you what I think you should know."

"If she wouldn't tell me, then why are you telling me?"

She shrugged. "That's a good question. I owe Lucy my life. Same with Ting and Ruth, we all do. So many bad things happened when Lucy's husband was murdered, along with our husbands, yet Lucy made sure we all weathered the storm. That's a saying in English, right?"

"It is."

"Well, I'm her friend—no, more than that—she's like my own sister. And I think it would be good for her that you know."

"That I know what?"

Min squeezed his hand and pressed her lips together. They walked in silence for nearly a minute before she said, "Now that I'm here with you... I'm feeling a bit hesitant. She would be furious with me, and I don't want that."

Levi remained silent, giving her space. They soon turned another corner, dodging a couple pedestrians walking in the opposite direction. Finally Levi said, "If you're not comfortable telling me, that's okay. If it's very important that I know, hopefully she'll tell me herself."

Min looked up at him and shook her head. "You don't know her, do you? You're very nice. I can tell. Too nice."

"What is it with you girls? Lucy said the same thing to me. I don't think you understand how *not* nice I can be."

Min nudged him again with her hip. "I'm not talking about your work. I mean inside. You care. I can sense it. And you have feelings for Lucy. Don't you?"

"I don't know," Levi replied honestly. He looked Min in the eyes as they passed the entrance to his apartment, completing a lap around the block.

"When she looks at you, it reminds me of how she looked at her late husband."

Tap tap tap.

Levi turned in the direction of the tapping to see Tony looking at him from the apartment's entrance.

He refocused on Min. "I'm not sure I understand what you're getting at."

"You understand perfectly well. In fact, you understand everything I'm saying."

"Yes, I do, but…" Levi paused on the sidewalk, realizing he'd just been duped. Min had just switched her last two sentences to Cantonese, and he'd responded without hesitation.

Tap.

Levi looked ahead, but couldn't see anything or anyone. Then again, that one was a weak signal, and with Denny's invention, it wasn't uncommon to get some false positives.

Min smiled mischievously. "I was watching you at the apartment. I could tell you were following our conversation. You were able to understand what we were saying. You and Lucy are the same people. Untrusting, but faithful. Harsh, but kind. She'd never tell you this, but I think she cares very deeply about you."

Tap.

Again it came from up ahead. But Levi still saw nothing.

"Okay, but—"

Tap tap.

Without even thinking, Levi pulled Min behind him just before the first bullet struck. It was like a sledgehammer hitting his chest, pushing him off balance. The only reason he didn't fall over was that Min was right behind him.

And then the second bullet hit, slamming into the side of his chest.

The only warning he could give was a grunt. He tasted blood in the back of his throat.

Min screamed and lifted him in a fireman's carry.

The world became blurry as someone nearby gunned an engine, tires screeched and people yelled.

Before he knew what was going on, Min shoved him into the back of the black SUV.

He coughed up blood.

She screamed at the driver in Cantonese. His mind was a jumble and he couldn't make out what she said. Something about a hospital.

His vision flickered and his chest felt heavy, as if a weight was sitting on it. He struggled to breathe.

His life didn't flash before his eyes. But the important people in his life did. His only thoughts were of his mother, and of the kids she was taking care of.

His kids.

Dying wouldn't be so bad. But he regretted not having the chance to say goodbye to them.

The world dimmed. He felt a hand on his face, and heard the soothing sound of words spoken kindly. They held no meaning.

And then the world went dark.

CHAPTER TEN

"This guy must have an angel watching over him. What did the tech say they dug out of his vest? A .338 Lapua round?"

Levi heard the voices talking, but he couldn't even open his eyes to look around. It was like he was floating in space, a mind without a body.

"Yup, I've never heard of such a thing. One of those is supposed to be enough to take down a rhino, yet this guy takes two to the chest and only has a broken rib and a posterior dislocation of the SC joint."

"Doctor Campbell." This voice belonged to a woman. *"Our patient's toes are twitching. He's not all the way down."*

"Shit, I've already put enough into him to knock out a horse." The man's voice was right next to Levi's face. *"It's like he's metabolizing the anesthetic at a ridiculous rate. I can't support putting anything more into him right*

now—his BP is eighty over forty. John, what's the story on the SC reduction? How much longer?"

"Trust me, I'm trying to get this guy off the table as soon as I can. I'm starting to see random muscle spasms as well. Are you sure you can't give him anything?"

"I'm sure. Too risky." The voice near his head changed to a soothing tone. *"Levi, just relax. We're almost done. You're one tough bastard, that's all I can tell you. You managed to come in here with a collapsed lung and a broken rib, and you dislocated the part of your collarbone that attaches to your sternum. And even with all that, and under anesthesia, you're still fighting. You'll be okay. I'm right here watching over your vitals. Doctor Spears is almost done, and we'll have you back on your feet dodging bullets and jumping over tall buildings in no time. Just relax..."*

Even though Levi couldn't feel his body, he willed himself to be calm.

"Whatever you're doing, keep it up. I'm closing." The voice sounded pleased.

Levi slowly became aware of the beeping of a machine. It was keeping pace with his heartbeat. And as soon as he had that thought, it dawned on him that he could feel his heart beating. It was the first sign of his body coming to life.

As the sounds of the world around him grew stronger and more precise, feelings and sensations reappeared all over his body, like pinpricks. He shivered with discomfort as he noticed the cold of the operating room against his skin. A moment later, someone lay warming blankets across his legs.

After some time had elapsed—Levi had no idea how long—he finally managed to open his eyes. A man in blue scrubs and a surgical mask was standing over him.

"Mr. Yoder, are you awake?"

Straining to bring the man's face into focus, Levi nodded weakly. He was about to try to speak when the man shook his head and shushed him.

He extended his arm toward Levi and said, "If you can, grasp the end of this coin."

Through a blurry haze, Levi could see the large coin between the man's thumb and forefinger. There was something familiar about the design, but he couldn't quite place it. The drugs running through his system made his thoughts sluggish. Without thinking any more about it, he lifted his hand and grasped the edge of the coin.

Suddenly, he realized the coin was glowing. It hadn't been doing that before, had it? His mind was a swirl of confusion.

And then, as the man put the coin away, it came to him. This guy was with the Outfit.

"Mr. Yoder, you don't have to worry. You're in a safe place, and we're watching over you."

Levi closed his eyes for what he thought was only a second, but when he opened them again the man was gone.

He was lying in a hospital bed, his left shoulder and chest wrapped in some contraption that prevented him from moving his arm—which was probably wise. The fog affecting his senses was slowly clearing; he knew his body was fighting against the drugs that had put him to sleep.

He hadn't always been this way. But ever since he'd fought back against cancer and won, it was as if his body just… processed everything faster. It was why he couldn't drink alcohol anymore. One shot would almost immediately make him nauseated—the alcohol rushing to his head and making his face flush hot—but within seconds, the effects would dissipate, leaving him with only a headache.

As his senses returned, he felt the pain growing in his chest. Beads of sweat popped up on his forehead. He closed his eyes and took slow, deep breaths. He'd practiced meditation as a means of expanding his senses, but it also helped isolate the pain. It couldn't remove it, but it helped. As he fell deeper into himself, he imagined his body trying to recover.

He'd been shot. He'd never been shot before. Electrocuted, yes. Poisoned, yes. Attacked with a bat, many times.

Being shot sucks.

Footsteps sounded outside his room. Levi opened his eyes again. His vision was much clearer than before.

With a quick knock, his door opened, and a bald man walked in, smiling warmly. The name "Dr. John Spears" was stenciled on his white lab coat.

"Oh good, you're awake. You're looking much better now than when I first met you. How are you feeling, Mr. Yoder?"

"Like I've been run over by a truck." Levi winced as he shifted in the hospital bed.

"Whoa there, killer. Try not to bust any of my stitches." The doctor lightly placed his hand on the sheet covering Levi. "I'm just going to check your dressing."

As the doctor examined him, Levi asked, "Can you fill me in on what I'm dealing with? I mean, I remember getting hit, and I remember tasting blood. What's the damage?"

"It's a lot less than it would have been if you hadn't been wearing body armor." He pointed with one hand just to the left of the center of Levi's chest, and with the other he pointed at a spot on Levi's left side. "You had two shots coming in almost perpendicular to each other. I'm thinking you got hit, turned, and got hit again. It had to be at a distance for you to have survived. But even so, you're a miracle man. I've seen lots of people shot by a heavy sniper round, and very few lived to tell the tale. In fact, I don't know anyone who's taken two shots from a .338 and lived, armor or no armor."

Levi observed the man's expression, demeanor, the way he carried himself, the way he spoke. "You sound like someone who'd know. Let me guess, you're not just a doc. Former SEAL? Army Special Forces?"

The doctor chuckled. "The latter. I'm an 18D, sniper, and yes, I've played a time or two with that type of round."

An 18D was a medical sergeant in the Army's Special Forces. Experts in medical trauma and emergency response.

"Ah," Levi said. "That would explain it. Glad to see

an 18D take care of me. I should have been a cakewalk compared to what you've dealt with in the past."

The doctor smiled—a genuine smile that reached his eyes. Levi sensed a good-naturedness about him and immediately took a liking to him.

"Oh, sure," the doc said. "In fact all you got was a cracked rib, plus part of what connects your collar bone to your chest was popped out of alignment." He pointed to a spot on the left side of his own chest. "You can't see it right now, but I put in a chest tube that's still hanging out of you. That was to treat your collapsed lung."

"Collapsed lung?"

"It's not serious. The tube helped bleed out the air that had collected between your lung and the wall of your chest. But your oxygen levels are back to normal now, so I think that'll be the least of your concerns. I'll have the nurse remove the tube before you leave."

Levi recalled the mysterious blue-smocked man who'd assured him he was being watched. It gave him a feeling of anxiety. "When can I get out of here?"

The doctor scribbled something on the whiteboard hanging on the wall. "You may not realize it, but you were loaded up with a bunch of stuff to keep you under, and we want all of that to works its way out of your system. I'm keeping you overnight to make sure you're managing the pain."

Levi had a very good sense of himself, and despite just having a saline drip hanging from the IV pole, he could feel the presence of the pain-dulling drugs still in his system. "Okay, Doc. Do you have an idea how long before I can start—"

"No exercise with the shoulder for at least two weeks. And then only stretching and light use. Six weeks before you're good to do whatever you're used to doing." He glanced at the clock on the wall. "Any other questions?"

Levi shook his head. "I'm good. And thanks for stitching me up. I won't forget it."

The man patted Levi's knee. "Word of advice: next time, kill them first."

A half hour had elapsed since the doctor's visit, and the pain from Levi's wounds was intense. Whatever drugs had been in him were completely gone, and now he was being accosted by the full ramifications of what had been done to him.

His skin was flushed, and despite the room being kept very cool, he wiped the sweat from his forehead and gritted his teeth.

A woman peeked through the door and smiled. "Oh, good. You're awake."

She walked in, sat on a stool and rolled it over to the side of his bed. She was carrying a clipboard, which she set in her lap. "Mr. Yoder, I'm Karen, the admitting nurse. Doctor Spears has you staying overnight, so you're stuck with us until we can check you out tomorrow. I wasn't here when you were brought to the ER, but it seems like whoever brought you in didn't speak English and disappeared before we could get a translator. We did collect your insurance information from the card you had in your wallet, but as you might expect, we've got some more paperwork to fill out." She smiled ruefully. "Can I ask who brought you in?"

"I don't remember. I think I might have been unconscious." The truth was, Levi remembered exactly who had brought him in, but he wasn't about to tell the nurse anything about Min.

The nurse scribbled something down. "And do you have family members or friends that you'd like me to call?"

"There's no need for that, nurse," said a familiar gravelly voice from the doorway.

Levi looked up and smiled as Vincenzo Bianchi and Frankie Minnelli walked in. They quietly but firmly escorted the nurse from the room.

"It's good to see you, Vinnie." Levi clasped hands with the don of the Bianchi family.

Paulie's six-foot-ten-inch frame appeared at the door. "Don Bianchi, there's a lady heading this way. I'm thinking she'll want in. You want me to—"

"Just give me a minute or two with Levi."

"You got it." Paulie turned to face the hallway, blocking the possibility of anyone getting in.

Vinnie eyed the tubes and wires hanging off of Levi. "Man, when Tony told me you got shot, I thought that was it. Your ticket got punched." He carefully laid his hand on Levi's good shoulder, leaned closer, and whispered, "We looked into who it was that shot you. There was an empty apartment about a block away that had a perfect view of our place. We think the scumbag who got you couldn't have been a professional hitter, because he was careless as fuck. Paulie found a spent shell in the bushes below the apartment's window. A pro wouldn't have let that happen."

Levi shifted in his bed and winced. "Hey, Paulie."

Paulie turned his head to look over his shoulder. "Yeah, Levi?"

"Please tell me you still have that shell and you didn't touch it with your hands."

"What kind of *stunad* do you take me for? Of course I got it, and I used the end of a pencil to pick it up, then had one of the boys bring me a plastic baggie to put it in. Frankie's got someone fingerprinting it and stuff."

"Don't worry about none of that now," Vinnie said. "We'll have you out of here soon enough. I'm making arrangements to get you a nurse and any of this equipment you need."

"Not so fast, there, Mr. Bianchi," said a voice from the hall. Lucy was standing on the other side of Paulie, trying to get a peek into the room, but Paulie kept shifting slightly to block her view.

"Oh, step aside, you giant meatball. I'm not going to hurt him."

Levi couldn't help but laugh—then wince in response to the shooting pains the laughing caused.

"Oh, damn. Don't... don't make me laugh."

Vinnie hitched his thumb toward the door. "That girl of yours has got some moxie." He leaned over and patted Levi on the cheek. "Whatever you decide, just let me know. I'm leaving two guys behind just in case. I don't want to take any chances, if you know what I mean."

Levi clasped hands with Vinnie. "Thanks, man. I appreciate it."

"Forget about it. You're a brother to me. And I promise you one thing: whoever that asshole is that shot you, his ancestors are gonna feel it when we get ahold of him. This *will* be avenged." Vinnie turned toward the door. "All right, Paulie, let the beautiful lady see her man."

Paulie stepped aside, and Lucy shoved her way past him and made a beeline for Levi's side. Levi noticed what looked like real emotion in her eyes.

As soon as Vinnie and Paulie had left and closed the door behind them, that emotion broke through. Lucy's chin quivered, and she grabbed his hand, kissed it, and held it close to her chest. Her voice was thick as she said, "Min told me if you hadn't pulled her out of the way, she would be dead."

Levi had replayed the shooting in his mind, and he couldn't disagree. But why in the world would someone want to shoot Min?

As if reading his mind, Lucy continued, "I'm positive that whoever did this figured they were aiming for me. Those bastards were after *me*." Tears dripped down her cheeks. "And you put yourself in harm's way."

"It's for the best." Levi gave her an evil grin. "I think you knew I was going to help you with your problem even if you didn't want me to. But now, with the don involved, well... whoever's behind this, they're all going to be grease spots."

Without letting go of his hand, Lucy rolled the stool closer with her foot and sat. She rested her head on Levi's good shoulder and whispered, "I don't want to see you hurt."

Levi kissed the top of her head. "Then start listening to me. I'm going to help with this. It was personal before, but now I owe them payback."

"But you're injured. You can't—"

"I'll get better, and *then* we do this."

Lucy lifted her head to look at him, their faces only inches apart. "I'll wait, but only if you come home with me and let me take care of you. I owe you my life."

"No, it was Min I—"

"Levi, shut up." Lucy leaned in and pressed her lips against his.

As they breathed each other's air, it felt to Levi as though she'd taken off a veil that had been obscuring his ability to sense her feelings. There was a connection that hadn't been there before. Something had changed.

She broke off the kiss, and her eyes shined with unshed tears. "Are you going to let me take care of you, for once?"

Levi lay his head back against the pillow as exhaustion washed over him. He closed his eyes and squeezed her hand. "Only if you answer that nice nurse's questions. I hate doing paperwork."

Lucy laughed and then cursed in Cantonese. "Just like my husband!"

Levi struggled to form words, but managed to say in Cantonese, "Is that a proposal?"

She gasped. "You know Cantonese?"

Levi's only response was a light snore.

CHAPTER ELEVEN

Even though Lucy's apartment building was still under construction, there were now armed security guards checking IDs before anyone could even get near the elevator. And when the elevator opened onto the eighteenth floor, Levi was immediately greeted by two more armed guards. They bowed as Lucy, holding Levi's right arm, escorted him down the hall, followed by two made men from the Bianchi family.

As they entered Lucy's apartment, three beaming Asian women were waiting to greet him. All wore red *cheongsams*, a traditional Chinese body-hugging dress. The apartment smelled of home-cooked food, which gave the place a homey feel that hadn't been there earlier.

Lucy barked out in Cantonese, "I'll go prepare his bed. Min and Ting, please help with the congee. Ruth, I need..."

As Lucy continued issuing orders, Levi turned to the two mobsters, Tony and Gino. He gave Tony a friendly smack on the shoulder. "Thanks for coming along."

Levi's first encounter with Tony hadn't been a friendly one. Levi had been forced to almost break the large man's wrist. But since then, they'd become friends. Tony was someone Levi trusted.

Tony shook his head. "Levi, by my mother's soul, when I saw you go down, I thought you'd been whacked for sure. I can't believe that barely a day later, you're up and walking around." He nodded toward the three *cheongsam*-clad women, who were all departing to do their assigned jobs, and winked. "Though I think I know why you chose this place instead of ours. I like the scenery here."

Lucy looked amused by this remark, but she raised an eyebrow at Levi as if daring him to comment on the "scenery" as well.

"I'll be fine here for a bit," Levi said to Tony. "Go ahead and tell Frankie where I am, and if he really needs me, I've got my phone. I especially want to know if anything comes up on that asshole who shot me."

Tony nodded. "I'll pass word to Mr. Minnelli. Is there anything else you need?"

"Nah, I'm good."

Tony and Gino departed, and Lucy closed the door behind them, then turned to face Levi.

"I don't want you to argue with me," she said. "At least for a little bit. Let me do this my way."

"Do what?"

Lucy wrapped her arm around his, pulled him into the dining room, and sat him down. "Sit here and don't move. I'll go check on your room and sort through your bag of personal possessions from the hospital. We'll probably have to get rid of some of your clothes."

"Don't get rid of the suit jacket or my vest."

"But they're ruined."

"Trust me, Esther will kill me if she doesn't get a chance to take a look at how that stuff performed."

Lucy laughed. "Okay, I won't throw anything out. Now just sit here, and I'll be right back. We're going to get some nutrition into you and then into bed. You need time to heal."

Levi was about to argue about being babied, but instead he simply nodded. "I'll be right here."

Lucy smiled—an expression he wasn't used to seeing from her.

When Levi was left alone, he pulled out his phone. First he texted Lola Minnelli, Frankie's aunt. She was the closest thing to a den mother the mob family had, which put her in charge of all the housekeeping workers that were on contract to the family. He would need her to arrange to get him at least a couple days' worth of clothes.

Then he switched screens and hit a hotkey. The phone rang twice before Denny's voice came through.

"Oh, shit. Levi, which hospital they got you at, I'll come—"

"I'm not in the hospital anymore."

"But I heard you got shot... twice!"

"Believe me, I'm well aware. I'm fine. The suit and my vest took the brunt of it. I need you to do me a favor."

"Anything."

"I need a complete forensic workup on that detective from the police report that doesn't exist anymore. John Carter."

"I can do that. Anything in particular you're looking for?"

"I'm not sure. But he's the one who claimed to have taken the testimony from Mindy Cross—and I'm now certain he was lying about that, because Mindy has now gone missing. Her wife filed a missing persons report and is losing her mind with worry. It all seems really convenient, if you know what I mean."

"Damn, that's some serious conspiracy stuff going on. I'm getting a little paranoid about this case. And I'll bet you that Mindy suddenly electronically disappears from everywhere, too. Hey, I assume you don't mind if I lean on these Outfit guys to help? I know you're a little iffy on them, but I don't have access to some of the historical snapshots of the internet databases that they do."

Levi suddenly recalled from the drug-blurred recesses of his memory a scene from the hospital. A scene involving a glowing coin. And he remembered what the blue-smocked stranger had said.

We're watching over you.

Min walked into the dining room and laid a steaming bowl of white rice porridge on the travertine table's lazy Susan.

"Sure, Denny, do what you have to. I'm not sure what

to make of those guys, but they haven't yet screwed me over."

"Okay, I'll dig on Carter and see where it leads. And while I'm at it, I'll poke around to see if anything pops up on Mindy Cross. Is there anything else I can do? I mean, I assume you're not one-hundred percent right now."

Ting appeared with a tray of grilled whole mackerel, and Ruth trailed behind with a tray of cut-up watermelon and cantaloupe, along with an assortment of spoons, bowls, and chopsticks.

Levi felt his mouth watering. "No, I'm not one hundred percent, but working my way up to it. If you can, have Esther Rosen—"

"There's no need," Lucy said as she entered. "I just called her. She'll be over tomorrow to take a look at the damage."

"Never mind, Denny, Esther's taken care of. So, no, I don't need anything else. Just get me the data as soon as you have it."

"Roger that. Take care of yourself."

As Levi hung up, he surveyed the spread laid out on the table. "You girls are going to spoil me," he said in Mandarin. He looked at Min, Ruth, and Ting, who had all taken seats on the opposite side of the table. "This looks and smells fantastic."

The three women smiled and said, "It's nothing," in unison. A typical Chinese response to any compliment.

Levi reached for a bowl, but Lucy stepped up beside him and lightly smacked his hand. "You only have one working arm. Let me do this."

Levi sat back, trying hard to keep his amusement

from showing on his face. It had been a very long time since anyone had taken care of him, and it wasn't something he was used to.

Lucy turned the lazy Susan so the rice porridge rotated into reach, ladled a bowl full, and placed it in front of Levi. "Start with that. It should be easy on your stomach."

"My stomach is just fine."

Levi picked up a spoon. He felt the stares of all four women as he sampled some of the plain hot congee. No pressure.

It had the consistency of watery oatmeal, but it was very smooth going down, and he detected a hint of ginger and soy sauce mixed in for flavoring. It was plain, but good.

He took several more spoonfuls before looking around at the others. "Is anyone else going to eat?"

Lucy gathered some steamed white rice into another bowl, piled on a few pieces of grilled mackerel, then added some vegetables that might have been steamed or pickled. It wasn't until she had placed that next to his bowl of congee that the rest of the women began serving themselves.

Ruth held a piece of the mackerel in her chopsticks and pointed it at Levi. "You need to eat a lot of this. It has special oils to help keep your bones strong."

Ting sipped at the congee and nodded in agreement. "Also the congee is full of protein. It'll help your healing."

Min reached across the table with her chopsticks and placed several more carrots and cabbage into Levi's bowl.

"You need more of the pickled vegetables to help keep your muscles healthy."

Lucy covered her mouth as she laughed. "You poor guy," she said in English. "The look on your face says it all. Having four Chinese mother hens clucking over you has to be stressful. I'm sorry. You'll learn that every Chinese person is an amateur doctor, and special food is always on the list of cures."

Levi shrugged—then winced as his immobilized shoulder complained. Eating was not a problem for him. In fact, he'd been starving, and the food, though it wasn't exactly his favorite, was fresh, palatable, and appreciated. True, he wasn't accustomed to being watched over by four mother hens. But he had to admit, it wasn't the worst way to recuperate.

Levi forced himself to eat until he truly couldn't take another bite, but it was nearly an hour before the women concluded he really was full.

As Ting, Ruth, and Min cleared the dishes, Lucy helped Levi up from the table and led him from the dining room. "We got you some pajamas and basic clothes. I'll help you with your bath before you get into bed."

Levi stopped. "I can bathe myself just fine."

Lucy gave him a stern look. "I heard what the doctors said about your drain tube. You shouldn't bathe for two weeks until your skin is healed. And you can't exactly sponge-bathe yourself."

For the first time in ages, Levi felt himself blush. She had a point.

Lucy pulled on his arm and led him to a bedroom with an attached bathroom suite. She shook her head. "Really. Who'd have thought someone like you would be bashful?"

Levi sensed her amusement. "You're enjoying making me uncomfortable, aren't you?"

She began unbuttoning his shirt. "Absolutely. Now be quiet and stop arguing."

Levi lay comfortably on the bed, his hair still damp from being washed by Lucy, who'd taken her task very seriously. In fact, she'd taken the whole bathing thing quite seriously. She didn't stop until she'd ensured that every square inch of him had been scrubbed to her satisfaction. After a minute of awkwardness on his part, Levi just pretended that she was a nurse.

Afterward, feeling a bit warm, he'd opted for only boxers and a thin sheet, but even that was too much.

He wasn't feeling warm from a fever. He'd had fevers before—maybe not in a long time, not since his bout with cancer, but he knew what they felt like, and this felt different. His eyes didn't have the sticky feverish feel that he remembered having. And he wasn't woozy; in fact his mind was clear as a bell.

But ever since the surgery, he'd felt anxious. As if something within him wasn't exactly right. Maybe that anxiety was manifesting itself in his body as heat.

He flipped off the sheet, let the cool tendrils of air-conditioned air float across him, and closed his eyes, forcing himself to relax. He employed a form of mediation he'd learned from a guru in India. The deeper he fell into himself, the more he could get a sense of everything around him.

The sound of his heart beating grew louder in his ears. He heard the flutter of a piece of paper as the air circulated through the room.

And then, nearby, he heard the sound of soft footsteps.

He breathed deeply, and took in the smell of jasmine as his door opened.

It was Lucy.

Even with his eyes closed, he felt her presence, standing in the doorway, watching him.

Without opening his eyes, he said, "Thank you."

She entered the room and approached the bed. Levi felt the mattress give slightly as she lay down beside him.

Levi opened his eyes. She was wearing silk shorts and a loose pajama top.

She put a finger to his lips and said, "Shh." She nuzzled her face into the crook of his neck and draped her right leg over his. "I have to wake you in two hours for your antibiotic."

"I have the alarm set for it."

"Good." She draped her hand gently on his stomach. "Get some sleep."

He took in a deep breath. The pain in his chest was still substantial, but not nearly as bad as it was earlier. As

Lucy's scent wafted over him, he focused once again on his breathing.

And as he lay there, counting the seconds as they went by, he wondered why Lucy was suddenly so different around him. Less sex kitten and tease, and more… more something else.

He didn't even get to forty-five seconds before he was sound asleep.

CHAPTER TWELVE

"Okay, Denny. What have you got?"

"That detective you had me look into. He's definitely on the take. He got four payments of seventy-five hundred dollars last month from some account out of Argentina."

"That's an odd amount." Levi sat up on his bed and winced as he stretched the muscles around his ribcage.

"Actually, not that strange if you're trying to avoid reported income. Money transfers under ten K won't get flagged by anyone. The thing that's odd is, we can't exactly tell who owns the account where the money came from. There's a lot of hinky stuff going on in that country's banking system, especially if you're in political power and pull some favors from the banking regulators. Either way, the guy's got some financial skeletons in his closet that I managed to dig up, besides the recent strange payout. Seems our guy isn't exactly being honest with the

IRS about lots of his past payments. You and yours might be interested."

Levi nodded. "That's good. Send me everything you've got and I'll see what kind of leverage that gives us."

"Will do."

~

"I know it sucks, Levi, but the fingerprints didn't lead anywhere. We even gave copies to Denny to do his magic, and he didn't get anything either."

Levi gritted his teeth in frustration as he absorbed what Frankie had just said.

Lucy walked into his bedroom with a glass of water in one hand and his dose of antibiotics in the other. She paused, a look of concern on her face.

"Frankie, I appreciate the effort. And as to the car, I don't need a driver. I can make it on my own just fine. I'm almost back to one hundred percent."

"Levi, I know you're a badass and all that, but Vinnie would kill me if anything happened to you and he found out I'd let you go without any backup."

Lucy's furrowed brow almost made him laugh. She was giving him the stare of death.

"Fine. Who's coming and when?"

"Paulie should be there any minute."

"All right, Frankie. Thanks again."

"Sure thing. And say hi to all the ladies for me."

"Will do."

Levi hung up, and before he could say another word,

Lucy snapped, "Where the hell do you think you're going? You're not even a week past your surgery."

Levi buttoned his shirt over the new vest Esther had just delivered that morning. "Can't talk. Paulie's going to be here any minute."

Lucy gave him a withering glare. "You're not going anywhere without me."

He shrugged and took the antibiotics and water from her. Downing both, he looked her up and down appraisingly. She was wearing a silk robe, with likely nothing else underneath. "Fine. If you want to come, then come. I'm leaving in five minutes."

"Five minutes?" Lucy's eyes widened. "Don't leave without me." She hurried out of his bedroom.

Levi chuckled as he reached for his loafers. The pain along the left side of his chest was still there, but it was no longer so bad that it prevented him from moving. He slipped his shoes on and was walking toward the front door when his phone buzzed.

"Hey, Paulie. You downstairs?"

"I'm about a minute away."

Lucy came running into the foyer. Min trailed after her with a belt, yelling in Cantonese, "You forgot this."

"You didn't tell me where we're going," Lucy complained to Levi as she threaded the belt through the loops of her curve-hugging skirt.

Levi saw that she was dressed a bit more upscale than was appropriate for where he was heading. But he merely opened the door and smiled. "It's a surprise."

Lucy smacked Levi's leg. "Why didn't you tell me you were visiting your mother and kids? I wouldn't have dressed like this."

Levi laughed, but Paulie glanced back at her from the driver's seat and said, "If you don't mind my saying so, I don't think any mother would care what you're wearing."

"Bah." She waved dismissively at the giant mobster. "None of you men understand. I shouldn't be wearing such a short skirt to see his mother."

Levi gently placed his hand on her leg. The skirt reached the top of her knee, which, as far as he was concerned, was perfectly acceptable for any occasion, business or otherwise. He leaned in and whispered in Mandarin, "My mother isn't exactly aware of fashion trends. She wouldn't know what's proper or not proper for a city girl. And I told you before, you look fine."

Lucy curled her lip with disdain. "'Fine.' I hate that word."

Levi smiled.

The SUV bounced lightly on the uneven dirt path leading to the house. The unusual sight of a car driving onto the rural Pennsylvania property caught the attention of some of the kids, who began running over. By the time Paulie parked, a crowd had gathered, with more kids on the way.

Levi opened the door and was greeted by shouts of "Daddy Levi! Daddy Levi!" Within seconds he was surrounded by kids ranging in ages from six to eleven, all wearing modest, dark dresses with white prayer caps. They jostled each other trying to give Levi a hug.

Ignoring the pain in his shoulder and chest, Levi

hugged them all back. The muscles in his cheeks grew weary from smiling so much.

Of course, none of these kids were biologically his, but to him that didn't matter in the least. He couldn't have loved them any more if they'd been his own. In fact, these girls were a relief to his aching soul—the one wholesome and pure thing in his life.

He'd rescued them from the streets of the city. All of them were foreign-born, and all had become victims of the slave trade. Many had been sold by their own parents in countries scattered throughout East Asia. Some had even been placed in underage sex rings.

No more.

It had nearly broken his heart to see them in the conditions they'd been put in. But now, seeing their happy, smiling faces, he hoped that eventually their troubled pasts would be a dim memory divorced from their current life.

He'd already made arrangements for their long-term well-being. He'd prepaid their college expenses and had set up trust funds so that when they turned twenty-two, they'd receive modest monthly stipends. They'd never be dependent on anyone ever again—no matter what happened to him.

"Miss Lucy?" Mei, one of his nine-year-olds, ran up to Lucy and gave her a big hug. She began chattering in Pennsylvania Dutch, and Alicia, Levi's eldest, translated into Cantonese for Lucy.

Lucy knelt so that she was face to face with Mei. She asked in Cantonese, "How are you doing?"

Mei gave Lucy a puzzled expression and shook her head. She looked uncomfortable.

Alicia said, "Mei lost her words. She doesn't remember much about before."

"But Mei, you remember me?" Lucy asked in English.

Mei smiled and nodded. In surprisingly good English, she said, "You came to visit before, and you were very nice. I remember that."

Hugging a kid in each arm, Levi felt guilty about not visiting more often. He'd heard of kids blocking out painful memories of abuse, and it sounded like Mei had done exactly that.

"Levi!"

Levi turned in the direction of the voice. His mother, dressed very much like the kids, wiped her hands on her apron as she stepped onto the front porch of the house he was born in. She held out her arms, and he jogged over to her with a smile.

She clasped his face in her hands and squeezed his cheeks. "It's so good to see you. Are you here for long?"

Levi heard the trudging of many feet, and looked back to see Lucy being pulled forward by Mei and a gaggle of kids, all smiling and excited.

He motioned to Lucy. "Mom, this is Lucy. I think—"

"Oh, yes. I remember you. You came several months ago, but that was without my boy." Mom shook hands with Lucy, then turned to Levi and asked in Pennsylvania Dutch, "Is she a *special* friend?"

Levi laughed, then whispered loudly to Lucy, "She wants to know if we're courting."

"Oh!" Lucy blushed.

Levi had to fight to keep his mouth from dropping open. A blush? From Lucy?

Apparently that reaction was answer enough for his mother, as she smiled broadly and clapped her hands with delight. "That's lovely. You're both able to stay for dinner, right?"

"Mom, I'm sure I don't need to ask, but is there enough food for one more? He's in the car."

"Of course there's enough," Mom said with indignation.

Levi waved at the car, motioning for Paulie to join them. The big mobster got out and jogged over. Several of the kids gasped as he approached.

"He's a giant," one kid said.

Levi laughed. "Kids, say hi to Mr. Romano."

"Hi, Mr. Romano," they all said in unison.

Mom clapped her hands to get the kids' attention, then began barking orders like a drill sergeant, except in Pennsylvania Dutch. The kids scattered to finish chores or help with dinner.

Then Levi's mom looked up at the giant mobster. "Welcome to our home. Please wash up, and I'll have dinner ready in fifteen minutes."

"Yes, ma'am."

Levi led Paulie and Lucy through the Yoder home, dodging kids and feeling a warmth inside him that he could only translate as happiness. He needed this. Family. Home. Even though he lived elsewhere, some small part of him would always live here.

Two weeks had passed since he'd been shot, and Levi was absolutely done being a patient. With the shoulder brace long gone and his flexibility at nearly one hundred percent, he was ready for the argument Lucy was going to give him about going out.

What he wasn't expecting was her throwing a karate gi at him and saying, "The doctor said 'six weeks,' and it hasn't even been half that. You're not going out there on your own until you can show me that you're healed."

Levi held up the gi, feeling amused. "What? You're going to fight me?"

Lucy gave him a stern look he was all too familiar with. "If it comes to that, yes."

Levi removed his shirt and jeans and began putting on the karate outfit. In his time living here with Lucy, he'd lost any sense of shyness or modesty. There was nothing she hadn't seen. It was almost like they were married, even though they'd never actually been intimate in any real way. They had a very different kind of closeness now... one that was hard for him to label.

When he was dressed, he followed Lucy to the workout room, where the floor had been laid out with gym mats. These were much softer than the tatami mats he'd trained on in Japan.

It suddenly dawned on him that he and Lucy had never worked out together, and she had no idea what his level of training was. He had to assume hers was extensive, given she had once served as her husband's bodyguard.

Lucy was barefoot, with loose white pants and a long pink shirt with a Hello Kitty logo on it. Not exactly workout clothes, but they allowed for unrestricted movement. She stood without a ready stance, just like any normal person would be standing on the street, and said, "Prove to me you're okay to go."

Levi felt awkward as he stretched, watching her watching him. Her eyes were focused on his feet, which was smart, because the feet often gave away an opponent's next move.

He tested her reaction time by flipping out a quick jab, aimed at her face.

She dodged with her upper body, not even using her hands. But she did shift her stance slightly.

Levi was also watching her as he tossed a quick snap kick to her midsection, testing her blocking.

With a sweeping motion of her arm, she pressed the kick aside and launched into a volley of attacks. Kick, kick, jab, back fist, all in rapid succession.

All of which Levi blocked—eliciting a smile from her.

Lucy yelled as she dove low, attempting to sweep his legs out from under him.

Levi hopped out of reach, and before she could completely reset, he charged, slamming himself into her and then dodging as she swung an elbow to his shoulder, barely missing her mark.

His heart was thudding loudly, and he felt a rush of adrenaline. He was ready for the fight.

And then he realized Lucy was grimacing and holding her chest where he'd hit her.

She was in pain.

Nothing else mattered as he ran toward her. "Are you—"

She swept his legs out from under him and was on him like a tiger. Punch, block, punch, block, and on her third punch he trapped her arm under his and wrapped his other arm around her in a bear hug.

As they rolled on the floor of the gym, Lucy began to laugh. It was obvious Levi had her in a compromising position. She couldn't attack him, but he couldn't do much either without changing grips. Then she rested her forehead on his, angled closer and gave him a sweaty kiss.

"You're much faster than I thought you'd be," she said.

They separated, lying on their backs, staring up at the twelve-foot ceiling.

"So, you're convinced I'm all better?" Levi said.

She put her hand on his and gave it a squeeze. "You're not all better yet, but I suppose you're good enough."

"Gee, thanks."

"That was a compliment."

Levi smiled. "So, what are you going to do today?"

"The three of us are going to be stalking our prey." Before Levi could comment on that, she put her hand over his mouth. "I don't plan to do anything more than observe, at least until you're with me. I promised you that. So what's your plan?"

"Oh, nothing too serious. Remember that police report the Cohens had gotten?"

"Yes."

Levi lifted one knee to his chest and then the next, stretching his hamstrings. "Turns out the detective who did some of the witness interviews was dirty, and he'd falsified witness testimony. Some of the boys have gotten some other interesting data from him, so I'm going to take a small team and see what we can learn about whoever is behind this Cohen murder mystery."

Lucy gave his hand a kiss. "Be careful."

"You too."

Levi stretched his arms above his head and felt only the slightest tightness around his chest. He was definitely not yet one-hundred percent, but like Lucy said, it was good enough.

It was now time for Levi and some of the Bianchi boys to take advantage of the mysterious dead drop they'd just learned about.

On West 54th Street in Hell's Kitchen, Levi used a piece of chalk to place a mark on the red brick building adjacent to an empty lot. Then he calmly crossed the street and joined Tony and Gino inside an auto glass shop. The owner of the shop wasn't a mafioso, but he was friends with Gino, and was more than willing to host an operation without asking any questions.

"Now we wait," Gino said with a heavy New York accent. He was seated on a stool, looking out the window. It was just past ten in the morning, and there weren't many pedestrians on the quiet, mostly residential street.

Gino was one of the Bianchi family's second-story guys—a short, muscular brute with a buzz cut and a scar running along his jawline. Levi hadn't worked with him before, but knew his reputation. He was an expert with locks, security systems, and gathering information. Those abilities had earned him the honor of becoming a member of *La Cosa Nostra*, the mafia. A trusted member of the Bianchi crew.

"Gino, tell me again what the detective told you about the pickup," Levi said.

Gino didn't take his gaze from the window. "It's a simple dead drop. When he wants to leave a message, he drops it behind the barrier that's blocking off the empty lot, and marks the building with white chalk."

"It's like something out of a spy novel," Tony said.

"How do they make sure nobody else takes whatever gets dropped behind the barrier?" Levi asked.

Gino snickered. "Believe it not, he gets a dead rat, guts it, sticks whatever message he wants inside its body, and then sews it back up. Nobody's gonna fucking pick up some mangy rat even if they saw a cop drop it."

Levi nodded with appreciation. "That's smart."

"I don't like smart," Tony groused. "It's trouble."

Tony was the muscle for today's operation. With a powerlifter's body and a streak of impatience, he was dangerous—but loyal. And since Levi hadn't fully healed yet, he was okay with letting Tony take the point position.

It was almost noon when Gino hissed, "Hey, we've got something."

Levi hopped off his chair and walked over. A tall man

in a threadbare shirt and worn, faded pants was peering over the barrier into the empty lot. The man then glanced up and down the street as if looking for somebody.

"Are you sure he can't see us?" Tony said.

"Nah." Gino shook his head. "We're behind one-way glass. But is that the guy? He looks like a bum."

"He's no bum," Levi said. "Look at his hiking boots Those are probably worth ten times more than the rags he's got on. This guy's playing the bum, but I'd bet you a hundred bucks he isn't."

"No way," Gino said. "That's a sucker's bet."

The man gave one final glance their way, then slipped into the empty lot. Ten seconds later he re-emerged, his gaunt face looking angry, and walked briskly off to the west.

Levi patted both men on the shoulders. "Ears in, let's go."

All three men inserted what looked like in-canal hearing aids.

"Test one, two, three," Levi said.

"I got you," Tony whispered, but it came through loudly in Levi's ear.

"Same here," Gino said.

The devices were working perfectly. Another one of Denny's specialty items.

The three men stepped outside, and Gino climbed over the barrier into the empty lot. *"I'm heading to Fifty-Fifth Street so I can approach from a different angle. Tell me which way the guy's going and I'll catch up."*

Levi was wondering how the hell Gino was going get

through the buildings behind the lot, but then he spotted him climbing a fire escape and vanishing onto the roof.

He and Tony took opposite sides of the street as they began following their mark. Levi opened up a map, making it look like he was a tourist.

Up ahead, their quarry took a turn. "Gino, he's hanging a right on Tenth Avenue."

"Gotcha, I'm jogging up Fifty-Fifth."

Levi crossed the street and caught up with Tony, who had just turned onto Tenth.

Gino voice broke in, *"I see him. He's heading west on Fifty-Fifth. I'm on him. Wait—he just turned into the GMC parking garage."*

Levi snapped his fingers and pointed at where Tony had parked on the corner of Tenth Avenue and West Fifty-Sixth. "Tony, go get the car and come around."

Tony nodded and raced north, while Levi dodged traffic to get across Tenth Avenue.

Gino voice broke in again. *"Hey, buddy. I can fix that dent really cheap. No, no... hey, I'm talking here. Bastard!"*

Levi hurried left on Fifty-Fifth. "Gino, what's going on?"

"Hold on, I'm writing his plate down. He's in a beige older-model Camry. And I got close enough to slap a tracer on his roof."

Tires squealed as Tony turned hard at the intersection and pulled up in front of the parking garage. Levi and Gino hopped in.

The second-story man pointed west. "He's heading toward the riverfront."

As Tony accelerated, Levi pulled up the tracking app on his phone. A blip showed their quarry's location. "We have a fish on the line," he said. "Now to reel him in."

CHAPTER THIRTEEN

As Dominic walked into the *Intelligencer*'s war room where all the editorial staff had been summoned, site security was eyeballing badges and repeating, "Turn off all cell phones." Dominic quickly grabbed a spot at the conference room table. The room didn't have enough seats to accommodate everyone, and he didn't want to be one of the ones stuck standing.

The place was indeed packed when, at five minutes past nine, Raul Vicente, the *Intelligencer*'s executive editor, walked in. In Dominic's opinion, the guy was a real asshole. Fortunately the only times Dominic had had to deal with him directly were when he was appealing an editorial decision made by the managing editor about one of his desk's articles. Though he didn't know why he even bothered with the appeals—the guy always rubber-stamped the managing editor's decision, no matter how idiotic it was.

Vicente walked to the front of the room and began pacing. "I think you know why I've called the entire editorial staff together. It's because of the egregious mistakes made in last Wednesday's issue. I go on vacation for one week and you guys fuck shit up so badly that you cost us nearly a hundred thousand subscribers! If you nimrods haven't done the math yet, that's over fifteen million dollars just in subscription fees alone—and that's before we talk about the impact to advertisers. That's *your* salaries being flushed down the toilet. If something like this happens again, I will have no problem replacing each and every one of you with a goddamned trained monkey who knows how to follow directions. I hope I'm being clear."

Dominic felt himself getting hot under the collar. Everyone in the room knew exactly what article had gotten subscribers so upset. He himself had been shocked when he saw that the paper had actually printed something favorable about Israel. Although the *Intelligencer* had always claimed to be fair and evenhanded with the news, that had never been true. They were always slanting things in ways that catered to their audience's preferred narratives. Even their hard news reporting had ways to tilt the narrative to maximize profits.

Vicente continued. "Honestly, I don't know how you could even fuck this one up. Seven innocent Palestinian kids were murdered by the Israeli army... and we actually sided with the fucking Israelis? Are you shitting me?"

One of the women in the room raised her hand. "Sir?"

"What is it, Cheryl?" Vicente snapped.

"Mr. Vicente, the Israeli government released video

footage showing that group of kids attacking two Israeli soldiers at a checkpoint. The soldiers were defending themselves, and there was also corroborating video footage from—"

"We don't portray Israel as the victim, *ever*!" Vicente's voice echoed in the room, his face red with anger. "And we're certainly not going to say that *above the fold*—even if those kids were a horde of screaming banshees led by the ghost of Yasser Arafat. Our readers don't want to hear that narrative, and you know it! What's wrong with you people?"

With his hand in his pocket, Dominic pressed a button on his old-school mini-cassette recorder and began recording. This was too much. He'd been at the Intelligencer for years, and he'd watched as the paper gradually skewed further and further away from even-handed narrative. But now, the old man had totally lost his mind—and it was time for that to come out into the open. Dominic had gotten into journalism to bring information to the people, not to spoon-feed them a carefully constructed narrative.

"Let me repeat, our readers don't want to hear about the righteous killing of kids near the Gaza Strip. We shape the news to the audience—"

"Are you suggesting we lie?" asked one of the younger editors, sounding concerned.

"No, you retard. We never lie. But the emphasis we place on news items should match what our readership wants to hear. That keeps them renewing their subscriptions. We're not devoting inches of print to the Israeli government being the good guy—not ever. We're selling a product here, people."

The executive editor stopped pacing and glared at the room for a full ten seconds before continuing.

"Let me also remind you about our policy regarding transparency. You have a problem with our editorial decisions? You have a problem with how your copy was treated? You leave that shit inside these walls. You don't *ever* use Twitter, or any other social media, to give your own narrative. Your time is the company's time. If you don't understand that, you can get the fuck out. Am I clear?"

Dominic bobbed his head like all the others, but he tuned out the madman as he ranted about how great a responsibility they all had to shape the news for the people. To manage the truth. To be the official record of what really happened.

All without lying, of course.

Dominic knew better. People were sheep who only read the headline. Maybe the first few paragraphs. That was it. Hardly anyone read more than that, because they were lazy. They depended on people like him to deliver the truth in bite-sized pieces.

He looked around the room at all the editors listening attentively to the top guy spewing his propaganda, and he began to wonder if it was it even possible to deliver the truth anymore.

The meeting continued, but for Dominic, it was all a buzz of nonsense. He felt a hollow pit in his stomach, and his mind wandered to Mendel Cohen. How many of his articles had been sacrificed because of the bullshit this guy was talking about?

Maybe it didn't matter. Mendel was dead, and—

Suddenly he thought of that intense mafioso he'd met with twice before. That guy had really left an impression. Sure, any time he sat down with a member of the mob it gave him the willies, but this guy was different. It felt like this Levi person could see right through all his bullshit and bluster, and read Dominic's mind.

Levi's words came floating back. *What would you say if I told you that the cops claim Mendel had an affair with her?*

Mindy Cross. God, she was pretty. And now her cubicle was empty, with no word whatsoever on where she had gone, or why. Had she quit? Nobody on the floor seemed to know.

He wondered if the two events were related in some way. Mendel's death, and Mindy's disappearance. Levi had asked about the girl the last time they'd met, but that was before her cube had been cleared. He should probably let the guy know about that. It couldn't hurt to be on the good side of one of Don Bianchi's men.

The rant, and the meeting, ended ten minutes later, and everyone made their way out of the room. But as Dominic exited, a security guard stopped him.

"Mr. Maroni, may I see your phone please?"

Dominic turned to the guard, who looked like he'd been hired straight out of central casting for the role of Chief Legbreaker. "My phone?"

The man held out his hand. "Yes, your phone, please."

Dominic pulled his phone from his suit pocket and handed it over. The guard powered it on, studied it for a moment, then handed it back.

"Sorry, just a routine check."

Dominic frowned as the guard walked toward the security office.

What the hell was that about? Routine check? The man didn't "routinely check" anyone else's phone.

Feeling anxious, Dominic took the escalator to the ground floor, walked outside, and dialed a number. After four rings, Levi's recorded voice came on the line. *"Leave me a message."*

"Mr. Yoder, I think we need to talk. Miss Cross seems to have either quit or been fired—no one's sure which, but her cubicle has been cleared out. And I also have a recording that I'm somewhat reluctant to share, but I think you should know about it. It may be related to the stuff you were asking about."

Dominic had just stepped around the corner, intending to take a walk and clear his mind, when something hard smashed against the back of his head. His knees buckled, and he collapsed to the pavement.

He was so overcome with sudden nausea that he barely noticed the hands rifling through his pockets. And then everything went dark.

Lucy glanced at the clock on the dashboard of the parked, darkly tinted Town Car. It was another fifteen minutes before the mass would start. "Are you sure

Xiang is going to be coming this way?" she asked in Cantonese.

"Yes." The driver, who had been one of her paid neighborhood informants for years, nodded emphatically as he looked through the windshield at 41st Avenue, a busy mixed-use street. "He and his two nephews go every day for mass. Always at the same time, except on Sunday. On Sunday they go for the early mass, which is done in Mandarin. Then they sometimes bring others."

Beside Lucy, Min frowned. "How many?"

"Sometimes it's just the three of them. Other times, one or two more from the local *tong*."

A *tong* was literally translated as a gathering place or hall, but in this sense, in the criminal sense, it could also be a secret society of sorts. A sworn brotherhood not much different from the Italian mafia. Xiang was the type who'd probably enjoy the stylings of a mafioso.

Lucy studied the street. On one side was Saint Michael's Catholic Church, standing on the corner of 41st and Union, and on the other were apartment buildings and small businesses. This was a bad place for a shooting to occur. So many windows.

And so many opportunities to be spotted.

A few people approached on foot from the apartments, dressed in what passed for church clothes in this neighborhood, moving slowly in the direction of the church. They were small families—Asian, Hispanic, and others. The mix she'd expect to see in this part of Flushing, part of the borough of Queens.

"When does he normally arrive?" she asked.

"He likes to get there just as it's starting. Last one in, first one out."

That sounded like Xiang. He was always careful. Nobody knew where he lived. But he had one idiosyncrasy that ruined his otherwise cautious behavior. He had been a devout Catholic for years.

Ruth, who was sitting in front, turned and scowled. "How can someone so religious be such a bastard?"

"No idea," Lucy shrugged. "I'm pretty sure that confessions can only go so far to cleanse one's soul."

Lucy turned her attention to the Chinese restaurant across the street. She remembered eating there when it first opened. But the owners had since moved, and the place was now covered with tags, graffiti from the local street gang. Tags that no doubt meant something to the teenage gang members, but was largely ignored by the real gangsters in the neighborhood.

Gangsters like Xiang.

He'd been her husband's right-hand man in China, before she got married, and before they moved operations to Hong Kong. But when her husband realized how much Lucy could help with the business, Xiang lost influence— and so he "retired" from the Chinese end of things.

Since then, Lucy had always done her best to keep track of the old man. She remembered the look he'd given her at her wedding. Behind that smile and the red envelope with a sizable check, she saw the seething hatred. That was over twenty years ago, but now here he was, in America, seeking revenge.

It hadn't taken her long to figure out who had put out a contract on her. The old man was a creature of habit.

The same bank account that he'd used to fund her wedding gift so long ago had more recently been used to wire one hundred thousand dollars to an escrow account to fund the contract on her life.

There was no question about it. Xiang wanted her dead.

Which meant he was ultimately responsible for Levi getting shot. If for no other reason than that, she was going to end that man—and anyone loyal to him.

"But first, the head of the snake needs to be cut off," she murmured to herself.

In the front seat, Ruth whispered excitedly, "Is that him?"

Lucy followed her gaze. Up ahead, on the opposite side of the street, three men were heading east on 41st. The tall man in front wore dark stylish glasses, a brown fedora, a green-checkered suit hung loosely on him, along with a gaudy purple tie. He had to be in his seventies.

But it was him.

His stride was purposeful, and a shiver ran up Lucy's spine as she recognized that gait.

Other details came unbidden to her mind. The scar on his chin. The birthmark on his belly. The image of him over her. Memories long buried came flooding back from whatever mental box she'd locked them in.

Her hands trembled with fury.

There were so many people on the street right now. Kids, churchgoers, innocent bystanders. But Xiang was right there, practically in front of her, taunting her... again.

"No, Lucy. No." Min grabbed Lucy's wrist. "Not now."

Lucy looked at her hand as if it wasn't attached. She was tightly gripping one of the guns she'd gotten from Esther. She forced her fingers to release it, to set it next to her on the seat.

Min quickly grabbed it, her face filled with concern.

"I'm fine," Lucy said. She tried to smile reassuringly. "Really, I'm fine. That's definitely him."

The driver looked at her in the rearview mirror. "So are we done here?"

Lucy let out a shuddering breath and nodded. "Let's go back to the apartment. We need to plan."

As the car pulled away, the memories returned. Those memories… that secret… a secret she'd kept hidden from everyone. Including herself.

But now she remembered it all.

She remembered sipping the drink.

She remembered feeling woozy.

And she remembered her soon-to-be husband's trusted partner leading her away from a party.

But mostly, she remembered that face—Xiang's face —as he forced himself on her. Violating her. Raping her.

Lucy clenched her hands into fists… and smiled.

Xiang was going to die in a most horrifying way.

Levi sighed with frustration as Tony and Gino spilled out of the Cadillac.

Gino motioned toward an old Camry parked across

the tree-lined street. "Well, that app of yours said he stopped on Morris Avenue in Elizabeth, New Jersey, and sure enough, there's the car."

"But no guy," Tony growled.

Levi felt exposed and was about to give an order for them to disperse when Gino snorted and said, "Well, look what the cat coughed up."

Levi followed the man's gaze. Stepping out of a doorway between a mobile phone store and a Latin market was a guy in his thirties, dressed in sweatpants and a dingy and completely unbuttoned dress shirt that exposed a belly and hairy chest. He was smoking a cigarette and staring directly at them.

"You know that guy?" Levi said.

"Oh, yeah." Gino roll his eyes. "We grew up in the same neighborhood. That's Johnny Guarino. He's a total loser, but his cousin was a connected guy."

"Connected with who?"

"The DeCavalcante family, I think. Johnny was always talking about his cousin Ralphie."

"Oh, *that* scumbag," Tony said. "Ralphie, the piece of shit who turned state's evidence and basically brought down a bunch of made men and connected guys? I should whack this guy on pure principle."

Johnny tossed his cigarette and started toward them, stepping into the street and almost getting himself run over in the process.

Levi put a hand on Tony's shoulder and shook his head in warning. Tony had a reputation for being a hothead—which took some doing in their line of business —and the last thing they needed right now was trouble.

"Hey, Gino!" Johnny yelled as he approached. "What are you doing slumming over here? It's good to see you, man. It's been ages."

Gino shook hands with the wannabe associate. "Don't worry about why I'm here. It's got nothing to do with you."

Johnny barely glanced at Tony and Levi before lowering his gaze and focusing strictly on Gino. He evidently knew better than to even ask who they were. There was a code among those in the mafia, a code that was understood even by would-be associates. And according to that code, a scumbag like this guy didn't even get an introduction to someone in *La Cosa Nostra*.

Johnny started to button his shirt. "Is there anything I can do to help? I've been here for almost ten years, so I know just about everyone in the neighborhood."

Gino pointed his chin across the street. "That gold-colored Camry. Whose is it?"

Johnny turned and pointed at the car. "What, that?"

Gino immediately smacked Johnny's arm back down. "Did I fucking tell you to point at anything? I asked you a question."

Johnny paled. "S-sure, Gino, i-it's, um…" His face scrunched up as he struggled to find an answer. Suddenly his eyes lit up. "Lonny. That's his name. He's got some German or Jewish last name like Manschitz or Manische-witz or something. He doesn't talk much. Mostly keeps to himself."

"Where's he live?" Levi asked.

Johnny was just about to point across the street, then slammed his own arm tightly to his side. "In my building, right here on Morris Avenue, above the Spanish market. Apartment three, two doors down from mine."

Gino patted Johnny on the cheek. "That's all we needed to know. Now, you get out of here and don't say a word to anyone that you saw us."

"Oh, no way would I do that." Johnny's tone was pathetically weak and nasal. "And I'm really sorry about that pointing thing, it's just—"

"Shut up, Johnny. You talk too much." Gino waved him away. "Get the hell out of here and forget you saw us."

Johnny opened his mouth, closed it, then hurried toward his apartment.

"What a fucking weasel," Tony said under his breath.

Gino nodded. "Even as a kid, he was a suckass. Some things don't change."

Levi's phone buzzed. Dominic. Levi let it go to voice-mail. He'd call him back later.

Just then their target, Lonny, stepped out the apartment building, passing Johnny going the other way.

"Guys, don't move," Levi said. "Don't turn your heads. Our fish just left his apartment."

Tony scuffed his shoes against the sidewalk, careful to not even look up. "Should we get ready to go after him?"

"No. I've got an idea."

Levi waited until Lonny got in his Camry and pulled away, the quarter-sized tracker still on its roof. Then he turned to Tony.

"Okay, he's gone. Tony, you stay in the car and keep watch. Gino, you do your thing and let's check out the apartment and see who this Lonny character is. Earpieces in."

As Tony returned to the Cadillac, Gino and Levi crossed the street and entered the apartment building. The place smelled like rotten milk.

Johnny was just down the hall, at the door to Apartment 1. He started to open his big mouth to say something, but shut it when Gino snapped his fingers. His eyes widened at the sight of the gun in Gino hand, and he disappeared into his apartment.

"Tony, you hear me?" Levi whispered.

"Yup, loud and clear. Nothing going on out here."

"Let me know if that changes."

"You got it."

Gino pulled a set of lockpicks from his inner suit pocket and began working on the door to Apartment 3. In seconds, Levi heard the snick of the deadbolt disengaging and then the sound of metal sliding across metal. Gino wriggled a pick in the lock while twisting it slightly. The doorknob turned, and the tiny man pushed the door open with a smile.

"Shitty apartments like this, they almost always have shitty locks."

Levi patted the man on the shoulder.

They both put on latex gloves as they entered, then Gino flipped on the lights.

The place was small. It was practically a one-room apartment, no more than four-hundred square feet. The bedroom was nothing more than a glorified closet. On a nearby card table was a bowl of cinnamon-scented potpourri fighting against the smell of mildew. It was losing.

Levi's attention was immediately drawn to a military-style hat made from a faded green cloth with a black visor and black band. At the middle of the black band was a silver skull and crossbones, and just above that was a German eagle, wings outspread, perched on a swastika.

Levi recognized the design. It was a Nazi SS cap.

A chill ran up his spine.

Gino noticed the hat as well—along with several other pieces of Nazi regalia. "Is this shit real?" he said. "What the hell was this guy into?"

Levi gritted his teeth. "Looks real to me. Maybe the guy's a collector. Or maybe his granddad was a Nazi and he wants to remember the good ol' days. Either way, it's time to find out who this guy is."

CHAPTER FOURTEEN

Levi watched as Denny scanned the two dozen fingerprints he'd captured from the apartment in New Jersey, entered them into the computer, and submitted them to compare against IAFIS, the FBI's centralized database for fingerprints.

"I can't believe you ran across a real Nazi," Denny said. "You always hear about neo-Nazis and white supremacists in the news, but I don't think I've ever seen any. What all did he have?"

Levi flipped through some of the photos he'd captured on his phone. "Lots of vintage Nazi paraphernalia, mostly. An obligatory *Mein Kampf*, of course. Freshly printed posters of Hitler and a few other Nazis I didn't recognize. The question is how he afforded all that stuff. He must have a connection to someone with money, because judging by the way he lived, I doubt he had much of anything other than dreams from Germany's 'glorious' past."

Levi had placed bugs in the room as well as on the guy's phone line. Hopefully they would reveal who that connection was.

"I got a hit," Denny said, tapping on the screen. "One of those prints is coming back for a Lonny Manheim."

Levi nodded. "Sounds right. The neighbor said his name was Lonny. What's the system say about him?"

Denny pulled up a screenful of text. "He's thirty-five, born in Coeur d'Alene, Idaho, and is an ardent follower of Pastor Jerald O'Brien. Looks like he was busted for check fraud, but he's been off the radar for almost a decade. Still, the FBI has a case file on him. And he's got associations with—no surprise here—the Aryan Nations. I'll go ahead and run financials on him, see if he's been wired something. But that'll take a while."

Levi leaned back in his chair and looked up at the ceiling. "Okay, so we've got an Orthodox Jew who is dead and was pissed off at his employer. We've got a lady he was wrongly accused of sleeping with, who's now gone missing. We have some dirty cops who we think were tracking anyone who visited the Jew's family. A now we have a Nazi sympathizer somehow mixed into this."

"Oh, shit!" Denny bolted upright.

Levi leaned forward. "Another match?"

"Yeah, but not from the FBI database. That casing Mr. Minnelli sent to me—the one from whoever shot you? I pulled a latent off the brass, and it matches one of the fingerprints from this Nazi's apartment."

Levi felt the heat rising up his neck. "Our Nazi knows the shooter. How the hell are those two connected?"

With his heart thudding loudly in his ears, he pulled out his phone and dialed a number.

"Hey, Levi."

"Frankie, I've got a lead on my shooter. Can you help arrange a pickup team? I want to do the questioning."

The line went silent for a second, then: *"Just give me an ID and I'll do the rest. When do you want to do it?"*

"Tonight. I'll text you the address. It's the same guy Gino, Tony, and I followed earlier today."

"Okay. I'll talk to them and call you back with a location."

"Perfect. Talk to you soon."

Levi hung up. The tips of his fingers tingled as anger washed over him. He wanted to punch something.

Denny looked up at him questioningly.

Levi got up and put his hand on Denny's shoulder. "Use everything you've got to get that Nazi's connections. Anyone he's ever talked to or collected a check from. Pull out all your tricks. I want this asshole."

Back in his apartment, Levi paced in anticipation. There were so many loose ends in this weird case. It started with a religious Jew who'd had an affair and killed himself, and it should have ended there, too. But with every thread he pulled, things got more complicated.

Denny had called and confirmed that Detective Carter, the one who'd supposedly taken Mindy Cross's statement about the affair, was on the take, but not from the same bank account that had paid off the other two cops. And this guy had been on the take for years, since he was in the academy.

Finding dirty cops was generally a good thing for the mob. Guys like Frankie knew how to leverage such cops to gain influence. But to uncover three in the span of a month? This was getting out of hand.

He suddenly remembered the earlier call from Dominic. He checked his voicemail, and sure enough, there was a message waiting.

"Mr. Yoder, I think we need to talk. Miss Cross seems to have either quit or been fired—no one's sure which, but her cubicle has been cleared out. And I also have a recording that I'm somewhat reluctant to share, but I think you should know about it. It may be related to the stuff you were asking about."

He hit a button to return the call. It rang three times, then voice mail picked up. Levi opted not to leave a message.

Just as he was putting the phone away, it buzzed with an incoming call.

"Hello?"

"Hey, Levi." It was Lucy.

"Hey there. How did your morning go? Did you manage to find your prey?"

"You bet I did." She sounded icy and serious. *"It took a bit, but we found him."*

"Did you…"

"No. I promised you that I'd let you be there when I put an end to his—"

"Careful, Lucy." Levi was always cautious about what he said, even on these special cell phones that Denny had set up with location-spoofing and military-grade data scrambling. He knew no technology was fool-proof. "Do you know when it will happen?"

"This weekend." He detected an odd tone to her voice. *"When are you coming back? We can talk more about it then."*

"Are you okay? You sound upset."

"I'm fine. I was just... I'm just thinking how my guy's responsible for you getting shot."

Levi shook his head. He knew now that his shooter was some type of Nazi collaborator, which made it almost certain he was unrelated to her guy. The Triad gang members were many things, but Nazi sympathizers, not so much.

"Don't be so sure about that," he said.

"I'm sure of plenty of things when it comes to this guy," Lucy snapped angrily. Levi heard her take a deep breath and let it out slowly, and when she spoke again, her voice was softer, more controlled. *"When are you coming over?"*

He looked out the window. It was already evening. "I'm not sure. I've got some stuff to do, and it'll be a long night. I'll call you tomorrow."

"You left before I could think to give you a key card." Her voice grew even quieter, almost like she was embarrassed. *"I'd like you to think of this place as your own. I'd like you to..."*

Levi's phone vibrated, and he checked the screen. Paulie was calling.

"Lucy, let's pick this up tomorrow. I'm getting the call I was waiting for." He switched to the other line. "Paulie. Tell me something."

"The boys are taking the fish to the butcher. I'll pick you up in five."

Paulie's giant silhouette stood before an ancient, rusted door attached to a rundown building in Jersey City. Levi shifted his weight from one leg to another, waiting impatiently for his companion to finish fiddling with the lock on the door. With a metallic snick, the giant man grunted with victory, turned the handle and to Levi's surprise, when the door opened, it did so soundlessly—as if the door was actually new, but had been designed to look like a century-old relic.

The two men walked into a cavernous room that held the musty smell of age. Across a vast concrete floor stood dozens of fifteen-foot-tall generators that were obviously from another era, and in the distance was a large pile of steel beams—no, railroad tracks, and next to them was a Jenga-like pile of wooden slats that reached almost to the thirty-foot ceiling.

"What is this place?" Levi asked.

Paulie led him through the maze of generators. "Used to power the subway between Jersey and Manhattan. It's been closed for ages."

He made his way to the far wall, opened a door and ushered Levi into a back hallway that was stifling hot, despite the mild evening outside. This place appeared to have no air circulation whatsoever. Levi prepared himself for a brutal night as he closed the door behind him.

When Paulie opened the next door, the smell of human waste—and the sounds of sobbing—assaulted Levi's nose and ears. Levi stepped in and took in the scene.

Lonny Manheim was bound with leather straps to a metal chair. His wrists were cuffed, and those cuffs were pulled tight by a rope that was attached to a metal ring on the far wall. If he weren't strapped so tightly to the chair, he'd look like he was ready to dive into a pool. The chair itself was riveted to two lengths of metal on the floor—more of the railroad segments that had been in the other room. Levi wondered how they got in here; they probably weighed several hundred pounds each.

Two mobsters Levi had worked with in the past, were standing at the far corners of the room, looking at the back of the Nazi with a look of mild amusement. Carlo, a tall thin mobster, and Angelo, a shorter, husky guy with huge bushy eyebrows, were the family's cleaners. They'd dispose of the body and all the evidence. They probably had buckets of chemicals nearby to take care of that business.

Paulie patted Levi on the shoulder. "You remember Laurel and Hardy, right?"

Levi nodded. When he'd first met the two cleaners, he'd started jokingly calling them Laurel and Hardy, and the moniker had stuck. In front of a captive, nobody was going to use real names. The guy would probably end up dead in the end, but sometimes things worked out differently.

"I thought you were going to wait for me before starting," Levi said.

Laurel shrugged. "We didn't lay a finger on him, I swear. This guy just crapped himself when we strapped him to the chair."

Lonny strained to look behind him, but he was bound too tightly. So instead he looked up to Levi, his chin quivering. His voice was surprisingly deep. "I didn't do nothing, I swear to you. This has to be a mistake. I have no beef with anyone. Really."

Levi pulled forward a metal folding chair and crossed his legs, assuming a relaxed position. "Who are you?"

Lonny blinked as if the question surprised him. "Um, I'm Lonny Manheim."

Levi made a rolling motion with his hand. "Tell me more. Where are you from? What are you doing here?"

"Um, I was born in Idaho, but I moved here about six years ago. I'm not really doing much other than collecting some unemployment right now. Before that I was bagging groceries and stocking shelves at the Pac-and-Save."

Levi leaned forward, trying to ignore the stench of the feces that had stained the man's pants. "Tell me about that collection you've got in your apartment."

"Collection?" Lonny looked confused for a second, then winced. "Oh, that. My grandfather was a member of the SS during World War II. Most of that stuff is from him. None of the rest of my family wanted to have anything to do with it, but I didn't see the big deal. I suppose it's bad to have, but it's my grandfather's stuff. I couldn't just throw it away."

Levi sat back and studied the man. He was haggard-looking, and could easily pass for ten years older than thirty-five. He was overly thin, unkempt, and literally scared shitless.

"Not everything in there was from your grandfather," Levi said. He spoke with a menacing growl. "Let me give you a fair warning. Tell me the truth, and you'll walk away. Lie to me just once, and you'll wish you were never born."

"I swear." Lonny's eyes bugged out with fear, and his voice was a pathetic whine. "I'll tell you anything you want."

A new stain appeared on Lonny's pants, and urine began pooling at his feet.

"You're right," he continued. "Some of that stuff, the posters, some of the other letters and stuff, I got that from friends back in Idaho. They were collectors, and I sort of traded a few things that didn't really mean much to me for something I could hang up."

Levi growled. "So you're a fan of Hitler."

"Well…" Lonny's face was a mixture of fear and confusion. "I mean, kind of. He did some amazing things. He was a great general, and he really loved his people and his country. That isn't so wrong, is it? We're taught to do the same thing in school here, right?"

Levi took a deep breath, blocking out the revolting smells, and slowly let it out. He couldn't let himself get angry before he got what he needed. This guy wasn't physically strong. He'd probably collapse from a heart attack before he got very far into the "coercing" stage of the interview.

Levi drummed his fingers on his knee. "Over six million Jews, dead. Over nineteen million civilians and prisoners of war, dead. Over twenty-eight million more soldiers and civilians throughout Europe, dead. This is the man you admire."

Lonny closed his eyes and shook his head. "I know. That was all terrible. But it was war. And I was always told those numbers weren't true. That those numbers were—"

"They're true." Levi clenched his fists and continued his slow breathing. "I walked through Auschwitz. Through Bergen-Belsen. Through Dachau. I saw the bones. The shoes. The pictures. I've spoken to elderly survivors of those camps. People who lived through a nightmare nobody should ever experience. You've been lied to. But that's not why we're here."

Lonny looked at Levi with wide, desperate eyes. "What do you want?"

"You were in Hell's Kitchen earlier. Why?"

"It's a brotherhood thing."

"Brotherhood?"

"The Aryan Nations has friends in lots of places. Sometimes those friends need to reach out and not have anyone see them reaching out, if you know what I mean."

"How do they reach out?"

"Well, it's simple, really. If there's a chalk mark on

the wall at a certain place, I look for a dead rat and collect it. Inside it, there's some information."

"And what do you do with the information once you get it?"

"I call a number and leave a voicemail. I don't know who's next in the chain, but I get a little money to make sure the chain isn't broken. It's not like I ever hear back."

"What kind of information have you picked up?"

"Stuff that never makes sense. Sometimes it's just a name. Sometimes it's a long number."

Levi frowned. This guy was just a tool in a toolbox. A way for local resources to reach out. But reach out to whom? The last time Levi had read about the white supremacists in the US, they were more of a joke than a real threat.

"Did you have any visitors in your apartment recently?" he asked.

"Yes," Lonny said without hesitation. "I don't know his name, but a brother of mine—"

"Aryan Nations brother?"

"Yes. He called me and said someone was going to come, and he would need a place to bunk for the night. The next day someone knocked on my door and just walked right in. He barely spoke. Barely said a thing. He asked for water, milk, eggs. He had an accent."

"What kind of accent?"

"Well, he spoke English really good, what little I heard, but it sounded kind of like a Spanish accent, maybe? It wasn't like the spics I hear around Jersey or New York, though. I got a bunch of them from Puerto

Rico all up and down my street. Besides, he was pretty normal-colored, so I don't know."

Levi sat back and stared at Lonny. The guy was a piece of shit. And he was probably the most chickenshit guy Levi had ever interviewed. But Levi didn't think he was lying.

"When was he at your place?"

Lonny bobbed his head from side to side as if calculating. "Oh, hell. I'm not sure. Ten days? No, it had to be at least two weeks, because I get milk once a week and he drank all of it right around when I first got it, leaving me with none. And that was just about two weeks ago. Maybe a day or two more than that."

Levi got up from his chair and frowned. That timing lined up with his having been shot. "Who was the guy who called you, telling you to expect a visitor?"

Lonny shook his head. "I have no idea. When the brothers need to reach out, they use a phone tree. It could be any of hundreds of guys. I didn't recognize the voice."

"Anything else you know about your visitor? What did he look like? Age? I want to know everything you remember."

"I guess he was my age, somewhere around his mid-thirties. Tall, like a couple inches taller than you. Kind of average build. And he was kind of rich-looking—pretty decent clothes and stuff. When he left, he left behind the clothes and shoes he was wearing. I have no idea why, figured he'd back for them, but nope."

"Eye color? Hair color? Scars? Tattoos?"

"He had dark brown hair. I'm not sure what color his eyes were, but they were kind of light. Maybe blue?

Hazel? Could have been green." Lonny shrugged. "I'm a guy, I'm not so big on staring at another guy's eyes, if you know what I mean."

Levi glanced at Laurel and Hardy, who were standing like statues, waiting for the inevitable cleanup and disposal. He sensed Paulie behind him, but didn't look back. Instead he stepped forward and flicked at the Nazi's cuffed hands. "Extend your fingers."

"I didn't—"

"Extend your fingers!" Levi yelled.

Lonny's fingers fanned out widely, and he began to whimper.

Without warning, Levi grabbed both of the man's middle fingers and twisted them violently. He felt the bones snap.

Lonny howled with pain and bucked in his chair, pulling at the cuffs. His middle fingers were now at a forty-five-degree angle compared to his other fingers.

Levi walked over to the two cleaners. "Do you have some popsicle sticks and duct tape?"

Angelo—or Hardy, as he was the short and stout one —had to speak loudly to be heard over Lonny's wailing. "I don't have popsicle sticks. How about some wooden paint stirrers?"

"That'll work."

Minutes later, Levi leaned back and examined his work. He'd whittled the paint stirrers into proper-sized finger splints, then duct-taped them to Lonny's broken fingers.

"Lonny," he said, "you were straight with me, so I'm going to make a deal with you."

Lonny's chest heaved. He was clearly unused to dealing with pain. "Anything," he said, gasping.

"You've made a lot of bad choices in your life. I'm not the one that's going to help you make better ones. This you need to do for yourself. But while you work on that, we don't need your kind in our city. Do you get me?"

"What kind..." Lonny began. "Oh, you mean the brotherhood stuff?"

Levi nodded. "My friends will take you back to your apartment. You'll pack one bag, and they'll get you a bus ticket back to Idaho."

"But—"

"Shut up!" Levi barked. "Don't test me. I notice you don't have any Aryan tattoos or other nonsense like that. That's good. Maybe you'll turn your life around. But that's not my concern. I broke your fingers so you'd remember this conversation. And when you think of your friends in the brotherhood, just remember that most of proper society would give them, and you, the middle finger. Change your life and change your worldview if you know what's good for you. But regardless, your city privileges are revoked. Am I understood?"

Lonny nodded vigorously. "Y-yes, sir."

Levi turned to Laurel and Hardy. "Hose this guy off and take him to his place. Whatever fits in one bag, that's it. Then take him to the Port Authority bus terminal, buy him a ticket to Idaho, I don't care what city, and make sure he gets on."

They nodded.

Levi signaled to Paulie that he was ready to roll, then turned to Lonny one last time. "If we ever catch you in this city again, I swear to God I'll kill you myself. You hear me?"

Lonny gulped, and a fresh stream of yellow fluid dripped from the chair. "Yes, sir."

CHAPTER FIFTEEN

Levi sipped at his seltzer and let the cacophony of the bar's patrons wash over him. It was late in the evening, but for Gerard's, it was prime time. Denny was behind the bar, Rosie was taking a food order from two made men, and Carmen was clearing emptied tables.

Levi leaned back in his chair, staring off into space. He hadn't expected to be done with his interrogation so quickly. Normally those things took time, especially with the type of people he was used to dealing with. A person needed to be worn down, convinced of the futility of his situation, and only then, at the end of what's often a bloody and messy marathon, when the pain had finally cracked through the last of the interviewee's resistance, did the truth come tumbling out.

The front door opened, and Levi looked over to see two dark-clothed figures entering the bar. Menachem Shemtov and Rivka Cohen. He immediately set all four of the chair's legs back on the floor and stood as they as approached his table.

The elderly jeweler shook his hand. "It's good to know you are easy to find."

Levi gave the man a lopsided grin. "Actually, your timing is perfect. I got here just ten minutes ago."

The white-haired man looked up, presumably at God, and said, "As always, he's watching out for us all. Do you mind if we take a seat?"

"Please, go ahead."

He gave Rivka a nod, which she politely returned, and they all sat down.

"I'm surprised to see you here," Levi said. "Is there something you need?"

Through Menachem's bushy white beard came a look of concern. "I heard you were in the hospital, and I wanted to make sure you are okay. If it's okay with you, I'd like to say a little prayer for your health."

Levi chuckled at the thought of someone sincerely praying for him. "I'm doing much better. And only a fool wouldn't welcome a prayer on his behalf. Thank you."

Reaching across the table, Menachem put his wrinkled and slightly arthritic hands on Levi's, bowed his head, and said, *"Ha-makom yi-rachem ah-lecha be-toch cal cholei yisrael."*

Rivka repeated the same, then explained, "It roughly translates to 'May the Almighty have mercy on you, among all the sick of Israel.'"

"Thank you," Levi said. "It's very kind of you to think of me. But... I assume you have other reasons for meeting with me as well?"

Rivka pulled a box from her purse and slid it across the table. "While I was cleaning Mendel's office, I discovered a hidden compartment behind one of his bookshelves. This was inside."

Levi lifted the lid off of the box. Inside were nearly a dozen microcassettes.

"I listened to some of them," Rivka said. "It's mostly people's voices at work, I think. They say some terrible things in it. I figured these might be useful to you."

"*Boobaleh.*" Menachem raked his fingers through his beard as he looked at his niece. "Mendel wouldn't have hidden it if it wasn't important."

Levi jiggled the box and counted eight tapes. "What are the terrible things that are said on the tapes?"

Rivka frowned. "I can't repeat some of those words. But I heard lots of things that were very rude about black people. And many terrible things about Israel." She shook her head. "I don't know why Mendel would have such recordings."

The tapes were unmarked and looked innocuous, but Levi felt a surge of curiosity. "Thank you for this. I think it might be helpful. And," he hesitated, measuring his words carefully, "I can tell you for a fact that Mendel never did these things that the police report said. I talked to the woman."

"The woman he was supposed to have..." Rivka's voice trailed off and she lowered her gaze.

"She didn't even know who he was. And I also interviewed the woman's wife."

Rivka's eyes widened and her mouth dropped open.

"Wait." Menachem's brow furrowed. "Did you say her *wife*?"

Rivka touched her uncle's arm. "She was homosexual," she explained. She looked at Levi. "Right?"

Levi nodded. "Yes."

"*Oy gevalt*, such a thing." The old man looked puzzled. "Really?"

Rivka's eyes teared, and she patted her uncle's arm again. "It happens. I just wish the Social Security office would listen to such things."

Menachem put his hand on Rivka's. "*Rivka-le*, I told you before, the family will manage."

"Hold on," Levi said. "What is this about Social Security?"

Rivka wiped at her eyes. "I shouldn't have said anything. I was expecting... well, it's because we still have young children, we should have a Social Security benefit for them, for us. So much of Mendel's taxes have been going to that for years and years. But because Mendel's death is said to be a suicide, they are denying our claim."

"This is not Mr. Yoder's concern," Menachem said. He turned to Levi. "The family will be fine. We'll take care of our own. But it would be helpful if the police report is updated with this woman's statement. That will happen, yes?"

"Actually... that's complicated." It was hard to get a witness's statement when the witness in question had vanished. "I'll try. But either way, I want you to know that Mendel never strayed." At least not with Mindy.

Rivka pressed her lips together into a thin line. "If not

for guilt over such an act, then he'd have had no reason to take his own life. But the report said he'd died from being poisoned. It's just not possible. I mean, to be poisoned, that means he would have eaten something that wasn't *kasher*. Mendel never ate outside the house. Not ever. If he truly was poisoned, that means someone murdered my husband."

Levi nodded. He was familiar enough with orthodox Jewish custom to know they'd never eat something that had come from an unknown, possibly unkosher source. "I'm afraid it seems likely. I'm still looking into that."

Menachem stood and shook Levi's hand. "We don't want to take too much of your time. Thank you for all that you've done and are doing. I'll forever be grateful."

"As will I," Rivka said as she stood. She looked somber in her all-black dress and topcoat, but for just a second, Levi saw the pretty girl hidden in the mourning middle-aged woman.

As these two very out-of-place people left the bar, Denny appeared next to Levi. "Hey, Levi, I got an update incoming from Marty."

Levi shook his head, lost in thought. "We need to solve this thing, Denny. Those are good people. They don't deserve this hanging over their head."

Denny nodded. "Agreed, but first things first. I think Marty has the ID for your shooter."

Denny's computer screen had a Teams session running on it. The computer whiz had explained that Teams was a new computer-based conference call that allowed people to share images. Currently the screen was blank, except for a face at the bottom marked with the initials "MB." Marty Brice.

Levi had never met the man before, but he looked like what Levi expected. In his thirties, receding hairline, face slightly pudgy, a wistful smile. But when he spoke, it was with a youthful excitement.

"Mr. Yoder—"

Levi cut in. "Really, for someone Denny says is particularly bright, you're slow on the uptake. Mr. Yoder is my father, and he's dead. Again, just call me Levi."

"Sorry." Marty laughed nervously. *"I'm just really bad with names. It's not intentional. Anyway, when Denny forwarded me the fingerprint, we didn't get anything on our regular database searches, but as soon as he told me the guy might have had an accent, it hit me."*

Denny smacked his forehead with the palm of his hand. "I'm an idiot. I didn't think about the accent. The passport scanners in the airport. If the guy is a foreigner, he probably had his prints captured going through customs. Those scans have to be attached to some database."

"Exactly where I went with it. US Customs and Border Protection has its own separate database for the incoming and outgoing biometric scans. So I did some poking around and found a match to the fingerprint off that shell casing. Here's the facial scan of the man who matched, taken as he left the country soon after the shooting, on his way home to Argentina."

An image appeared on the screen of a man in his mid-thirties. He had the chiseled features of a guy who could have been featured on the back of a magazine, smoking a cigarette and wearing a cowboy hat, in days gone by. His eyes were pale blue, and just enough of his shoulders were pictured to see that he wore a well-made suit and perfectly knotted tie.

"What's his name?" Levi asked.

"Herman Gerhard."

"Doesn't sound very Spanish," Levi said as he memorized the face.

"No. In fact he's the grandson of Wolfgang Gerhard, a scientist and former SS officer who escaped through one of the ratlines established just after World War II."

"A ratline?" Denny said. "What's that?"

"I read about the ratlines." Levi felt nauseated at the thought of them. "They were secret escape routes for former Nazis. They called them 'ratlines' because those fascists were fleeing Europe like a bunch of rats scurrying away from justice. Lots of real scum managed to escape, and many ended up living in South America."

"Exactly right," Marty said. *"It was a complicated mess back then. It had to be chaos. The Soviet Union was scooping up all of the former German scientists it could, as were the Americans. Each trying hard to keep those resources from the other, and I can only imagine how hard it would have been for the allies to keep track of who was where and somehow prevent the bad guys from making their escape. Anyway, this Wolfgang Gerhard was both a scientist and a devoted crony of the infamous Josef Mengele."*

Levi pulled in an angry breath and held it. Mengele

was probably the worst of the worst that escaped. He was a legit medical doctor who was known as *Todesengel*, the angel of death. He did unspeakable human experiments at Auschwitz, and he made the determinations about who would go to the gas chamber and who would go to the work camp.

Marty continued. *"When Mengele eventually died of natural causes in Brazil, he chose to be buried under the name 'Wolfgang Gerhard.' That was likely to further evade post-death attention, but it might also have been a sick dedication to a former friend living fifteen hundred miles away.*

"But back to Gerhard. He became friends with Argentina's President Peron, he managed to accumulate a large amount of wealth, and he formed the Gerhard Group, a privately held company that holds deeds to many properties around the world, including close to a million acres of pastureland in the pampas of Argentina. Gerhard died in 2000, and his son, Juan, has been chairman of the Gerhard Group ever since. And our guy Herman is Juan's son.

"Herman, however, has almost zero public profile. I can see that he's traveled to Europe, mostly through Germany and the Scandinavian countries, and he occasionally visits New York and Los Angeles. Always first-class travel. Never for more than a few days at a time. But beyond that, he's pretty much a ghost."

Levi sat back in his chair. "Do we have an address for him?"

"Hold on a second, Mr.—I mean Levi. I don't think it's exactly wise to go visit him quite yet. Remember how I

said his father is wealthy? I don't mean just a little bit. Forbes doesn't recognize the Gerhard family holdings because they're all private and mostly undisclosed, but I have satellite images of the family compound, and it's larger and better protected than most army bases. Let's go ahead and figure out what other data we have before anyone goes anywhere. There's got to be something solid linking the two of you. Why would he want to take a shot at you?"

Levi raked his hand roughly through his hair. "Hell if I know. I was working on a job for the widow of a reporter who worked at a big newspaper. He was poisoned, but it was called a suicide based on a witness statement that, as I later discovered, was faked on the police report. The detective who supposedly interviewed that witness is dirty, so my folks talked to him, and we got some decent intelligence out of him."

He turned away from the monitor as he spoke. He was sick of seeing Gerhard's face.

"I was recovering from having been shot, so I didn't get this firsthand." Levi's visualized the handwritten report that Paulie had given him. "Denny figured out the guy was getting payoffs…"

Levi turned to Denny, his eyes widening. "Oh crap. Those payoffs were coming from a bank account in Argentina."

"Yup," Marty said. *"We knew about that. We're still trying to attach that account to the Gerhards. No dice yet."*

Levi's heart thumped a bit faster than before, and he felt a tingle at the tips of his fingers. He really needed some time with the heavy bag—or better yet, with this Herman Gerhard. "We also learned that the detective used a dead drop to communicate with some contacts. He didn't know who they were, and he wasn't the curious type. He was getting paid—that was all that mattered to him."

"What would he communicate?" Denny asked.

"That's the weird thing." Levi drummed his fingers on the desk. "He claimed that every once in a while, he'd get a call on his cell phone. It was always a digitized voice, and it basically would give him instructions. Usually they were looking for some information about a case. He'd write it down and use the dead drop to communicate the data. Evidently, he had no other way to contact these people.

"In the case of the death of the reporter I was investigating, this Detective Carter was told to fake an interview with some woman and put it in the official record. But he admitted to my guys that he'd never even met her."

"Hold on." Levi could hear Marty typing. *"How did this detective know it was a legit communication? Couldn't any moron with a voice scrambler call him and tell him anything?"*

"There was a code word being used," Levi said. Paulie's notes were pretty extensive. They'd not only had to threaten to kidnap the detective's kid, they had to literally send someone out to collect her before Carter finally broke. "What we learned was that the first word after 'hello' would always be 'everef.' Which doesn't mean anything in any language I looked up."

There was silence on the line for a good five seconds

before Denny leaned closer and said, "Marty, you still there?"

"I am. I'm just waiting on—aha! I just ran that phonetically through our computers. It's not a word, it's an acronym for Ein Volk, ein Reich, ein Führer, which literally translates to one people, one nation, one leader." His voice took on an uncharacteristic growl. *"It was, and I suppose still is, the motto for the Nazi party."*

Levi frowned. "This all stinks. And still, my only connection is this loose one with a dead reporter."

"Wait," Denny said. "You were in the *Intelligencer* building a bunch of times talking to people, weren't you?"

A chill raced up Levi's back. "You're right. I interviewed a lady who works there, a beautiful woman, and she's gone missing. I also talked several times with another contact in the building."

His natural instinct was to say as little about Dominic as possible. Any associate of the family was family business, and he wasn't about to talk family business to anyone outside the family. So he kept the man's name, and any identifying details, to himself.

"The last time I talked to him was in that building, and I kept getting the feeling I was being watched. When I spotted a security camera pointed directly at me, I left the building with him... and now that I think about it, I've called him several times and have gotten no answer."

"What the hell is going on over there?" Denny said, his eyes almost popping out of his head. "It's like the Bermuda Triangle in that building. One dead guy, one missing girl, and maybe another missing person?"

"I'll do some digging into that," Marty said. *"Maybe there's some connection I can piece together."*

Levi reached for the box of cassette tapes the Cohens left with him, and turned to Denny. "Do you have something that'll play microcassettes?"

"Sure… oh, you want me to look now?"

Levi nodded.

Denny got up from his chair and disappeared into the rows of shelves.

Levi leaned closer to the computer. "The wife of the dead reporter said she found a bunch of tapes hidden in a secret compartment in her husband's office. She said they have some 'terrible' stuff, but keep in mind that she's an ultra-orthodox Jew and pretty sheltered. I have no idea what's—"

"Sorry to interrupt, Levi. Is Denny still around?"

Marty's voice was loud enough that Denny poked his head out from behind the rows of shelves. "Yeah, what's up?"

"Denny, do you have a Graff 8x or 16x cassette digitizer?"

"No. But I made a 32x digitizer as a custom piece for… well, let's just say someone needed to copy a bunch of audio tapes really quickly. Hold on, I think I've got it back here somewhere."

Within a minute, Denny returned with what looked like a laptop case. He laid it on his desk and opened it to reveal another case, this one clear plastic, with a bunch of bare circuit boards and wires inside. It had slots for both full-sized cassettes and microcassettes.

He unlooped a cable. "Marty, you want me to dub and

spool to you, and you'll do signal processing on your end?"

"Ya, that's fine. I've got the CPU power here. Just use the standard mailbox, and I'll open up port twenty-three for you."

Denny plugged one end of the cable into his tape machine, and the other into his computer. A few keystrokes later, and a new screen popped up. "Okay, got an SSH connection to you."

He turned to Levi. "Is there a particular cassette I should start with?"

Levi shrugged. "I have no idea what any of them are, so no. I also, by the way, have no idea what you guys are doing. You two just said a bunch of words that don't mean anything to normal people."

"I'll explain," said Marty. *"It sounds like you might have something interesting on those tapes, and since time is sort of important here, Denny and I are converting them to a digital format, and I'm borrowing some time from Tempora to—"*

"Tempora?" Levi interrupted. "What's that?"

Marty chuckled. *"Well, strictly speaking, it's supposed to be a secret computer system the British use to process and evaluate Internet traffic. At least it was until that asshole Snowden blew its cover. Anyway, I'll steal a bit of time from Tempora to have it evaluate and flag keywords from the audio Denny will be spooling to me."*

Levi frowned as he thought of what that actually meant. "The computers can understand speech that well?"

"Not all of them," Denny said with a smile. He

plopped a cassette into his machine, and it started rapidly spinning the tape in its reel. "But some certainly can."

For the next couple of minutes, Denny quickly worked through all the tapes, repeatedly popping one cassette out and another in. Each time, the machine whirred, rapidly transmitting the contents.

"That's all of them," he said finally. "How's Tempora doing, Marty?"

"Fascinating..." Marty said.

Levi waited for more. When nothing was forthcoming, he got impatient. "Uh, can we get more than just the one word?"

"Here, let me share."

Several bars appeared on Denny's computer screen, moving from left to right on the monitor, and various keywords flashed on screen for a second before disappearing. Words like *Nazi, bomb, Democrat, Intelligencer, Republican, Führer, Jew, Israel, terrorism,* even *aliens.* Then *Intelligencer* popped up several times in a row, followed by *blacks*—and with a beep, the screen began scrolling through paragraphs of text.

"Okay, Tempora isolated the segments of speech that have the highest hit percentage for the keywords I fed it. Let's see what we've got."

A man's voice came over the phone while the computer highlighted the text like a closed caption TV system would.

"Raul, we can't have this kind of dissent from the staff editors." The man had a slight accent—vaguely Spanish, but muddled somehow. *"You need to get them in line and make sure they understand that what we're doing is for*

the good of the business. They'll accept doing things for the Intelligencer—*after all, it's how they get paid. This is a long battle in the war against the* Untermenschen. *For the police forces, we must emphasize the clashes they have with your minorities. The blacks and browns need to be shown as victims."*

"Victims?" This voice had an American accent. *"But—"*

"Listen to me. If we make it clear that these Africans are being victimized by the brutal police, it gets us what we want. Let the savages play the victim. Let them soak in it. It will help with our narrative against the authorities. By emphasizing these police encounters with minorities, we can weaken society's support for its police. Turn the public against them. And we can make the blacks and the browns dependent on those who truly do not have their best interest. We write stories about how welfare is just and fair for those poor victims. Abortion rights are especially important—already in some US cities, more black babies are aborted than born. This is excellent. We want more of this. And so do they! It's their right."

Both voices laughed, and Levi swallowed at the bile rising in his throat.

"We shape the stories. We weaken those who are truly our enemy."

"Like Israel?" the American said.

"They're the enemy. So many of the Untermenschen *escaped the final plan and have infested that part of the world. Obviously we can't have them shown in a sympathetic light. It's not what our readers want."*

The man laughed again, and Levi and Denny exchanged an expression of disgust.

"But we do have a large Jewish readership—"

"Raul, it won't matter. Be subtle. Don't print the things that are inescapably favorable to those Zionists. If you have trouble with your staff, change them. Move them. Let me know if there's any issues with anyone. Just remember, it's for the good of the readership, the Intelligencer, *and their jobs. Over the last fifty years, the public has slowly shifted to our way of thinking, and it will continue to do so. Trust me. My grandfather laid this plan out even before he left the fatherland. The Reich will be reborn. It will just take time.*

"And Raul, you're a big part of this. Our paper is referenced by many others as an authority, which means you have in your hands the reins to control the thoughts of millions of readers. Don't underestimate the power we have at our disposal.

"And be patient. The fatherland fell because we were overeager. Our plan is set, but it needs time to bloom. It's not yet that time.

"Remember, if you have any issues, the security team I've hand-selected should be able to take care of it. Anything more complex, get in touch with me and we'll talk."

The sound of chairs scraping against a floor was followed by the opening and closing of a door, and then silence.

Levi cleared his throat. "There's no way those two would have said that if they knew they were being taped. The room had to have been bugged."

Denny smiled. "Sounds like that Jewish reporter of yours had a little spycraft in him. That takes some giant brass balls."

"Especially considering who he was bugging," Marty said. *"I would have to assume that 'Raul' is Raul Vicente, the head guy at the* Intelligencer.*"*

"Then who was the other guy?" Levi wondered aloud. "He sounded like a total peach. Though he doesn't have a German accent, he's sure as hell sounded like a Nazi. Oh, by the way, what's an *Untermenschen*? He talked about being at war with them."

"An Untermenschen is what the Nazis called inferior people," Marty said. *"You know, Jews, blacks, homosexuals, and others that were sub-human to them. This is way more serious than I thought. I'm going to have to get Mason involved, and we'll call in some extra hands on this. I'll put a team on the* Intelligencer *and also get some resources on Herman Gerhard. We need to tie these people together. This has the feel of a national-level security issue. Levi, what in the hell have you managed to uncover?"*

Levi shook his head. "I have no idea, since this all start with some widow and her supposedly unfaithful husband. Anyway, there's one thing I insist." He lowered his voice to a deep growl. "If and when anyone moves against this Gerhard character, I want in on it. And I want some time with him when this goes down."

"I can't promise anything like that."

"Then I'll talk to Mason. I'm not taking no for an answer."

CHAPTER SIXTEEN

A handful of mob associates were working out in the basement of the Helmsley Arms. A variety of state-of-the-art workout equipment, ranging from stationary bikes to treadmills to weightlifting stations, was flanked by floor-to-ceiling mirrors that were mounted on the walls. Most of the crew were rotating through the weightlifting stations, but Levi found himself in the center of the gym, squared off against a 125-pound heavy bag hanging by a chain from the ceiling. Beads of sweat poured down his face as he performed a series of snap kicks, the heavy thwacks of his shin against the canvas echoing loudly across the gym.

Jimmy "The Truck" Gambino hopped off the bench press and moved his arms around in circles, having just benched four hundred pounds, then walked over to Levi. He was only about five foot eight, but he was easily two hundred and twenty pounds of solid muscle.

"Hey, you wanna go all crazy on it, I'll hold the bag for you," he said.

Levi gave him a nod.

Jimmy grabbed the bag and braced himself.

Levi sent a barrage of kicks, jabs, and punches at the now-steady target. The soreness in his chest was practically gone, and his hits grew in pace and intensity, forcing Jimmy to push forward against the onslaught.

After nearly two minutes of nonstop attacks, Levi finished with a spinning back kick that knocked Jimmy two steps backward and left Levi breathing heavily.

"Nice," said a woman from the far side of the gym, near the elevators.

His muscles aching, Levi grabbed a towel, wiped his face, and smiled as Lucy walked toward him.

Jimmy bumped fists with Levi. "You're a fucking beast, my friend."

Tony had also come down on the elevator, but instead of walking over, he just shouted across the gym. "I tried ringing the apartment and you didn't answer, so I figured you were down here. I gotta get back to the front, but I figured she was okay to come see you, am I right?"

Levi nodded, Tony disappeared back upstairs.

"How is it that you're able to do that?" Lucy asked.

"What do you mean?" Levi moved his arms back and forth, feeling the heat from the exertion making him less tense. "I've been doing that stuff for years."

"No, I mean how are you moving so well after only a couple weeks. The doctors—"

"Doctors don't know everything." Levi waved dismissively.

Lucy's sour expression faltered as a smile crept onto her face. "You're impossible." She leaned in, gave him a kiss on the lips, and whispered in Mandarin, "I wanted to let you know that it's going down tomorrow, first thing in the morning." She handed him a plastic keycard. "That's for you. I've got to run—there's lots of stuff I need to get ready. You coming over tonight?"

Levi nodded. "I'll walk you out."

As they started toward the elevators, one of the bull-necked mobsters asked, "Hey, Levi, are you okay to start up those lessons again?"

"Sure. I'll be right back and we can go over disarming techniques."

"Cool." The mobster called out to one of the men near the supply cabinet. "Hey, get those rubber knives out of there."

"You teach them martial arts?" Lucy asked as they got on the elevator.

"Nah, just some basic techniques to help out with their day-to-day stuff."

Lucy wrapped her arm around his. "Maybe we can teach each other some lessons."

Levi raised an eyebrow. "That could get interesting."

She gave him a sidelong glance and shook her head. "I'm not sure how to interpret that."

The elevator doors opened and they stepped into the lobby. "Well, I suppose we'll have to wait and see just how interesting it is." Through the lobby's glass entrance he saw a familiar vehicle idling in front of the building. "Is that yours?"

"Yes." Lucy gave him a quick peck on the lips. "Tonight?"

Levi nodded and watched as she walked out and hopped into the back of the waiting SUV.

Curiosity grew within him as he wondered what she had in store for tomorrow's assassination.

After his training session with the other mobsters, Levi headed to Lucy's apartment. As he stepped out of the elevator onto her floor, he was greeted by a beefy Asian guard who could easily have passed for a sumo wrestler. The man was a giant, almost as tall as Paulie, and probably weighed nearly four hundred pounds.

He gave Levi a polite nod and said in halting English, "Madam is home, Mr. Yoder."

"Thanks. What's your name?"

The guard looked confused for a moment, then with seeming reluctance said, "Zhang Wei."

Levi replied in Mandarin. "It is good to meet you, Zhang Wei. Please, just call me Levi."

The guard shook his head and responded in English. "No, Mr. Yoder. But thank you for asking."

Levi wasn't sure what to make of the humorless security guard. He chuckled and switched back to English. "Okay, smiley. Hope you have a good day."

Levi swiped the keycard that Lucy had given him over the reader on the apartment door, and the lock disengaged. He walked inside and was greeted by a scene he hadn't expected.

This wasn't the planning of an elaborate assassination plot. There were no street maps with arrows and well-choreographed movements. No array of weaponry being cleaned and prepped. Instead, four women sat on the sofa watching a movie on TV.

Charlie's Angels, of course.

Levi removed his shoes and took a seat next to Lucy. She leaned against him as the movie continued.

After a minute, it dawned on Levi that Ting, Ruth, and Min were all apparently understanding the movie, even though it was in English and there were no subtitles. He leaned closer to Lucy and whispered, "It's in English. How are they following?"

She patted his knee. "They all understand English."

Levi paused, realizing he'd fooled himself into making assumptions. He shook his head and smiled. He would need to stay on his toes around these ladies.

Lucy Liu's character appeared on screen, and Lucy nudged him. "You think I look like her?"

Levi bobbed his head to the left and right. "Sort of. You have a lot of the same intensity."

"I think she's prettier."

Levi looked at Lucy and shook his head. "I disagree."

She wrapped his arm around her shoulders and rested her head against his chest. "Good answer."

Levi leaned back and tried to relax. But with Lucy and these ladies planning an operation he knew nothing about, relaxing was pretty much impossible.

When the movie finally ended forty-five minutes later, the women clapped politely and began chattering in Cantonese about it.

Levi waited patiently for the critique to subside before asking, "Can you guys fill me in on tomorrow's plans?"

Lucy hopped up from the sofa and held out her hand. "Come, we'll show you. If you want, you can even be involved."

He looked at her quizzically as she pulled him up off the sofa. She'd previously made it clear to him that she wouldn't let him get involved in helping fix her affairs. This was a change in pace.

They all went into the dining room, and Levi saw immediately that this wasn't going to be a simple shot-in-the-back-of-the-head assassination. Arrayed on the travertine table were eight handguns, a loaded magazine lying next to each, and four sets of folded-up garments that looked suspiciously like nuns' habits. But it was the red canister with black writing on it that gave Levi pause. They looked like they were military issue, and each had a pull ring.

What in the world were these women doing with grenades?

It was well before sunup when Levi stepped out of his bedroom in Lucy's apartment. He was fully dressed, armed with one .45 caliber handgun in his shoulder holster, his SIG Sauer P229 nine-millimeter tucked into an in-waistband holster at the small of his back, and a couple of specially made throwing knives that were always with him.

He smiled as he walked into the kitchen and found Lucy standing there in a nun's habit—minus the headpiece.

"Is it wrong that I think you look sexy in that outfit?" he said.

Lucy smiled with uncharacteristically girlish delight as she looked at herself and ran her hands over the black material. "It's very roomy. That's why I picked it."

"I suppose it won't be so out of place outside of a Catholic church." Levi grabbed a carton of milk from the refrigerator and poured himself a glass. "No tea or coffee this morning?"

Lucy shook her head. "I don't do caffeine before a fight, especially if I'm using a gun. I need a steady hand for that."

As he drank his milk, he glanced toward the dining room table. The grenades and guns were gone.

Lucy noticed the direction of his gaze. She smiled and patted the billowing nun's habit. "I've got it on me."

"Ya, I guess you don't have to worry about any of that imprinting under that habit. Are you going to tell me why you need an incendiary grenade?"

"Nope. Just be thankful I'm letting you be our driver. I need you to understand that I'm just as capable as you in doing what needs to be done."

Levi finished his milk and put the glass in the sink. "Have I ever doubted your—"

"It doesn't matter." Lucy grabbed him by the chin and gave him a quick kiss. "You're a good man, but I know you have some unspoken doubts. Just get us out when it's time."

Levi stretched his back and heard a few comforting pops. "I'm just the getaway driver."

"Exactly."

Much of 41st Street had been lined with construction barriers, but as Levi approached, two Asian men in a work van removed the barriers directly across from a Chinese restaurant.

"Don't worry, they work for me," Lucy said.

The workmen motioned toward the now-empty spot, then hopped into their truck and drove away.

Levi pulled in, and the three women in the back seat of the Cadillac Escalade SUV got out, leaving behind just the clear plastic sheeting that was covering all of the seats but the driver's. Levi watched as Ruth, Min, and Ting, all dressed as nuns, raced toward the dumpster that had been placed on the street in front of the restaurant. One of them unlocked a control box attached to the dumpster, and using some form of hydraulics, the top of the dumpster yawned open.

"What's the dumpster for?" he asked. "You planning on putting the bodies in there?"

In the passenger seat beside him, Lucy smiled. "You'll see. It's about ten minutes before mass starts at St. Michael's." She leaned over, gave him a kiss, hopped out, and ran to join the others as they walked up the street toward St. Michael's.

The minutes ticked by, and Levi had nothing to do but watch the people who walked toward the church. Almost all were probably Chinese, since Lucy had told him the early morning mass was being given in Mandarin.

But then the action began. He spotted a group of five men walking toward the church, and at the same time, he spotted the four nuns walking, heads down, away from the church and toward the men.

Whatever was going to happen, it was going to happen now.

The older man leading the group wore dark sunglasses—even though it was early morning and over-cast—a brown fedora, and an expensive-looking suit worn sloppily. He was keeping a brisk pace. That had to be the guy.

Without thinking, Levi pulled his Glock from the shoulder holster. Then he stopped and admonished himself. "Levi, this isn't yours to do." He put the gun in his lap and gripped the steering wheel as the two groups approached each other.

His heart raced as he looked on.

Lucy counted five, with Xiang leading the group. Glancing at her companions, they nodded and walked west on 41st Street. Without having to look, she knew the women had both of their guns ready. They'd planned for up to eight opponents, but with five, she'd be able to what she'd hoped.

The four "nuns" walked with a steady pace, all of them with their faces focused on the ground just ahead of them. Lucy's hands were hidden by the dark garment of their costume.

With the cool fire of revenge burning in her veins, Lucy gripped her pistol in one hand and held ready a strip of duct tape in the other.

With just a glance, she caught the blur of the men approaching on the sidewalk. The clicks of Xiang's foot-steps rang loudly in her ears. They were about fifty feet from each other.

Forty...

Thirty...

Lucy's heart raced and yet the women maintained their pace, neither slowing down or speeding up.

Twenty...

Ten...

Lucy held her breath as the two groups passed each other on the sidewalk.

And just as they passed the last of Xiang's men, all four women turned.

For Lucy, it felt like everything was moving in slow motion.

Ruth, Ting, and Min selected their targets.

Ting was the first as her silenced weapon recoiled with practically no sound whatsoever.

And then Ruth pulled her trigger, following by Min.

Lucy pushed forward as the women continued firing

into their targets. The men collapsed like marionettes whose strings had been cut.

The one gang member who was just behind Xiang turned.

Without hesitation, Lucy squeezed off two shots, both slammed into the man's face, splattering Xiang with blood.

Xiang felt at the back of his neck and Lucy rushed forward, being careful to hop over the convulsing man she'd shot.

Aiming low, she shot three times, and rushed to Xiang as his legs gave out under him.

Slapping the duct tape over the man's mouth, he was still conscious, despite having had his spine severed by her gunshots.

Lucy heard the women struggling with the bodies, but her focus was on Xiang as she spit in his face.

"I remember what you did to me." She smiled at Xiang's widening eyes.

He recognized her, beneath the nun's habit and the blood spattered on her face, Xiang knew who she was.

Good.

Putting away her gun, she grabbed his arm and said, "I saved you from death by gunshot, so you could be awake to enjoy this."

With the help of the others, Lucy lifted Xiang up and tossed him into the open dumpster.

The women raced back across the street, while Lucy pulled the pin from the incendiary grenade and dumped it into the trash.

Lucy slammed the control box to the dumpster and its

top began closing as smoke and heat billowed up from within.

"Burn in hell," Lucy growled as she raced back to the SUV.

~

Levi had been holding his breath as he watched the action from his vantage point. Just as the last of the men passed the nuns, the women turned in a swirl of black and quickly mowed down the gang members.

Working quickly as a team, the women heaved the bodies into the dumpster and then raced back to the SUV.

Lucy was the last to leave the scene. She pulled the red canister from within her habit, pulled the ring, tossed it in the dumpster, and slammed the control box with the palm of her hand. The top began to lower as intense light flared from within.

Ruth ripped open the rear passenger door and dove into the back seat, followed by the others. Lucy climbed into the front, yelling, "Let's go!"

Drips of molten metal seeped from the edges of the dumpster, and Levi swore he could feel the rising heat even from thirty feet away. As he turned the wheel and slammed his foot on the gas, he asked, "What the hell was in that dumpster?"

"Two thousand pounds of thermite," Lucy said matter-of-factly.

"Two thousand *pounds*? How the hell... no, let me guess. Esther."

Lucy smiled as she used wet naps to wipe her face

from the blood spatter. "I told you women can take care of business, often much better than men."

Looking in the rearview mirror, all he saw was a brilliant blob of light as the dumpster was overwhelmed by an intense chemical reaction that no water would put out. He chuckled and shook his head. "I never doubted you for a second."

At a dingy hotel on 39th Street, the ladies, now changed into ordinary clothes, piled out of the car, grabbing a duffel bag from the back. Levi rolled down the window, and Lucy leaned in and said, "Don't worry, I've arranged to get a pickup after we shower."

"And you're sure about the car?"

"Yes." She blew a kiss through the open window. "Consider it a present."

Levi smiled as the women streamed into the Hyatt. Lucy really had planned every aspect of the operation.

As he pulled away from the hotel, he took out his phone and dialed a number.

"Yup."

"It's a 2019 Cadillac Escalade. Full cleanup and strip. Bring Laurel and Hardy in for the cleanup, part the rest of it out."

"You got it, boss. The cleaners are already here and the parts crew is getting ready. One hour from whenever you get here, there won't be anything left."

"Good. I'll be there in thirty minutes."

He hung up and battled morning traffic. He was almost at his destination when the phone rang. "Yes?"

"Levi." It was Doug Mason's gravelly voice. *"I've got some news for you on a few things. Are you able to talk?"*

Hearing Mason's voice sent a shiver through him. "Go ahead. I'm just sitting at a red light."

"I wanted to call you directly on this. Based on some of the work Marty and his team have done with the intelligence you gathered, we're putting together a case for an international operation. I want to make sure you're in a condition that—"

"I'm totally healthy, if that's what you're asking. Is this to Argentina?"

"Possibly. We're still working on some details. Before we get to that, I need help gathering some intel. We've confirmed there's been communication between our friends in Argentina and the security office in the Intelligencer building. Marty and his team managed to retrieve voice records of those calls, and the voice patterns picked up a match for someone known to us. He's ex-Special Forces. I'll forward you his records and the latest photos we have. We believe he can help confirm a few things. I'll send you a list of items we need. I'm assuming you'll be able to help gather the intel for us?"

Levi smiled as he turned right on Amsterdam Avenue. "I'll work something out."

"Just be careful. I know you're quite capable of handling yourself, but this guy's no slouch. He won't go down easy."

"Understood."

"One more thing. I have some rather unpleasant news about Mindy Cross."

Levi's heart sank into his stomach. "She's dead, isn't she?"

"I'm afraid so. Her naked body was found by a New York State Highway Patrol unit about four hours ago, just outside of Utica. From the initial police report, it looks like she'd been tortured, and most of the bones in her body were crushed. She was only ID'd through fingerprints."

Levi tightened his grip on the steering wheel as he pulled into the open bay of a repair shop. "Thanks for letting me know. Send me what you've got and I'll be right on it."

"It's sent. Good luck."

The rolling door lowered as Levi got out of the Escalade, and Angelo approached.

"Hey, Levi." He peeked inside the black SUV, then patted the roof with a gloved hand. "This is a totally sweet ride. You're sure you want a total cleanup and have it parted out?"

"I'm sure."

Angelo began bellowing instructions to the crew. One guy rolled over a giant red box of mechanic's tools while another lit an acetylene torch.

Levi stepped aside with his phone to look at the data Mason had sent him. It was clear this guy he needed to talk to was going to be trouble. Staff Sergeant Jerry Mixon was a former member of the Tenth Special Forces Group out of Fort Carson. He had three tours in Iraq and one stint as part of Joint Combined Exchange Training in the Negev Desert in Israel.

Among the info Mason sent was a scanned image of some handwritten notes by a Captain Lassiter.

During a desert terrain maneuver, Staff Sergeant Mixon had point, and was at the controls of the Humvee when he veered off course and plowed into an IDF squad, killing one Israeli soldier and injuring two others.

He claimed that he'd veered off course due to what he believed was an IED set on the trail as part of the exercise. He further claimed that he didn't see the squad he'd run into.

There were no obstacles officially placed on the trail as part of the exercise. Furthermore, testimony from Staff Sergeants Ramirez and Baxter, both of whom were in trailing vehicles, claimed to not see anything that would have prompted Staff Sergeant Mixon's actions.

It seemed that incident marked the end of Mixon's career. He was offered a chapter ten dismissal from the army, which allowed him to avoid a court-martial and thereby start his civilian life without a federal conviction. He was stripped of all military benefits, of course. For the past five years he'd been working as chief of security for the *Intelligencer*.

Levi hit one of his speed-dial numbers, and three rings later, Frankie answered. *"Hey, what's up?"*

"I've got someone I need to do a pickup on, but I need a little help."

"How much help?"

"I'm thinking a visit from the doc, a pickup crew, and one more."

"One more? This must be a big boy."

Levi looked back at the SUV and was surprised to see that it had already almost been stripped to the frame. "Ya, he's going to be a handful. It'll be just outside the *Intelligencer* building."

"Okay, my friend. I'll set it up. I'll have one of the capos give you a call when they're ready."

"Thanks."

Levi hung up and walked over to the remnants of the SUV. "Can one of you guys drop me off at Lenox Hill?"

One of the men winching the engine up from out of its mounting said, "I'm heading that way in a bit. I can take you."

"Thanks."

Levi turned back to his phone and pulled up an image of former staff sergeant Mixon. The man's stone-like face reminded Levi of some of the bruisers he encountered that time he was in Russia. The man's thick muscular neck, wide chest, and menacing stare were probably enough to scare most people off.

Levi smiled as he took in the image of the elite soldier. "The bigger they are, the harder they fall."

CHAPTER SEVENTEEN

When Levi opened the door to Lucy's palatial apartment, he was greeted by the sound of the four women enthusiastically saying "*Ganbei*!"—the equivalent of "Cheers" in English. He followed the sound of clinking glasses and laughter to the dining room, where Lucy stood, holding out a champagne glass.

"To our handsome angel in wolf's clothing," she said.

Min poured another glass and handed it to Levi.

Lucy stepped up to him, a devilish smile on her face.

"I came over just—" he began, but was cut off as Lucy gripped the back of his head and pressed her lips against his. The other women tittered and cheered.

Levi backed away and smiled. "I have to get going. I was just checking to see if everything's okay."

"Everything is really great," Lucy said. She pouted. "But I wanted to celebrate with you. Please?" She ran a finger down his chest and hooked it around his belt, pulling him closer.

He felt his heart thundering in his chest. Something with Lucy had completely changed. Was she drunk?

"I have to meet some people related to the Cohen case. Otherwise…"

Lucy ran her hands over the front of his suit jacket as if wiping away lint. "A rain check?"

"Yes, when I'm done with this." He turned away, trying to ignore the effect that Lucy was having on him. He needed his mind clear and on the task at hand—a task that involved a dirty ex-Special Forces soldier who needed to be broken.

Levi paid the owner of a hot dog stand twenty bucks to let him hang out behind him while he served customers. The man readily agreed—it was free money for the dirty water dog vendor—and the spot gave Levi a perfect view of the people coming and going through the entrance to the *Intelligencer*'s headquarters.

It wasn't a short wait. Nearly six hours passed, and it was on into the evening before Levi saw the tall brute of a man he was looking for.

As soon as the man exited the building, Levi jogged across the crosswalk and managed to hit the sidewalk just as Jerry Mixon approached the corner.

The head of *Intelligencer* security stopped short at the sight of Levi. "Mr. Yoder, I'm surprised to see you… looking so well."

An icy sensation crept up the back of Levi's neck. The man had for all intents and purposes just admitted that he knew Levi was shot.

Levi grinned. "Surprised the bullets didn't do their jobs, Jerry? I've got some questions that I think you have answers to."

"You won't get anything from me." Mixon started once again toward the street corner, but he got no more than two steps before Levi blocked the ex-soldier's way.

Mixon snorted, put his hands on his waist, and shook his head. "You have no idea who you're dealing with. Get out of my way." He puffed out his chest and let his suit part slightly, revealing the butt end of a pistol in a shoulder holster.

"Make me," Levi growled in return. Adrenaline dumped into his bloodstream and he felt his rage building.

"Little man, don't make me have to hurt you. It'll take a lot more than you to—"

As planned, Paulie had come up behind the man. The big mobster smacked the back of the ex-soldier's head with a rubber-coated baton.

And yet, despite the power behind the blow, Mixon didn't go down. His eyes unfocused for a mere moment. Still, that was long enough for Paulie to cover his face with a cloth doused in sevoflurane, a potent anesthetic.

A white-paneled van screeched to a halt beside them, and within seconds, Paulie, Levi, and the ex-soldier were gone.

In a sound-isolated room in an abandoned building, Levi stood back and watched the tiny bespectacled Indian man named Mohan do his work on Jerry Mixon. Mohan was legitimate—he had been a practicing anesthesiologist before he retired—but Vinnie's father had done him some kind of favor, and now the man was completely loyal to the Bianchi family. In fact, for as long as Levi could remember, this same doctor had always been brought in for specialized situations such as this.

"He'll be fully conscious, right?" Levi asked.

"Oh, most definitely," the doctor said confidently, with a strong Indian accent . He cut open Mixon's shirt, revealing a well-muscled torso and a tattoo of a swastika on his right pec. "He's one of those, is he?"

"Evidently."

Mohan placed several electrical leads on Mixon's chest, one on each arm, and one on each side of the man's waist. He had already intubated the big man, and the machine was in essence breathing for him.

Finally, he pulled out a syringe, cleaned the injection port on the IV with an alcohol swab, and plunged the syringe into it. He smiled at Levi. "This is Quelicin—the good stuff. It'll only be about a minute before he's totally immobile. I'll attach an infusion pump to the IV so that he gets a constant four milligrams per minute throughout the procedure. You tell me when you want him wiggling again, and I'll make it happen."

Levi dialed Doug Mason.

"Do you have the brain scan application installed?"

"Denny put it on my phone. It's running, but from what I can tell... Hold on." Levi turned to the doc, who was now attaching wires to Mixon's scalp with some type of adhesive. "When will we have a view into his head?"

"Any second now." Mohan attached one last lead and pressed a button on a machine. "That should do it. The EEG is running."

Levi looked down at his phone app. A bunch of wavy lines scrolled from left to right on the screen. "Doug, are you getting this?"

"Yup. Let's see if this guy is worth the trouble we've gone through."

Levi put his phone on speaker and set it down. "Let's wake him up, Doc."

They all knew that interrogating Mixon was pointless; the man would have died before he'd willingly tell them anything. And a standard lie detector would be no better —he'd probably been trained on how to beat one of those. But by monitoring the man's brain waves directly, Levi could get around any such training. This was a whole new methodology that worked better than anyone liked to admit.

The doc handed Levi a capsule, which he broke under the ex-soldier's nose. The smell of ammonia permeated the air.

The doc kept an eye on the EEG. "He's conscious."

Mixon hadn't moved even an eyelash.

Levi leaned in close. "It must be hell knowing I'm out here and you're stuck in an unmoving body. But like I said before, we have a few questions for you."

Levi held up one finger, which was the agreed-upon sign for when he was about to say something truthful. Just as with a standard lie detector test, they would need a few control questions to calibrate the responses. "Staff Sergeant Jerry Mixon, I hear you avoided a big chicken dinner by chaptering out of the service."

The doc checked the screen, then scribbled something on a notepad.

Levi held up two fingers. A lie was coming. "Staff Sergeant Jerry Mixon, you are currently fifty-two years old."

More scribbling from the doc.

They continued these control questions for the next couple minutes. Finally Mason said, *"Our guy says he's got a good lock on this guy's brain wave patterns. Let's move on."*

Levi picked up his phone, flipped to the playback application, and played clip number one.

"The fatherland fell because we were overeager. Our plan is set, but it needs time to bloom. It's not yet that time."

"Staff Sergeant Jerry Mixon. You know that voice."

The ex-soldier lay still, but the doc checked the screen, then nodded, indicating that Mixon viewed Levi's statement as true.

Levi frowned. "The voice on the phone is Herman Gerhard."

Again, a nod from the doctor.

"You are familiar with the name Mendel Cohen."

Yes from the doctor.

"You poisoned Mendel Cohen in some way."

Yes.

"You were ordered to do it."

Yes.

"Herman Gerhard gave that order."

No.

Levi mentally replayed the scene from Denny's back room when he first heard the name of his assassin. "The order came from Juan Gerhard."

Yes.

"Okay, that's enough," said Mason.

Levi took his phone off speaker. "You don't need more?"

"No, we have other intel that confirms the same kind of thing. What you're seeing at the newspaper has happened with a half dozen other places. These people are a risk to national security at the highest level. I've already tabulated a list of names, including judges and elected officials, that are in their pocket. Our friends down south are responsible for more than you can even imagine. I've got enough to justify an extraction team. We promised to give you a shot if it came up—this'll be it. You up for it?"

"Does a chicken have feathers? Hell, yes. Tell me when."

"I'll make a few calls, but keep your phone by your side. It'll be very soon. As for our sedated friend. I can send someone over to clean him up, or I can leave it up to you. Your choice."

"I got this," Levi said.

He hung up, disabled the transmissions from the brain-wave app, and returned to Mixon's side.

"Staff Sergeant Jerry Mixon. You know who Mindy Cross is."

The doctor again indicated yes.

Levi's fingers tingled with pent-up rage. "You killed her."

The doctor frowned as he nodded.

Levi took a deep breath. "Staff Sergeant Jerry Mixon. It was Herman Gerhard who ordered it."

The doctor shook his head.

Levi gritted his teeth. "Juan Gerhard ordered it."

Yes.

Levi closed his eyes for a second, then turned to the doc. "You can leave now."

The physician pointed at all the wiring and equipment. "What about all this?"

Levi gave as reassuring of a smile as he could muster. "I'll make sure he's taken care of. Thank you so much for everything."

Levi escorted the man out of the room and watched him as he walked down the lonely hallway and turned the corner toward the exit. When he was satisfied that the doctor was gone, he sent a quick text, grabbed some medical tape, and returned to the paralyzed ex-soldier.

He ripped off two pieces of tape, then pried Mixon's eyes open. The man's pupils contracted, reacting to the light. He was definitely in there.

"I want to make sure you can see me," Levi said as he taped the man's eyelids open.

The door opened, and in walked Laurel and Hardy.

Levi nodded at them before facing Mixon once more. "Jerry, that girl you left on the side of the road like a bunch of garbage, she was a good person. She didn't deserve that. And because of that, I want your last moments in life to come with certain... knowledge. I did

243

a little research on you, and I know that your wife died giving birth to twins, Harry and Harriet." Levi's heart pounded in his chest. "And when you go to hell, Jerry, I want you to remember this: I'll make sure that your kids get the same treatment Mindy got."

Levi took two steps back, drew his .45 caliber Glock from its shoulder holster, and shot the ex-soldier twice in the head. Brain matter and blood spattered across the bed and nearby electronics.

"Nice," Laurel said. He began putting on white plastic coveralls.

"Are you really gonna take out that guy's kids?" Hardy asked.

Levi smiled and shook his head. "Of course not. I just wanted that asshole to think that as his last dying thought."

"Whoa. That's harsh." Hardy began disconnecting the equipment.

"What he did to that woman was harsh. It's the least I could do for her."

As he walked out the door, his phone vibrated with a text from Mason.

I just sent you an address. Be there in two hours. Don't pack, the Outfit will handle all the logistics. Bring your ID.

CHAPTER EIGHTEEN

"I can't really talk about it," Levi said. "I'm in an Uber on the way to a meetup." He felt guilty that he probably wasn't going to be returning tonight.

"Let me guess," Lucy said. *"It's for the Outfit."*

"Yes."

"Levi, let me be honest with you. There's a reason why I separated myself from Mason. They always want more of you than you're willing to give. I was to them exactly what you are right now: an angel in wolf's clothing. You're one of their bad guys that they can work through. But eventually, that won't be good enough. And I'm afraid for you."

"I don't understand. When we first met, I thought you were in a pretty good place with them."

"I was. I am. But they'll eventually ask you what they asked me. They wanted my loyalty to the Outfit above all

else. And at the time, I was still trying to make my husband's business work, you know, rebuild his legacy. Now that I've completely obliterated it, I don't have that excuse to say 'no' to them anymore. Well, except for one."

"And what's that?"

All Levi heard was her breathing.

"Lucy?"

"It's hard for me to say this on the phone. I wanted to do this the right way..."

"Do what?"

"Levi, I can't imagine my life without you in it. I have no idea if you feel the same way—and that's not me trying to get you to say something back. In fact, don't..."

Levi felt a flush going up his neck. He couldn't believe this was the same stoic dragon lady he'd met only a handful of months before.

"My point is, I know you. You're dedicated to your family. Both your real one and the one you've sworn yourself to. You'll never quit, and that's one of the things I love about you. But it's also why I can't have anything to do with the Outfit. I can't offer them the connections I used to anymore. They'll want me all the way in or not at all. And if I'm in, that means I don't run my life anymore. I'd have to keep things from you and set them at a higher priority. I don't want that, I want to control my life. You, they'll push for more, but they'll settle for what they can get. Do you understand what I'm saying?"

"I do." Levi felt a strange regret. "Listen, you and I need to talk about us. But not now. I have to get going. I'm going to be out of town probably for a day or two. I'll call you as soon as I can. Okay?"

"Please be careful."

"I will."

As Levi hung up, the Uber pulled up to the corner of Lenox Avenue and West 127th Street in Harlem. Levi thanked the driver and hopped out. But as he walked toward his destination, he had to work to shove the conversation with Lucy out of his mind.

He needed to focus.

This neighborhood didn't strike him as one with a hot nightlife, but just up ahead, techno music hummed through a door surrounded by purple neon lights, and two bouncers outside were telling a couple of teenagers to move on.

Checking the address, Levi realized that this night club was his destination.

He approached the two bouncers. They were huge men, probably three hundred pounds each, but with a powerlifting, strong-as-an-ox sort of build. Levi would have said they were twins of Fat Albert, but only if Fat Albert worked out a lot more.

"I'm supposed to meet someone here," Levi said.

One of the bouncers said, "I'll need to see some ID, Mr. Yoder."

Levi hesitated. *How the hell does he know my name?*

But he said nothing as he pulled out his wallet and showed his driver's license to the half-ogre.

The man shook his head. "Not that kind of ID, sir."

It took a couple seconds before Levi recalled who'd sent him there. He dug the coin out of his pocket and held it out.

The bouncer grabbed the other side of it, and when

the coin's eye lit up, both men stepped aside and motioned for Levi to enter.

As Levi opened the door, he braced himself for an auditory onslaught. But despite the sound of techno music seemingly coming through the door, the inside of the building was utterly silent. And when he shut the door behind him, he heard only the muted sound of the music —coming from *outside*.

Or, apparently, from the door itself.

The whole thing was a ruse.

He stood inside a wood-paneled lobby, fresh with the scent of wood polish and pipe tobacco. A reception desk stood across the room, manned by a tall, thin, white-haired gentleman.

"Mr. Yoder, I was told to expect you tonight." The man spoke with a very posh British accent, and reminded Levi of the butler from *Downton Abbey*. "ID, please."

This time Levi knew what to do. He held out the coin, and when the attendant grabbed the other side, the eye began glowing.

"Very well, sir. It's very good to meet you. I'm Mr. Watkins, the proprietor of this establishment."

Levi looked at his surroundings. "I'm sorry, Mr. Watkins, but what is this place?"

"I suppose that's a simple question with a complicated answer. Let's just say that this establishment meets the needs of those who seek its assistance. And I believe you are here for just such a reason."

"I'm not really sure what I'm here for, to be honest."

Watkins motioned toward a hall on Levi's left. "Then let's see if we can figure that out. Please, follow me."

The hallway was lit by old-fashioned sconces with lightbulbs that flickered as if they were aflame. At the end of the hall a door stood slightly ajar.

"Sir, this is our quartermaster's domain. When you arrived, it was this wing that was unlocked." With a grand sweeping gesture, Watkins motioned toward the door. "After you."

As Levi pushed the door open, he was surprised by how slowly it moved. It was six inches thick and must have weighed hundreds of pounds. Nonetheless, it moved noiselessly.

As he stepped through the doorway, lights flickered on, revealing a locker room similar to the one Lucy had shown him in Seattle. At that location, he'd collected a variety of guns and cash. But this room was a hundred times bigger. He couldn't help but wonder what in the world it might contain.

Curious, he tapped on a few of the lockers. He didn't hear a hollow thud. Nor did he see any means of opening the doors.

Mr. Watkins motioned toward a pole in the center of the room. Affixed at about eye level was a visor, like one might see on a submarine's periscope. "If you will, Mr. Yoder, please peer into the biometric scanner."

Levi walked over and put his eyes against the visor. A green light flickered, followed by a series of clicks. And then nothing.

Levi stepped back and looked around. Several of the lockers had popped open.

"Sir," said Mr. Watkins, gesturing, "let's start with this side of the room, shall we?"

Levi's curiosity was undeniable as he looked into the first open locker. Inside lay a set of military fatigues.

"It's clear that the company has you going on a mission," said Watkins. "It would be wise for you to put those on."

Levi turned to face the man. With his almost-white hair and the wrinkles around his eyes, he had to be in his late sixties at least—but his voice was strong, he had perfect posture, and he gave off a youthful energy. Altogether, it gave him an ageless quality.

"How long have you been doing this?" Levi asked.

"This, sir? What do you mean?"

"I mean walking people through whatever it is I'm doing."

"Oh, you mean prepping for a mission?"

"Is that what this is?"

"Of course. And as to how long I've been doing this…" Watkins pressed his lips tightly together and hummed for a bit. "I suppose this would be my fourth decade. Yes, just about forty years."

Levi's eyes widened. "I guess I'm in good hands."

"Most certainly, sir."

"And you can call me Levi."

"That's very kind of you, sir, but I think after forty years, I'd be more likely to spontaneously combust than to fall out of proper protocol."

With a laugh, Levi pulled out the fatigues. "Should I change now?"

"I think that would be for the best." Watkins motioned toward a table next to the biometric scanner. "You can leave your possessions on the table. I'll keep them safe for your return."

Levi put on the fatigues. The name tape on the shirt was printed with the name *Yoder*, and on his arm was a patch with the wolf and halo insignia.

"They're not kidding around with this angel in wolf's clothing, are they?" he said.

"No, sir. Shall we continue?" Watkins motioned toward the next locker.

Levi moved one by one through the next several lockers, and soon he was almost completely kitted out as a soldier, from his military-issue combat boots to an advanced battle vest with ballistic inserts, load distribution system, and what Watkins called SAPIs and ESBIs— small-arms protective inserts and enhanced side ballistic inserts. The Outfit wasn't fooling around when it came to protective gear.

At the next locker, he picked up a Glock 19. It was a nine-millimeter pistol with a fifteen-round magazine, and it already had a round in the chamber. He also retrieved a wallet with military-issue ID called a CAC, a common access card.

Somehow or another, Levi found himself looking the part of a US soldier.

He turned to Mr. Watkins. "That was the last locker. Now what?"

The white-haired man smiled and motioned for Levi to follow him.

They went back down the same hall through which they entered, but instead of leading to the lobby, it took them to a set of stairs going down.

"Hold up. Where's the lobby?" Levi said.

Mr. Watkins gave him a sympathetic look and motioned toward the stairs. "Sir, the train is waiting for you."

"Train?"

Levi looked down the stairs. Somehow, someone was messing with him. He was certain that the lobby had been here. It was a straight hall—no way he could have gotten lost.

He heard a click somewhere in the building and turned back—only to find himself staring at a blank, wood-paneled wall.

"Wait a cotton-picking minute. Where's the hallway? And where's Watkins?"

The white-haired man was gone.

"What the hell is going on?"

Levi's mind raced as he wondered how he'd gotten turned around. Or maybe, the hallways were on casters of some kind and moved?

The entire place suddenly took on a haunted house vibe, which he wasn't exactly thrilled with.

With nowhere else to go, Levi descended the steps. A sleek railway car was waiting at the bottom, its doors open. Levi stepped on board.

A disembodied voice announced, *"The train will be leaving in ten seconds. Please hold on to a rail or you will likely be thrown backward. This is your only warning."*

"Lovely." Levi took a seat and gripped one of the poles.

"Five seconds. Four. Three. Two. One."

Levi slid backward as the train accelerated at a pace rivaling that of a race car. Within seconds, the wind was keening wildly as the train flew through the darkness.

Whatever tunnel it was that Levi was in, it must have been very long, for despite the train's speed, Levi traveled for nearly forty minutes before the train began to decelerate.

The disembodied voice returned. *"We will be arriving at Joint Base Andrews in approximately five minutes. Please disembark only after the train has come to a complete stop."*

Levi shook his head at the sheer stupidity of that message. "As if I were going to jump off."

Then it struck him: Joint Base Andrews? That was in Maryland, over two hundred miles from New York City. How the hell had he gotten all the way here so fast? He did the math in his head and supposed it could be possible —if the Outfit had a train, for its own personal use, that rivaled the speed of Japan's bullet train.

And evidently they did.

The train doors opened and Levi stepped out. A young military officer greeted him. "Mr. Yoder, can I please see your cack?"

"Cack?"

The diminutive woman looked up from her clipboard. "Your Common Access Card. CAC."

"Oh, sure." Levi fished the laminated smartcard out of one of the seemingly endless pockets of his new outfit.

Lieutenant Humphries inserted the card into a reader, an LED flashed yellow several times and finally gave off a solid green light. She handed it back and hitched her thumb toward the stairs to her left. "Hoof it up those stairs. The mission crew is gathering already. Departure is at 0300."

"Yes, ma'am."

Levi chuckled as he bounded up the stairs. This was certainly not what he was expected to be doing when he woke up this morning.

The stairs led up to the tarmac of an airfield, and the moment Levi stepped onto the asphalt, he felt a vibration as the stairs were slowly replaced by a slap of matching asphalt. Thirty seconds after having climbed up from a hidden subway, there was absolutely no sign that it even existed.

Levi blinked in a amazement and turned his gaze toward the few lights on the runway. Nearby, there was a jet with white lights on its landing gear penetrating the darkness.

"Yoder, get over here."

Levi followed the voice to a crew of about twenty people in uniform who had gathered at the base of the jet. As he approached, he heard a voice that was oddly familiar.

"Hey, Levi. How's the ribs?"

When Levi spotted the speaker, his jaw nearly hit the tarmac. "Doctor Spears?"

Spears's squint-eyed look of amusement was unmistakable. This was the guy who'd patched Levi up. "In the flesh. It's good to see you. I hope you're ready for this."

"I'll be honest, I don't even know what *this* is."

"Don't worry, we'll get everything squared away on the way. We've got about nine hours before we've got wheels down in Buenos Aires. Besides, I think Brice is still gathering the latest satellite photos and arranging for ground transport. I'd guess we aren't striking the target until oh-god-thirty tomorrow."

Levi's attention was drawn to the morale patch on Spears's shoulder. Unlike his halo-wearing wolf, the doctor's patch featured an eagle capturing a snake.

John noticed Levi's gaze and patted at the patch. "I know what you're thinking, and yes. We're all part of that same unit that doesn't really exist."

Levi scanned the others, and sure enough, they all wore the same patch. He was the only one with the wolf. He wondered what that might mean.

"Oh, hey gorgeous," said a woman's sultry voice. "Fancy meeting you here."

Levi turned to see a face that gave him a distinct feeling of unease. "Hey, Annie."

The Outfit's dark-skinned assassin walked over and gave him a hug. "You look cute in a uniform." She nodded at Doctor Spears. "Hey, Johnny."

Spears rolled his eyes and gave Levi a pat on the shoulder. "Just like with a spider, don't let her crawl into bed with you." And with that he walked back toward the rest of the crew.

"Don't listen to him," Annie said. "He's just sore from the last time he and I played together. I do like to play, if you know what I mean." She brazenly wrapped her arm around his waist and bumped her hip into his. "But I'm also serious when I need to be, and I don't want to wear you out ahead of the mission. You and I have point."

"Speaking of the mission, do you know—"

"Okay everyone," a man's voice bellowed in the night. "We've got intel updates from HQ and have clearance to take off. Everyone get your asses on board and find a seat. We'll talk mission parameters in the air. Operation *Kristallnacht* is underway."

CHAPTER NINETEEN

It was two a.m. in Argentina, about seventy-five miles south of the capital of Buenos Aires. About a quarter mile from Levi's position was the center of the Gerhard compound. A guardhouse stood at its entrance, and about a hundred yards of paved driveway led from there to a mansion complete with east, west, and north wings. The compound was surrounded by a twelve-foot concrete wall topped with razor-sharp concertina wire.

There was no moon out, and it was almost pitch black on the grassland surrounding the compound. But Levi's vision was much better than most, and with only starlight to guide him, he was able to watch as nearly a dozen men from the Outfit's tactical engagement unit silently rolled equipment onto a slight hill overlooking their target.

Levi felt the tension building around him as the team set up for the assault on the compound. The team had split responsibilities, and the other squad was nowhere to be seen. The other squad's job was to ensure there was sufficient distraction such that no military attention was brought to bear on them during the assault.

Levi adjusted his Kevlar helmet. It had some heft to it, thanks to the various night vision devices attached to it, making it feel like more of a hindrance than a help at this point, especially given his own natural visual ability. He tilted his head to the left, cracking his neck, and some of his stress abated.

"You seem pretty comfortable with the low light," Annie said, squatting next to him. "How are you doing that without the night-vision goggles?"

He suppressed an urge to laugh as he saw her wearing her own NVGs. They made her look like some sort of bug.

"Once my eyes adjust, I have pretty good night vision. Better than most. Anyway, I have a lot of experience tracking stuff at night, so I've rarely ever needed to use them."

"You might give it a shot. They really do help." She flipped up one lens. "I'm using a Hoplite, which lets me set the NVG to infinity, and when I flip down the lens, I can shift focus so I can see clearly up close. You and I will need close-quarter stealth."

With a shrug, Levi lowered his goggles from his helmet. The world did indeed brighten immediately—but he quickly flipped them back up. "I don't care for them— they mess with my peripheral vision. And I don't need them out here, not with the starlight and the city light reflecting off the clouds."

Annie looked up at the sky and shook her head.

"You're nuts. But that makes you sexy as hell. Makes me wonder more and more what you're like under the sheets."

Levi chuckled. "Are you always like this?"

"Like what?"

"Such a blatant flirt. It's not exactly endearing, you know."

Annie sighed. "It's a personality flaw, but I've learned to live with it. Though *you* are actually someone I probably wouldn't regret fucking. Are you with someone?"

"Are you?"

"Hard to say. There's one guy I don't flirt with, because I actually care what he thinks."

"I'm thinking it's not Doc Spears. He's not exactly your biggest fan."

She waved dismissively. "He's just pissed that I used him as a one-night-stand."

"Girls don't like it when guys do that, so why would a guy like it when a girl does that?"

Annie shook her head. "You really are naïve. Most guys would love no commitment, just some raunchy sex."

"Clearly Spears didn't. And regardless, it's kind of an asshole thing to do."

"An asshole thing to do? I'm not normally a back door kind of gal. Why, is that your thing?"

Levi shook his head. "Maybe you should flirt a little with the guy you like and not so much with the rest of the male population. Have you considered that strategy?"

"Oh, shut up. I'm thinking you're too stuffy to be that much fun."

Levi's hearing protection crackled and he heard the

squad leader, Captain Roscoe, grumble through the headset.

"Everyone, make sure you've got your ears on at all times. Brice's directional noise amplifier is gonna fuck up their ability to hear what's coming, and if you're not protected... well, we don't need anyone on the team getting their eardrums blasted to hell.

"Charlie Team is ready with the distraction on a five-minute countdown, and Gamma Team is ready to pull the plug on the compound's power as well as block all incoming and outgoing signals. That includes our comms channel. We need everyone on their targets and rendezvous at the extraction point at 0300.

"Sanchez, you copy what I'm laying down?"

"Copy that, sir."

"Spears?"

"Roger that, I'm on board."

"Brown?"

"You bet your sexy ass I'm ready." Annie's tone suggested she was trying to sound sexy, but Levi suspected most people on this frequency were rolling their eyes.

"Yoder?"

"Roger, I'm ready."

The captain rattled through the rest of the names, then said, "I just got word from Charlie Team. We've got thirty seconds."

Levi saw several of the men taking aim through high-powered rifles with silencers attached.

"You've got your copy of the house plans memorized?" Annie asked.

"Yes."

"Then you saw the underground tunnel. I think the Gerhards will try to escape that way. The entrance to it is in the north wing. The bedrooms are in the east wing. Which one do you want?"

Levi studied the T-shaped home. "The east wing is the closest—let's clear it first. Gamma Team has people stationed at the tunnel's exit anyway."

Annie nodded.

Roscoe counted down. *"Five... four... three... two... one."*

Suddenly, it was as if dawn had come hours too soon, but from the northwest. Charlie Team had just blown up a little-known munitions storage facility west of the capital. The distraction was on. That would draw the attention of the authorities for a while.

"Steady... hold your fire..."

Levi tensed as several members of the team hoisted scaling ladders onto their shoulders. The lights in the compound flickered and died. And then everything happened at once.

A half dozen shots rang out in the night. Three scaling ladders were positioned against the compound's wall, and the team began climbing. More shots rang out, and within the compound, a flashlight lit a small patch of ground near the guardhouse.

Someone said *"Idiot,"* another shot was taken, and the flashlight fell to the ground. Yet another guard had been taken out.

Levi raced up his ladder and over the wall. The

concertina wire had already been cut away. He slid down the other side and landed inside the compound.

An armored vehicle's lights had turned on just inside the compound when Levi spotted Spears yell something to one of the men. Seconds later, the doc had one knee on the ground with a large device hoisted onto his shoulder.

Annie yelled over the gunfire, "That's one of those new M3E1s. Latest variant of a Carl Gustav. I wonder what kind of ammo he's—"

At that moment, a huge belch of fire blew out the back of the weapon's tube, sending a projectile streaming at the armored vehicle.

Levi shielded his eyes as the heavy round slammed into the vehicle and almost immediately blew the vehicle up with an impossibly bright explosion that damaged the guardhouse, and set fire to a patch of the nearby landscape.

"Awesome." Annie nodded with appreciation.

Levi motioned toward the compound. "Let's go."

He felt the vibration in his chest before he heard the sound. His hearing protection clamped the noise significantly, but it could only do so much. Someone had activated the directional audio projection device, and he both felt and heard the rhythmic sound blasting over the compound. It was an old song, sung low and slow as if it was part of a Gregorian chant—ominous-sounding, almost gloomy, with a medieval feel.

.   .   .

God rest ye merry gentlemen
  Let nothing you dismay
  Remember Christ our Savior
  Was born on Christmas Day
  To save us all from Satan's pow'r
  When we were gone astray
  Oh tidings of comfort and joy
  Comfort and joy
  Oh tidings of comfort and joy

As the song repeated, Levi was struck by the immensity of the power being transmitted through the air. The giant sound array wasn't even aimed in their direction, yet it rattled the nearby rocks in the soil. He could only imagine how loud it must be for those it was aimed at.

He smiled at the irony of having a song about Christ being broadcast at these godless monsters. They deserved no less.

Lucy sat with Rivka Cohen at her kitchen table, where they'd been catching up over a hot cup of tea. Rivka looked exhausted. She had seven kids, and now she had no husband to help with bills or anything else.

"Rivka, please let me know what I can do."

"There's nothing that can be done. We've filed our final appeal with the Social Security Administration, though I don't expect much to come of that. We both know Mendel didn't take his own life, but that's not what the official record says, and unless something changes with that, I don't think we'll have much choice but to move. We can't afford a lawyer's time to intervene and force justice to be served, and even if we could, we could do nothing without new and solid evidence."

Lucy looked over at the stack of flattened moving boxes. The Cohen family was planning in anticipation of the inevitable. Without the monthly Social Security payment they were owed, savings could only go so far.

Rivka reached across the table and gave Lucy's hand a squeeze. "It's okay. We'll move in with family and sell this place. It'll be tight, but *Hashem* will provide. You and Levi have done a lot to soothe my aching heart. I can at least go to bed at peace knowing that the lies about my husband are just that—lies. It's really all that I hoped for."

The front door opened and a stampede of kids raced into the kitchen, hugged Rivka, and just as quickly vanished into all corners of the home.

"Remember, chores first!" Rivka yelled after them.

Two of the older girls walked into the room more calmly. "Mom, should we start the challah?"

Lucy stood. "I have to get going."

"Are you sure you don't want to stay for dinner?" said Rivka.

Lucy shook her head and they exchanged a kiss on the cheek. "I'll look into what we talked about. You never know what miracles can happen when you set your mind to things."

Rivka walked Lucy out while the girls began assembling the ingredients to make the dough for the Sabbath bread.

Lucy felt a pang of guilt as her driver pulled away from the curb, and she clacked her fingernails nervously on the hand rest. Despite all logic, she felt responsible for the Cohens' situation. This woman and her family were innocent victims of heinous circumstances, and it was bothering Lucy more than it should.

Back at her own apartment, she waved off the greetings from the ladies, headed straight to her bedroom, and began pacing. Anxiety was eating at her—not just due to the Cohens' situation, but also because of her own stupidity in laying bare her feelings for Levi.

She soon decided there was nothing she could do about Levi. He was off doing whatever task the Outfit had set for him. But the Cohen thing... that she could do something about.

The solution was a mere phone call away, but there would be a price to pay. A price of freedom that she'd worked hard to achieve. Before she could think too much about it, she made the call she'd said she'd never make again.

Doug Mason answered. *"Yes?"*

"It's me."

"Lucy!" His voice was surprisingly upbeat. *"I'm so glad you decided to call. I suppose I should congratulate you."*

"Congratulate me? On what?"

"On the contract being dissolved. Was that your doing, or our illustrious Mr. Yoder?"

"No, that was me." Lucy took a deep breath and

reminded herself that this guy was always up to something. "Doug, I called for a reason. I have a favor to ask."

"Oh? The last time we talked, you said you were done with us and going out on your own. Are you finally asking to come back, this time as a full member?"

"No, I'm not. I don't want to have anyone dictate what I do and where I do it."

"Then what do you expect from us?"

With pent-up frustration, she barked, "I'm expecting you to be a human for once, damn it. Does everything with you have to be some form of barter? There's a woman Levi and I have been working with who needs help with some red tape."

"You're talking about the Cohen widow."

"Yes. I'm the one who convinced Levi to help her. And it seems that it's gotten him sucked into something that you're undoubtedly profiting from. The least you can do is help this woman out by correcting the coroner's findings. She's got seven kids, for Christ's sake."

"Why don't you just buy her life? You can afford it."

Lucy's blood began to boil. "You're a real asshole sometimes. This is more than just the money to these people. Until the record gets straightened out, this family won't know for sure that their husband or father wasn't a cheating scumbag coward. I know that this Cohen guy was tracking down all sorts of Nazi crap that you're probably all over now. Mendel Cohen was a good guy, and you know damned well he was murdered. He doesn't deserve to have his family's memory of him tarnished like this. I know you're pure lizard, just wearing a human skin to get along with people, but for once can you do something that doesn't earn you a stripe in whatever board room you Outfit people hang out in?"

Mason chuckled before answering. *"I miss your way with words, dragon princess."*

"And I miss nothing about you. Can you help the Cohens or not?"

There was silence on the line for a few seconds before Mason responded. *"How about this. You promise me to keep an open line of communication, and I'll see what I can do. Do we have an agreement?"*

Lucy frowned. "I suppose. You'll look into the Cohen thing?"

"I will."

"Doug..." Lucy sighed with frustration.

"What?"

"Nothing. Just do what you can."

She hung up and opened her nightstand drawer. She pulled out a coin and looked at the image on its face: a wolf with an angel's halo. It had burnt into it a large X, invalidating it.

Her former ID.

She smiled only slightly. "Well, I got what I wanted, and I didn't have to sell my soul. I just hope he delivers."

CHAPTER TWENTY

God rest ye merry gentlemen
Let nothing you dismay
Remember Christ our—" .

Levi tapped a button on his headgear and the deafening singing almost completely vanished. An amazing feat considering that he still felt the vibrations in his chest. One of the science officers on the team had explained it on the plane—something to do with narrow-band noise cancellation that was tuned to the sound generator—but it was impressive all the same.

Now that he could hear himself think, Levi focused on the house around him. The interior rivaled the world's finest hotels, with marble and gold everywhere, engraved wood, and a smell of lemon polish. But it was dark enough inside the house that even Levi needed the night-vision goggles. He had one eye focused out to infinity and the other adjusted for close quarters. He panned the M4 carbine down the first-floor hallway, which ended at a T. His weapon's infrared illuminator bathed the area in an invisible light that shone brightly in his viewfinder.

Annie stepped up beside him and used hand signals to indicate that she'd take the left. Levi slowly advanced to the right.

As he moved down the adjoining corridor, a door opened and a man staggered out with an AK-47 slung over his shoulder, he grimaced with pain as he clapped his hands to his ears. Levi put two shots into the target, one in the chest and the other in the jaw, spinning him around and dropping him. A widening pool of blood spread from the man's crumpled body.

Continuing his advance, Levi brought up a mental image of the floor's layout. This was the residential wing. Bedrooms flanked both sides of the hall, with the master bedroom at the end.

From somewhere in the distance came the sound of automatic weapons fire, followed by a loud *whomp*. A grenade?

Levi rapidly cleared each room as he passed. When he arrived at the ornate double doors to the master bedroom, he broke them open with a smash of his heel, then ducked as gunshots erupted.

"*¡Quítate! Geh weg von mir!*"

A panicked old man was yelling in both German and Spanish for Levi to go away. He wore plain pajama bottoms and a T-shirt, but a gold Rolex on his wrist and a heavy gold braided necklace told Levi that this was probably the man he was looking for.

It was still pitch black, and the man was staring wide-eyed in all directions as the sounds of war grew closer. Levi smiled as he heard the continued trigger pulls of an empty revolver.

"Mr. Juan Gerhard, I presume." Levi yelled as he drew closer.

"Who is that?" the man responded in heavily accented English.

"Mendel Cohen," Levi growled as he stood only ten feet away.

The man froze for a moment, then sneered. "A good joke. But your joke is over. I've already called the authorities. They'll be here any moment."

Levi felt a surge of rage boil through him. "Bullshit." He glanced at the bed, a cellphone lay on it. Keeping his M4 trained on the old man, he leaned over, picked up the phone and it showed no signal. Giving Gerhard a chilling smile, he shook his head and tossed the phone away. "We're blocking your cell signal, and your landlines have been cut, *Herr* Gerhard."

"Whoever you are, I see that you're with the American military. You have to bring me in—I'm unarmed." He tossed aside the empty revolver and held out his hands. "My lawyers will have me out in less than twenty-four hours, and you'll regret that you were ever—"

A gunshot exploded from behind Levi, distributing the top of Juan Gerhard's head across the bed. The old man's body collapsed, twitching spasmodically.

"Were you hit?" Annie said with concern.

"No." Levi looked down at the old billionaire—now dead, just like his victims.

"Well, let's go. The rest of the bedrooms are clear."

As they turned and moved toward the north wing, Levi's thoughts turned to the billionaire's son, Herman Gerhard. One down, one to go.

As they entered the hallway that led to the escape tunnel, shots rang out. Annie and Levi threw themselves to the ground, aiming and connecting with one of the guards, each of them riddling him with a three-round burst.

They advanced once more, and Levi growled, "I owe the son some payback."

Annie nodded. "You can have him as long as you don't let him monologue at you. That's how all the good guys get shot in the comics. Just don't do it."

"Yes, ma'am."

The door behind the now-dead guard was easily eight feet tall and heavily engraved with images of German military figures, including Hitler at the top, with a swastika underneath him. It was also locked.

Levi was about to shoot the lock when Annie put a hand on his arm. "Wait."

She fished through the guard's pockets and came up with a large ornate key. She shoved it into the lock, twisted it, and the door unlocked.

Leading with the M4, Levi pushed open the door. It led to a plain room filled with file cabinets and smelling of dampness and the lingering scent of cologne. At the far end a door stood open, leading to stairs going down.

"This is the place," Annie whispered.

Levi led the way down the stairs. The stairs connected to a tunnel that had been carved out of solid stone. Only occasionally did a root peek through a crack in the bedrock.

Levi noticed that the vibrations in his chest had vanished, so he tapped at his headgear, disabling the narrow-band filter. Now he only faintly heard the chanting from above. Otherwise the tunnel was silent.

Breathing deeply, Levi pushed forward. Annie was like a shadow beside him, utterly silent.

The scent of cologne was getting stronger.

They reached a Y in the tunnel, and the cologne made it clear that someone had taken the path on the left, which was surprising. According to their maps, that way led to a storage chamber—a dead end. The exit was to the right.

Levi motioned for Annie to wait, then slowly advanced down the left-hand tunnel.

When he reached the curve in the tunnel that led to the storage chamber, he unclipped a tear gas canister from his belt, pulled the pin, and tossed it around the corner.

In response, a spray of bullets ricocheted off the tunnel wall, sending rocks and dust through the air.

Levi took position on his stomach, ready to fire. The hiss of the canister echoed down the tunnel, followed by coughing and the sound of footsteps. Some of the smoke came around the corner, but Levi was back a safe distance.

Suddenly a man stumbled blindly around the corner.

Levi took his shot. A direct hit under the jaw, blowing out the back of Herman Gerhard's head.

It was over.

Levi looked over the edge of the MH-60M Black Hawk that hovered fifty feet over the Atlantic Ocean. Dangling from a rope beneath the chopper were two blood-stained bodies wrapped in chains.

The pilot's voice came across his headset. *"Whenever you're ready."*

Levi pulled the release lever, and the bodies of the Gerhards hit the water with a splash. They sank beneath the surface and began their descent to the ocean floor twelve thousand feet below.

"Levi." It was Mason's voice.

"Yup. Just disposed of the package."

The helicopter gained altitude and began racing away from the coast.

"Excellent. We've got a bit of trouble buzzing around now that the teams have left, so we're on plan B for your extraction. The pilot's taking you to USS Stout, *which is about sixty miles east-northeast of your location."*

"What's a USS *Stout*? And is that how I'm getting home?"

"The Stout *is the nearest vessel I could make arrangements with that could take your helo. It's an Arleigh Burke-class destroyer, so you're in good hands. As soon as they're in range of a country that's less annoyed with us, the Black Hawk will transport you to*

*an airport and we'll have you home quickly. Don't
worry."*

Levi sat back and shrugged. Two evil people had been
dispatched, and probably a bunch more. These were good
things. But he wondered if it would end up making any
difference. The world was still a shitty place.

"Please tell me we got some intel out of that place
that you guys are going to do good with."

Mason chuckled. *"We got everything that could be
had. We'll be analyzing it within the next twelve to
twenty-four hours. One thing we know for certain, you
guys just chopped the head off of a group that's been
financing and infiltrating the media for decades. Oh, and
coincidentally soon after you left for burial duty, the
entire place somehow caught fire."*

"Somehow, eh?" Levi smiled.

*"Oh, and a few more things. The Gerhard Group is
no more. Some of our forensics guys cracked the banking
puzzles with that company and... let's just say they're no
longer liquid.*

*"That being said, since this mission cost you in many
ways, we've arranged for you to get a stipend. Let's just
call it a 'pain and suffering" expense. That's being
deposited into an account you'll be able to draw from.
Also, for housing and protecting one of our own, I've
arranged for payment to your landlord, who I assume
doesn't take checks. I'll call you back with those
arrangements."*

"My landlord... oh, okay." Levi presumed Mason was
referring to the don, but he was somehow a bit surprised

that the Outfit was going to pay him money. It made sense, but he hadn't expected it.

"Levi, just remember. These were bad guys, and they'll never again be able to stir the pot like they had been. I'll make sure good comes out of this mission, but I can't promise that it'll be the end of these kind of troubles. We'll fight the good fight, and you should know that you did good today. Just relax, and I'll have you home before you know it."

Levi laid his head back and closed his eyes. Just before he drifted off to sleep, he wondered how Lucy was doing.

CHAPTER TWENTY-ONE

On the way home, Levi had to stop over in Harlem to swap out his military gear for his civilian clothes. This time, nothing bizarre happened in that hotel that wasn't a hotel—no disappearing Brits, no vanishing hallways, and absolutely no stairs leading down to high-speed trains. Levi was relieved. The Outfit was a mystery wrapped up in an enigma, and he just didn't have the mental energy for that.

The truth was, he wanted his life to go back to where it had been before the whole Cohen case and the Outfit had gotten into his head.

Now, at Gerard's, he clinked glasses with Lucy. Hers was a scotch and soda, his was a seltzer, and everything was good in the world again.

She took a sip of her drink, then reached across the table and took his hand. "I really did miss you. That feels weird to say, since you were only gone a few days, but it's the truth."

As he looked back at her, it suddenly hit him what had changed about her. Initially, she'd always been unreadable. Her face might as well have been the face of a porcelain doll. He couldn't sense her emotions, her thoughts, nothing. But now, as he looked into her dark brown eyes, he saw everything. Vulnerability. Contentment—that had certainly not been there before. And more. So much more.

The front door opened and two people walked in— Rivka Cohen and her uncle, Menachem. And for the first time, they were both wearing huge smiles.

"What's with the happy faces, you two?" Levi asked.

Rivka hugged Lucy, and Menachem grabbed Levi and kissed him on both cheeks. Menachem declared for everyone to hear, "This man is a miracle worker."

Confused, Levi motioned for them to sit. "Please, a bit less enthusiasm. What have I missed?"

Rivka, beaming, pulled out an envelope and slid it toward him. Levi pulled out the contents.

Inside were two items: a report from the New York coroner's office, and a report from the Social Security Administration.

Before Levi could read them, Menachem jumped in enthusiastically. "It seems someone initiated a coroner's inquest, and as a result, the cause of death was labeled a homicide. A man named Jerry Mixon had the same poison at his home that was used to kill Mendel. Evidently it's a rare poison. The police are now pursuing charges against him—though he's gone missing."

Rivka nodded. "And when we gave that to the Social Security people, they had already gotten the report and were changing their verdict."

"Like I said, a miracle worker!" Menachem said.

Levi opened and closed his mouth. He had no idea how this had happened. He looked to Lucy, who merely smiled and gave his thigh a squeeze under the table.

Levi turned back to the Cohens. "I'll be honest. Some of that may be luck," he tilted his head toward Lucy, "or you might thank her. She's been working lots of different angles. She's probably the miracle worker more than I am."

Lucy elbowed him gently and shook her head. "He's overly modest. This was his doing." She reached across the table and squeezed Rivka's hand. "Either way, I'm thrilled for you both."

Rivka stood, as did Menachem, who said, "Tonight's Shabbat, and I have to get things ready, now that we're not moving. Do you think you could come for dinner tonight? We'd love to have you celebrate with us."

Levi looked at Lucy, who nodded. "We'll be there before sundown."

"Fantastic." Rivka clapped her hands together enthusiastically. "We'll see you then."

Levi felt genuinely happy for the first time in a long while as Rivka and Menachem walked out of the bar. He held up his glass to Lucy. "We did good."

Lucy wiped a tear from her eye, nodded, and clinked glasses with him. "We did."

"I have to meet with the don before the dinner, though. Do you want to meet me at the Cohens?"

"How about I come over in a couple of hours? I'll just get dressed at your place, okay?"

"That works for me." He glanced at the clock above the bar. "I better get going."

She drained her drink and they both stood.

Lucy's driver was waiting outside, and he dropped Levi off at his place before taking Lucy to hers. And as Levi watched the SUV disappear down the street, he realized something.

He'd really missed her, too.

"I'll sign for Mister Bianchi." Levi replied as he scanned the armed guard's delivery clipboard and noted the package was for Vincenzo Bianchi, care of Levi Yoder. He leaned over to look past the armed guard. An armored truck was parked in front of the Bianchi crime family's apartment building. Tony, who was front door security that afternoon, stared at the scene with a look of confusion as Levi signed the receipt on the guard's clipboard.

"Thank you, sir." The guard handed Levi the heavy briefcase and a key.

Seconds later, the armored car pulled away and Tony rolled out the x-ray scanning device while Levi lay the briefcase on the table under the call panel.

After a minute of scanning, Tony nodded and said, "Nothing that will go boom. Looks like a bunch of paper. No wires, nothing else."

Levi tapped a button on the call panel and heard the sound of a phone ringing.

After the second ring, Don Bianchi's voice echoed through the lobby. *"What's up, Tony?"*

"Hey, it's Levi. A briefcase just arrived for you in an armored truck."

"A briefcase? Did Tony—"

"It scanned clean, Don Bianchi." Tony said emphatically.

"Okay, Levi. Come on up, I wanted to talk to you anyway."

"I'll be right there."

Levi stepped off the elevator and walked down a short hallway. Two mobsters hopped up from their chairs and opened a set of double doors to Don Bianchi's parlor.

As Levi walked in, he smiled at the warm opulence arrayed in front of him. It was very different than Lucy's place. For all he knew, Lucy might actually be richer than the don, he had no idea. But somehow, the don's taste felt homier to Levi. It held a warmth that felt more lived in, while Lucy's taste tended toward the feel of a museum.

The two fireplaces were lit and glowing with a welcoming warmth. Vinnie's large desk, wet bar, chairs, ornately-carved wood paneling, paintings, and even the replica of the *Venus de Milo*. This is what home felt like.

Nobody else was there.

Levi walked over to the pair of chairs by the fireplace and set the briefcase down on the table between them.

Pulling in a deep breath, Levi wondered what Vinnie wanted. Lately, the don's attention had been pulled to a variety of issues that Levi was only barely aware of. Some of it was a beef with another mob family in Jersey, but the other stuff, he knew nothing about.

For Levi, it was odd to think of Vinnie as the head of a Mafia family. After all, he'd known him since they were both kids. Vinnie's dad had actually gone to bat for Levi, and as far as he knew, he was the only non-Italian in *La Cosa Nostra*.

With his head resting against the back of the chair, Levi had his eyes closed when Don Vincenzo Bianchi, head of the Bianchi crime family, and Levi's lifelong friend, walked in. Their eyes met, and Vinnie's familiar crooked smile brought back childhood memories of them on the streets of Little Italy.

Those were good times.

"Levi!" Vinnie walked quickly across the room, and they hugged and kissed each other's cheeks. Like always, the don poured himself an amaretto sour. "Can I get you a seltzer?"

"Sure, why not."

Levi walked over to the bar just as Vinnie squeezed a CO_2 cartridge into a large metal canister, and moments later the two of them were sitting around the fire, sipping their drinks.

"Where's Frankie?" Frankie was almost always around, as head of security, and he was Vinnie's cousin.

"I wanted this to be just you and me." Vinnie smiled and pointed at Levi with his drink. The sweet amber liquid sloshed in the etched crystal glass. "So, you got the key to this thing?"

"Oh, yeah, I forgot." Levi fished the key out of his pocket and handed it over to the don.

The don stared at the key, turning it end over end in his hand, and then tossed it into the fireplace.

"What?" Levi sat up and stared back and forth between the key and Vinnie. "What'd you do that for?"

Vinnie waved dismissively at the question and pointed at the key. "Look."

The key had landed under the grate where the natural gas blew flames through the lava rock. The key was shining brightly, shimmering in fact, like it was about to move. And then it did. The key began melting, turning into what Levi had to assume was a puddle of molten lead.

"The key is a *fugazi*."

"A fake? The key was a fake?" Levi frowned. "But that's the only key I got."

Vinnie laughed, leaned forward and patted Levi on the knee. "My friend, I've got a confession to make to you. You were right a couple months back. I'd slipped up, and you caught me. I of course wouldn't otherwise admit it, but you got me."

"Vinnie, I have no idea what you're talking about."

The don motioned toward the briefcase. "Look for the keyhole."

Levi picked up the briefcase and ran his hand over where he'd have expected there to be a keyhole or a combination lock. There was nothing. He tried popping open the latches, but they weren't budging. "I don't get it. How are you supposed to open this?"

With a grin resembling the Cheshire Cat, Vinnie said,

"It would take a pair of real angels in wolf's clothing to pop that open."

"I don't get—" Levi froze, his eyes widening as he stared at Vinnie. His mind raced back to the last time Levi had mentioned that turn of phrase in Vinnie's presence and replayed the scene in his head.

"Remember when you called me an angel in wolf's clothing?"

The don wiped his eyes. "I guess, maybe." He patted Levi's chest and chuckled. "Though that fits you to a T, my friend." He turned to Frankie and pointed at the trunk. "You'll need to talk to the Rosenbergs about…"

Levi noted how Vinnie had changed the subject pretty quickly, but now…

Levi's mouth dropped open as he watched Vinnie dig something out of his vest pocket and extended his hand. Grasped in the don's fingers was a coin.

"No goddamn way…" Levi leaned forward and grasped the other half of the coin. A second passed and a light began glowing from the eye of the pyramid.

Levi hopped out of his chair and raked his fingers through his hair as he stared at the man he'd known most of his life.

Vinnie pointed to the empty chair. "Sit. I know you're freaking out, but let's talk."

Levi sat and asked in a hushed tone. "Who else knows?"

"Nobody. I've got a contact at the Outfit. I don't do much for them anymore, but occasionally I do a thing here and there. I was told two days ago by my contact that you're now *in*."

"Wait," Levi's mind rushed through a million thoughts at once. "So, did you know back when I was dealing with the Japanese mobsters?"

Vinnie nodded. "Yeah, in fact, I thought you'd be the right type to do this kind of thing. Sorry, but they knew about you because of me."

Levi blinked as he sat against the back of the chair. Shocked. "How long have you been with them?"

"It happened soon after you disappeared. After your Mary died. My pops was sick, and they wanted an *in* with the New York City families." Vinnie drained his glass and set it on the table. "You may or may not have heard that it was a bit rough on the streets when pops passed. The Outfit helped me consolidate power. Don't get me wrong, that place has its own agenda, but I think they're out there for the good of our country. Maybe even for the world. We're certainly not legit, at least not all the way, but we're keeping things calm." He pointed at the briefcase. "Well, let's open her up."

Levi glanced at the briefcase and said, "How?"

Vinnie leaned forward put a finger under the latch on the right side of the briefcase. "Under the latch, they've got some kind of scanner. It takes two members to open one of these. And if someone tries to pry it open, it'll self-destruct just like in those Mission Impossible movies."

Levi stared at Vinnie, still having trouble comprehending that the leader of the Bianchi crime family was a member of the Outfit. He leaned forward, put his finger under the remaining latch and almost immediately the briefcase popped open.

"Well, let's see what we have here." Vinnie opened the briefcase and nodded as he collected bundles of cash. Each ten-thousand-dollar bundle was marked with VB on it.

Levi frowned at the box that had an envelope taped to it. "I thought the x-ray only showed paper. What's that?"

"Knowing these guys, that thing is probably invisible to x-rays or something." Vinnie picked up the box and nodded appreciatively. "The envelope has your name on it."

Vinnie handed it to him and as soon as Levi separated the envelope from the box, a chill raced up his spine. He'd seen that kind of box before. Opening the envelope, he was surprised to see that it contained a handwritten letter.

Levi,

I'm sure you're a bit shocked right now. But I told you when we first met, that this is a highly select group of people you are joining. We don't extend invitations lightly, and betrayal is repaid with excommunication from the group.

We have deposited a fairly sizable credit into your account for a mission well done. Thank you again. However, I should note that we take security very seriously in our organization, so we keep tabs on everyone.

We expect much, and we believe the benefits are commensurate to what you put into it.

Like always, we've been watching. I reviewed video footage of the operation which you participated in just outside of St. Michael's Church. Lucy and her team performed admirably. I'd mistakenly assumed you were a large part of that operation. I've reconsidered my cancellation of Lucy's membership in the Outfit.

Enclosed is an identification template. She knows how to use it, and if she so chooses, she'll be welcomed back as a member of my unit. The same as you.

Oh, and you can tell her something for me.

Tell her that I'm not asking her to sell her soul to the Outfit. I understand that's not for her. We just want to rent it on occasion.

Mason.

Levi hefted the lacquered box in his hand and smiled.

Vinnie asked, "Is everything okay?"

He nodded. "Things are looking up. I have a few things I need to talk to Lucy about tonight."

Levi was freshly showered and, in a robe, when the doorbell rang. He opened the door to find Lucy in the hall with a newspaper in one hand and a garment bag in the other.

She looked him up and down and smiled. "Tony let me up. I hope I didn't catch you at a bad time."

"No, of course not. Hey, I've got something from Mason for you."

"That can wait." She walked in and laid her garment bag on one of the chairs. "Have a seat."

Levi smiled and took a seat, noting that the bossy side of Lucy had made its reappearance.

She tossed him the newspaper. "Check out that headline."

He read the headline aloud. "*Israel Fends Off Attack From Palestinian Terrorists*. That's definitely a headline I didn't think I'd ever see." He skimmed the article, which described how the Iranian-backed Hezbollah had set up an attack using Palestinian children.

Lucy sat in his lap, crushing the paper and smiling. She looped an arm over his shoulder, touched his chin, and pulled him closer for a kiss. As their lips touched, Levi's hand accidentally settled on her waist, and he quickly pulled it away.

She whispered, "Touch me again."

Levi's heart raced as he placed his hand on the back of her shoulder and trailed his fingers down until they reached the small of her back.

Then he leaned back, his eyes widening. "I don't understand. You normally freak out—"

Lucy put her finger on his lips, and her eyes grew glassy with unshed tears. "Let's just say I learned about some emotional baggage I didn't know I had, and once I threw it away, I got over some things. Besides, I told you going into business together would be a good thing for everyone involved."

He put his hand on her leg, shocked she wasn't

jumping out of her skin. "So what's next with this part-nership?"

Lucy's face flushed, and she pulled at the knot of his robe. "Let's go to your bedroom and discuss things."

"I thought that wasn't in your plans," Levi said with a lopsided grin.

"I lied."

AUTHOR'S NOTE

Well, that's the end of *Never Again*, and I sincerely hope you enjoyed it.

Since this is book three of a series, I'll presume that I've introduced myself to you before and won't make you suffer through that sort of tedium again.

However, I did want to talk a bit about my contract with you, the reader.

I write to entertain.

That truly is my first and primary goal. Because, for most people, that's what they want out of a novel.

That's certainly what I always wanted. Story first, always.

Now, don't get me wrong, there are all sorts of perfectly valid reasons to be reading, and in fact, I get a huge kick out of it when people tell me that they kept on having to look things up to see if they were real, and being shocked to learn that many elements in my stories are real.

For me, I take pride in trying to give people entertainment, while attempting to stay as true to science and technology as possible. And if the novel is inspired by real events in some way, like this one, I try to provide verifiable excerpts that allow readers a bit more insight into the facts of the subjects covered in the story.

When my stories contain topics that have possible controversy or ones with potentially polarizing opinions associated with them (e.g. GMO) I never take a position as the author. I let the characters play out their roles and make no advocacies. However, I do endeavor to lay out the facts as they exist for the reader to ultimately draw their own conclusions.

So far, I've covered broken arrow incidents (See *Perimeter* for that), child sex trafficking (*The Inside Man*), and in this novel, the dangers behind media bias.

Some have called my choices eclectic, unexpected, but the vast majority of feedback I've received to date has thankfully been positive. So, thank you for that. Posting reviews is, of course, the easiest way to let me and others know what you thought of this novel or any of my work. Word of mouth is precious to us poor authors.

However, even though I enjoy writing about events, history, science especially, my primary goal always circles back to entertaining.

As always, at the end of this book, I have an addendum where I cover certain details regarding the creation of this novel, the research that went into it, and of course, I go into the science and technology—mostly because I can't help myself.

I do hope you enjoyed this story, and I hope you'll continue to join me in the future stories yet to come.

Mike Rothman

September 20, 2019

If you enjoyed this story, I should take a moment to introduce you to another one of my titles that I think you'd enjoy. It is book 4 of the Levi Yoder series, and it's called The Swamp.

If you'll indulge me, below is a brief description:

As a fixer for one of the New York Mafia families, Levi would rather keep a low profile. That changes when the Outfit, a mysterious organization, reaches out to him for assistance. Threats to a set of world leaders have been traced back to members of organized crime and their connection with government insiders from DC and Moscow.

When dealing with criminals, Levi knows what to do. However, when he finds himself immersed in a world filled with smiling officials, political apparatchiks, and deceit beyond compare, he learns why some people think of government as The Swamp.

In THE SWAMP, Levi finds himself taking on an almost unattainable goal: stop an impending threat that, if successful, could destabilize much of Western society and give rise to something much worse.

With threats emerging at a frantic pace on two continents, Levi can't be everywhere at once.

It may already be too late to do anything about what's going to happen.

PREVIEW – THE SWAMP

With his heart beating through his chest, John pulled the minivan into the parking spot nearest to the third-base line of Simpson Field. It was early morning and the dew still glistened on the grass. He had a clear view of the congressional baseball practice, and they'd already fielded the players.

In his rearview mirror, he saw someone approaching on the driver's side. The man rapped his knuckles on the window and motioned for him to lower the window.

John glanced at the badge clipped to the man's belt and complied. "Yes?"

The man leaned down, his eyes quickly roaming across the interior of the late-model Toyota minivan before settling on the driver. "Sir, I'm Agent Sanchez from the Capitol Police. We have some congressmen practicing on the field today, so if you want to watch them that is certainly within your rights, but you and your vehicle will need to be searched ahead of time."

John was twenty, and he looked like an innocent white kid from the upper-middle class—but he didn't trust the cops. He tried to keep his voice steady as he turned off the car and unbuckled his seatbelt.

"Is there a problem? I used to come here with my brother and we didn't have to be searched." He unlocked the doors and stepped out of the minivan as another agent appeared at the passenger-side window. John looked over his shoulder at the other agent. "The door's unlocked. I have nothing to hide."

Sanchez motioned for John to lift his arms. "We had an update to our security policy after the congressman was shot in 2017. Arms out to the side."

After a quick but thorough pat-down, Sanchez looked over to his partner, who tossed him a thumbs-up as he slid the minivan's door closed.

"Okay, sir, you're good to go. Enjoy the practice."

John smiled as he walked past the bleachers and pulled out a newspaper clipping from the *New York Times*. He looked back and forth from the article to the players on the field. At least one of the men—no, two from the article were on the field. One red-headed and fifty-something, the other with a drooping left eyelid. There were probably more, but he'd have to get closer to get a better look.

No way was he going to risk it.

Besides, he didn't need a closer look. These men were all traitors to the country his father had fought and died for in Afghanistan. These congressmen were living large on the taxpayers' dime. They were liars and cheats, all of them.

He gave his surroundings a quick scan and saw that the cops were clustered around the press box and the dugout, just as he'd expected. They were out of his way for now.

Stuffing the article back in his pocket, John walked over to some shade trees just out of sight of the field. At the base of an oak tree he found the little patch of dirt he was looking for. He took another quick look around, then used his hands to move the loose dirt until he uncovered the item he'd buried here two days ago.

He pulled the ammo box out of the ground, flipped open the latches, lifted the lid, and smiled.

Inside were an old Smith & Wesson revolver and a Heckler & Koch MP5 submachine gun. Both had once belonged to John's father.

He slipped the revolver into his waistband, then slammed the filled magazine into the MP5, pulled back on the gun's charging handle like he'd seen his dad do countless times, and chambered the first round.

As he flipped the fire select to "auto," he recalled the details of the *New York Times* article, and his face burned with anger. The headline had read: "The Citizens of the World Are One Day Going to Feel the Effects of Today's Vote in DC." The article had gone on to identify the traitors who'd crossed party lines to join the opposition.

John muttered under his breath, "Some citizens will feel those effects today."

Slinging the MP5's carrying strap over his shoulder,

John tucked it under his windbreaker and strolled toward the field.

The game was in session. A pitch was thrown, and the batter at the plate made contact with a resounding *whap*. As the ball sailed into the outfield, heads turned to follow it.

With the loud thudding of his heartbeat drowning out all the other noises on the field, John pulled out the submachine gun, lined up his first shot, and pulled the trigger.

Sitting on a park bench on the north side of Lincoln Park, Levi Yoder waited for his contact to arrive. It was the middle of a bright and sunny day in DC, and though the risks of COVID infections were almost nonexistent in the open air, most people wandered through the park wearing their face masks. It was a strange time he was living in, one where politics and science were often confused.

Levi hadn't had so much as a cough since beating cancer a few years back, but he too wore a mask. Not because he thought it would do him any good, but because if he didn't, he'd stand out—and that was the last thing he wanted.

As one of the only made members of the Italian mafia who wasn't actually Italian, Levi had long ago embraced a life of obscurity and shadow. But today he wasn't doing anything for the Bianchi family. In fact, if Don Marino knew what he *was* doing... well, there'd be a lot of uncomfortable questions.

His phone vibrated and he tapped the Bluetooth receiver on his ear. "What's up?"

"Levi, it's Brice. I'm calling to give you a heads-up that the FBI's gunshot monitors just triggered an alert in your area."

Levi pressed his lips into a thin line. "I haven't seen anything out of the ordinary."

"Shots were fired just across the river from you, around two miles from your current location. The computers say it was automatic weapons fire. I don't have any police scanner traffic yet, but the Capitol police are going to lose their minds over this. Don't be surprised if all public venues around DC get slammed shut in the next fifteen minutes."

"Does this change my plans?"

"No, that's still on. Just wanted you to know that there's some stuff going down nearby and you might see a surge of activity in the area."

"Roger that."

Levi hung up and sat back against the park bench with his senses on high alert.

Brice was the chief tech guy for a place called the Outfit, a part of the government nobody ever talked about. The Outfit was also his second "employer"—in a weird sense of the word. He didn't exactly pull a regular paycheck from them, but occasionally they had things they needed done that required Levi's more unconventional skills and resources.

Today was exactly such a day.

He glanced at his watch and frowned. It was two minutes past the scheduled meeting time, and that told him a lot about the person the Outfit had sent him to meet up with.

In the society of which Levi was a member, you were never late to a meeting without having a really good reason. And if you were late to a meeting with someone of a higher rank, that was equivalent to a slap in the face. People had gotten whacked for less.

But this wasn't some mafia capo he was meeting with, or even a business acquaintance. This was a DC stooge of some kind, and like most federal government workers, they always thought they were the most important people in the universe.

His phone vibrated again. "Yup?" he answered.

"Walking toward the statue of Mary Bethune and the two kids." The man's nasal voice reminded Levi of Paul Lynde, the voice of Templeton the rat from the *Charlotte's Web* cartoon—and perhaps a bigger star from game shows in the seventies.

"You're late."

"I know, sorry. I just got—"

"I'm sitting on the northernmost bench."

Levi hung up and scanned the park for his contact. In the distance he heard multiple sirens.

A minute later he saw a thin man dressed in a dark suit fast-walking in his direction. The man was in his forties, and the suit lay well on him—it was tailored and likely above the price point of the typical government worker.

The two men's eyes met, and the contact gave Levi a nod as he approached.

He sat on the other side of the park bench, then turned

to Levi and said with a grin, "What's your favorite way to hide a corpse?"

"Medium rare, slathered with garlic butter and paired with a nice Chianti." Levi glared at the man. "What the hell kind of question is that?"

The man shrugged, thrust his chin forward, and looked down his nose at the mafioso. "I was just trying to break the ice. I know who you are, Mr. Yoder. I also know about your connections to New York and the other families on the East Coast. You've acted as a CI in the past, and I'm glad to hear that you're willing to help *us* out again."

It took everything Levi had not to throttle the man sitting just outside arm's reach. The only law enforcement he'd ever worked with in DC had been the FBI, and at no point had he ever been an informer. "I don't know what kind of stuff you think you know about me, but if you're implying that I've been a confidential informer for you or anyone in the past, you're sadly mistaken, Mister…"

"Smith. Just call me Agent Smith."

"Okay, Smitty. What is it you want?"

The agent frowned. "I'd assume your person would have told you what I'm here for. Do you have it?"

Levi sighed and shook his head. "I don't know what kind of training they're giving you people in the FBI Academy, but this isn't how it works. *You're* the one looking for a favor." He leaned forward and growled, "What the *hell* is it you want from me?"

Smith's eyes widened slightly, but otherwise he kept a calm demeanor. "I was told you have some photos for me."

"Very good, Smitty." Levi gave the man an icy stare. "Now tell me what kind of photos you think I have. You want the naked ones of you with your neighbor's daughter?"

"What?" The agent shook his head and snorted derisively. "I don't even know who my neighbors are much less whether or not they have kids. I was told that there's compromising photos of a certain congressman's wife."

"And why would you want such a thing?"

The agent lowered his voice to nearly a whisper. "I can bring the full force of the FBI to bear if need be. I don't need to explain why."

"Baloney. I don't care who you think you are, you don't have the authority to do jack."

Levi wasn't the least bit intimidated by the man's hollow threat. He couldn't imagine why the Outfit had okayed giving this pompous ass *anything*. But in the end, he had to trust their intel on the matter.

He pulled an envelope from a pocket on the inside of his suit jacket and handed it over. "There you go, Agent Smitty. Is that what you wanted?"

The agent peered into the envelope and pulled out a set of polaroids. As he flipped through them, a smile grew on his face. Levi couldn't fathom what might be so entertaining to an FBI agent about pictures of some woman snorting white powder.

Smitty put the pictures away and got up from the bench. "Thank you, Mr. Yoder. You've done a great service for your country." Then he turned and walked back the way he came.

Levi's phone vibrated, and he tapped his earpiece. It was Brice.

"I've been watching through one of the park's security feeds. You're all done?"

"That guy is lucky I didn't kneecap him, but yeah, he's got the photos. Was there something else before I head back to New York?"

"Yup, Mason wants to see you. Now. If you can head over to Georgetown, I'll meet you at a bar called the Rooster and Bull. I just texted you the address."

Levi shook his head as he got up and walked back to his rental. "I wouldn't have thought you to be the bar type, Brice. I'll be there in twenty minutes. What's this about?"

"Honestly? I have no idea. All I was told was that Mason wanted to meet with you today. Management, like God, works in mysterious ways. They don't always share their agendas."

"Well, whatever Mason has planned, I'm going back to New York tonight. I've got an appointment that I'm not going to miss. You tell him that."

"Roger that, Levi. I'll let him know."

There were cops everywhere along the route from Lincoln Park through the National Mall and past Foggy Bottom on the way to old Georgetown, where Levi was to meet Brice and Mason. Whatever the shooting was that Brice had told him about, it hadn't hit the airwaves yet, but Levi sensed the tension in the air as he drove through the heart of the country's capital. There were at least twice as many cop cars on the road as normal, and in Georgetown he spotted a pair of flatfoots walking the beat every other block. Something had definitely stirred up the hornets' nest.

Levi pulled into an open spot on the side of the road, hopped out, and put coins in the meter. As he did so, he caught the eye of an old man in dirty threadbare clothing staring at him from across the street.

"Do you have any food I can have?" the old man yelled.

Levi shook his head and walked south on 31st Street until he spotted what he was looking for: a faded sign featuring a profile of a rooster on the left, the head of a longhorn bull on the right. He opened the door beneath the sign, and the smells of stale beer and wood polish wafted from within.

The place was like any other dive bar. Dimly lit, a few tables and booths, a gray-haired man behind the counter toweling a glass dry. It was obviously a slow time of the day, as there was nobody else in this place but one pudgy man at the bar. The man Levi had come to see.

Brice stood and held out his hand, gripping the edge of a coin between his thumb and index finger. It was a challenge coin. Such coins were popular in the military, usually to signify that the person holding the coin was a member of a particular group or campaign. This one was a bit different. It served the same purpose, but mere possession of such a coin wasn't all that was required to be identified as a member of the Outfit.

Levi gripped the other side of the coin. For a moment, nothing happened. But after a second or two, the coin grew warmer. The coin featured a pyramid, much like the one on the back of the one-dollar bill, and when the eye in the pyramid began glowing—signifying that both holders of the coin had passed a biometric identification —Brice pocketed the coin and motioned toward the unoccupied stool next to him.

"Mason should be here any moment." He waved to the barkeep. "Get my friend a…" He glanced at Levi. "If memory serves me right, you're a teetotaler, aren't you?"

Levi looked up at the grizzled barkeep. "A seltzer would be great."

The barkeep placed a glass of sparkling water on the bar, and as Levi pulled out his wallet, the old man waved it off. "The drinks are covered. Your money's no good here."

Mason arrived a minute later, coming through a door at the back. "Levi!" he said as he approached with his hand extended. They shook hands vigorously, and the shorter man grinned mischievously. "I've been waiting for this day for quite a while."

"You have?" Levi frowned. "Brice did tell you I don't have much time, right? I've got a plane to catch."

Brice nodded. "I told him you have important plans."

The director gave Levi a lopsided grin. "Surely you have time to let me give you a tour of our headquarters."

Levi sighed. "I'm sorry, I only have time for a short meeting. You know the traffic is miserable out there."

"Then I guess it's a good thing we don't have to

drive," Mason said with a grin. "You're standing in our lobby." He stepped away from the bar and motioned for Levi to follow. "Well, hurry up. You said you don't have much time, right?"

The director led the two men through the door at the back of the establishment and down a plain hallway that ended at two restroom doors. Mason pushed open the door to the men's room and motioned for Levi to enter first.

Levi stopped short. "I don't understand."

Brice walked past Levi, looking amused. "You'll see."

With Mason still holding the door open, Levi stepped into the bathroom.

Three closed stalls and two urinals were lined up on one wall, with an "Out of Order" sign taped to the door of the farthest stall. Just past the sinks, a white-haired man sat on a stool, dressed in tan slacks and a plaid button-down shirt. He nodded at Brice, then looked over his John Lennon-styled spectacles at Levi, as if sizing him up for a fight.

"This the new guy?" the old man asked.

Brice shrugged as Mason came in, the door closing behind him.

"What is this?" Levi asked. "Why are we gathered in a bathroom with an old man giving me the stinkeye?"

"Who you calling old?" said the white-haired man, crossing his arms.

"I wouldn't recommend pissing Harold off," said Brice. "He might give you the wrong one."

"The wrong what?" Levi asked.

"The wrong towel. It's only happened once or twice," Brice said. He accepted the towel that Harold was holding out to him, then went into the stall marked "Out of Order." "At least, that's what I've heard," he added as the door closed behind him.

From inside the stall came a loud metallic click followed by a long whooshing sound.

"Those rumors were never substantiated," Harold said loudly over the din of the flushing toilet. He held out another towel.

Mason motioned for Levi to take it, so he did. It was heavier than he expected, but otherwise it was soft and fluffy and... well, a towel.

Mason pushed open the door to the out-of-order stall. Brice wasn't inside. The stall was empty.

"What the hell?" Levi said. He glanced at his towel. Was this some kind of bizarre entrance?

"Put the towel on the lever and flush," Mason said. "But make sure the towel is in contact with the lever when you press down."

Levi stepped into the stall and shut the door behind him. He inspected the toilet, looking behind the tank and around the underside of the bowl. It looked like an ordinary toilet. He felt the towel in both hands, running it through his fingers, feeling for anything out of the ordinary.

"Put the towel on the flushing lever," Mason said from outside the stall.

Levi did as he was told. "And just flush like normal?"

"That's the idea."

"He's kind of slow, isn't he?" said Harold.

Levi shook his head and pushed down on the lever.

I hope you enjoyed the preview of The Swamp.

ADDENDUM

This novel deals with the evil of racism, and especially focuses on anti-Semitism. And of course, if anti-Semitism is brought up, one only needs to look at the title of the book to realize that I'd borrowed a phrase rooted in a nightmare many people experienced as part of Hitler's reign of terror, the Holocaust.

I should probably give a little background on this topic, since my family has a personal connection to that time. Many of you may not know it, but I'm the first person in my family born in America. In many ways, I was raised at the knee of my Hungarian grandfather who'd fled Nazi occupation. Most of that generation of my family died in concentration camps. Of my grandfather's family, only he, his sister, and his mother survived.

I normally reserve the addendum to discuss and maybe go deeper into the science and technology referenced in the novel, and I will, but I also wanted to talk about why I wrote this particular book.

You see, I was raised to be very appreciative of the things afforded to me by my birth country. My grandfather, who emigrated to the US from Israel in the 1950s, he was a huge proponent of buying only American. Whether it was cars, building supplies, or school supplies for young M.A. Rothman, he was grateful to the country that he now called home.

My father, he enlisted in the Air Force during the Vietnam era, and later served for decades in the Army.

I have without a doubt been raised in a family that appreciates this country, but I'd also been brought up to respect history. I know where I came from, and I know what my grandfather's generation had been through. My grandfather's sister and mother were both survivors of Bergen-Belsen, an infamous Nazi concentration camp.

So, *Never Again* was born from what I find to be a problem in our society. It relates to the media. And sadly enough, this isn't just a problem in the US, it's worldwide. Unlike a century ago, where global news took weeks or months to reach people, we now have twenty-four-hour news and many more people are tuned into the current events of the day.

This would be great, if it were not so easy to manipulate audiences into a view of the world that may or may not reflect reality.

This is where media bias comes in.

And before I delve into examples of what I'm talking about, let me state something clearly about the topic.

Inevitably, when we talk about media bias, we'll uncover the ugly topic of politics. I don't ever purposefully write with a political bias in mind, but instead try to present things as they are, and allow the reader to come to their own conclusions.

So, when it comes to media bias, I believe there's two primary types of bias:

1. Bias that is purposefully misleading when it comes to headlines and lede paragraphs in an article.
2. Bias that omits key information that is germane to the article and naturally leads the reader to a conclusion that is likely different than the one they'd otherwise come to if they'd been told all the facts. This is what I refer to as the sin of omission.

An example of the first would be a study, initiated by the Council of Religious Institutions of the Holy Land and authored by professors Sami Adwan of Bethlehem University and Daniel Bar-Tal from Tel Aviv University, and overseen by Bruce Wexler of Yale. This study tried to scientifically evaluate how Israelis and Palestinians are educating their children with regard to the other side of the conflict.

Regardless of whether you agree or disagree with the results of the study, one thing is key: how did the media represent the results? I'll provide two examples:

1. The Associated Press carried the headline, "Textbook study faults Israelis and Palestinians."
2. While the New York Times carried this headline for the same study, "Academic Study Weakens Israeli Claim that Palestinian School Texts Teach Hate."

Clearly, in the latter headline, we have a stronger political bent toward the conclusion, focusing only on the Israeli claim being wrong.

Again, without debating the merit of the study, because trust me—I have strong opinions on it—the headline leaves the reader with a poor impression of Israel. And rarely do readers look beyond the headline or the lede paragraph.

As to the second type of media bias, the "sin of omission" continues to plague our society.

Imagine if a major newspaper told you that a male public figure had exposed himself to a woman at a party during college, as a joke.

You might be outraged, right? That would certainly be the intent of the article.

But what if I told you that at the time of writing that article, the authors knew that the alleged victim had absolutely no recollection of this incident.

You might think differently, right?

Well, just such a thing happened with the New York Times on September 14th, 2019.[1]

Again, media bias is about portraying the truth while shaping the narrative to suit a viewership or an agenda. In the above case, there was a book, written by the authors of the article in question, where they admitted that the victim didn't recall the incident. It was only after another reporter brought that to light, and after the ensuing uproar, that the New York Times added a minor revision stating that fact.

It would be very easy for me to write an entire book lambasting the media and enumerating their many failures, but that's not what I do. And I don't think it's what you, the reader, would likely want to read. I'll simply act as a person to point out the inconsistencies in narratives and possibly make people aware that not everything that's fit to print is telling you the truth.

My advice for everyone is to *not* get your news from a single source. You too can combat the sin of omission by getting your news from various sources.

Now, onto the nerdy and educational stuff, which is likely why most of you tuned into this addendum.

Even though this title is very much a mainstream thriller, like always, I sneak in various pieces of technology, some of which may exist in today's world, and others are simply adaptations of existing technology. In other words, things that *could* be made if someone were so inclined. Unlike in previous addendums, this time I've included a few bits of history and statistics, which I think are particularly germane to the topics covered in this novel.

Obviously, my goal in this addendum isn't to give you a crash course on college-level science or history, but instead give you enough information or keywords so that you have the data necessary to do more research, if you're interested.

Ratlines:

I made reference to ratlines in the novel, and they most certainly existed. And all things considered, it's easy to understand how such a thing can come to pass. All one needs to do is think about what it must have been like in Europe around 1945.

The aftermath of World War II was a chaotic mess for the citizens of the European countries as well as the governments. Both the allied forces and the Soviet Union were jostling for controlling positions, scooping up resources, which included scientists and anyone deemed useful to either side, and of course, there was bringing the guilty to trial.

Throughout the 1940s, there were a series of trials held in Nuremberg whose goal was to bring to justice those people who'd committed war crimes, high-ranking members of the Nazi party, and of course, the *Schutzstaffel*, otherwise known as the SS to most English-speaking people.

All totaled, only hundreds of people were brought to trial for crimes, yet the SS, the paramilitary wing of the Nazi party, they had numbered over 250,000.

It's easy to imagine how in the post-war confusion, there were many guilty parties who sought refuge anywhere but Europe.

And thus the ratlines were born.

The ratlines were essentially escape routes from Germany and from previously-occupied territories that mostly led to sanctuaries in Latin America. In particular, Argentina, Chile, Colombia, Brazil, and Central America were preferred targets for the escaping Germans.

The ratlines were supported by the one authority that had roots both in the Americas and in Europe, and that was the Catholic Church.

There were two main routes for those looking to escape Germany:

1. Flee to Spain, and then to Argentina
2. Flee to Rome and then to South America

The ratlines were the "underground railroad" for escaping Nazis. And some rather infamous names managed to escape. I mentioned one in the story, Josef Mengele. The so-called Angel of Death of Auschwitz. He lived his life happily until he died of natural causes in Brazil. Another example was Adolf Eichmann. This man was known as one of the major organizers of the "Final Solution to the Jewish Question" that resulted in the Holocaust.

Unlike Mengele, Eichmann was eventually found in 1960 by agents of the Mossad and brought back from Argentina to stand trial in Israel.

Antisemitism:

Nowadays, we don't really think much about antisemitism in the US. It's not in the media much, and as we know, if it's not in the media, then it isn't part of the public's social awareness.

Is there a antisemitism problem in the US? In the world? The novel implied that there might be. But is there?

Well, for that I'll go to the FBI. The FBI releases yearly statistics on Uniform Crime Reporting (UCR).

Quoting from the FBI's Uniform Crime Reporting web site:[2] "The UCR Program's primary objective is to generate reliable information for use in law enforcement administration, operation, and management; over the years, however, the data have become one of the country's leading social indicators. The program has been the starting place for law enforcement executives, students of criminal justice, researchers, members of the media, and the public at large seeking information on crime in the nation."

That being said, the media would have you believe that the victims of hate crimes are usually race-based. Movements like Black Lives Matters and such are certainly elements in today's media. And in this case, the statistics would agree that nearly a majority of racially-motivated crimes are against people of African descent.

For instance, in the US as of 2017, 48.6% of the reported racially-motivated crimes were shown to be anti-Black or due to African American bias.[3]

But if I asked you what religious group suffers the most religious-based hate crimes in the US, most people in the US would likely believe we as a society have an anti-Islam problem. Certainly, that public awareness has been prevalent since 9/11/2001.

Would it surprise you to learn that this wasn't even close to being true?

Let's look at the earliest UCR records that I have access to from 1996:[4]

- 79.2% were victims of crimes motivated by their offenders' anti-Jewish bias.
- 1.9% were victims of anti-Islamic (Muslim) bias.
- 2.5% were victims of anti-Catholic bias.

These numbers shocked me. Jews being more than twenty times more likely to be a victim of a hate crime compared to any other religion is disturbing. Interestingly enough, Muslims were less likely to be a victim of a religiously-motivated hate crime than Catholics. But, as a numbers nerd, I had to dig a bit deeper to see if I saw any trends.

Looking at the year before 9/11, the FBI statistics for 2000[5] showed the following:

- 75.3% were victims of crimes motivated by their offenders' anti-Jewish bias.
- 1.9% were victims of anti-Islamic (Muslim) bias.
- 3.8% were victims of anti-Catholic bias.

Not much different than four years earlier. Now, what about 2001?[6]

- 57.1% were victims of crimes motivated by their offenders' anti-Jewish bias.

- 26.3% were victims of anti-Islamic (Muslim) bias.
- 2.1% were victims of anti-Catholic bias.

Well, I suppose that isn't a surprise. There was an anti-Islam backlash, but I'd note statistically, Jews were still the majority of the US's boogiemen by a factor of two when compared to Islam, and a factor of twenty-eight when compared to Catholics.

Well, what about a year later? Things were a bit calmer, right? Actually, yes.[7]

- 65.3% were victims of crimes motivated by their offenders' anti-Jewish bias.
- 10.8% were victims of anti-Islamic (Muslim) bias.
- 3.6% were victims of anti-Catholic bias.

Jews were now six times more likely to be a victim of a hate crime compared to the next highest religion, and you'll find that the trend didn't change much up through the latest statistic we have for 2017 where Jews become only three times as likely to be a victim of a hate crime.[8]

- 58.1% were victims of crimes motivated by their offenders' anti-Jewish bias.
- 18.6% were victims of anti-Islamic (Muslim) bias.
- 4.3% were victims of anti-Catholic bias.

Let's face it, there will always be hate crimes. If the media was actually paying attention, there would be more emphasis on the antisemitism that's prevalent in the US, because that's what the statistics certainly imply.

Frankly, as a Jew, I don't play the victim card. I'm a big believer in pulling one's self up by your bootstraps and not using excuses. It's something I was taught by my grandfather and that lesson has stuck.

Either way, I think the numbers are fascinating. Whether they're an indictment on the media or not… that I'll leave to you to decide.

Okay, now onto the cool science stuff. I swear.

Shear-thickening fluid / Liquid Body Armor:

In the novel I have the following passage:

That Mr. Wu of yours gave me a bunch of shit about not messing with the suit's protective liner. Let me guess, it's some kind of STF material? That new liquid body armor the army's been experimenting with?

So, is this real, or is it not real?

It's real. At least, from an experimental point of view it is definitely in research phases across many companies, and with the military. The whole concept deals with something known as non-Newtonian fluids.

What is that, you might ask.

Well, Newton had postulated that liquids have a specific resistance to being deformed regardless of stress.

However, Isaac Newton may not have encountered

some of the experiments we now take for granted. For instance, if you mix something as simple as cornstarch with water, you can create a slurry that exhibits the properties of a non-Newtonian fluid.

Simply put, if you slowly put your finger into the cornstarch and water goop, it'll slowly sink in as if you were sticking your finger into a jar of peanut butter. Yes, there's some resistance, but not a lot.

The interesting thing about this slurry is that if you attempt to stick your finger in quickly, I don't suggest it, you're liable to break it. Your finger, not the slurry.

That's the basis of shear-thickening fluids. When shearing forces are applied very quickly, such as when a finger is rapidly being pushed through such a fluid, or better yet, a bullet, the fluid exhibits a much thicker viscosity at that moment.

So, in principle, it would be possible for a layer of liquid-like substance to become rock hard when a force is suddenly applied to it.

That's the basis on which the liner for Levi's suit is constructed. Combining layers of Kevlar soaked in polyethylene glycol and nano-particles of silica are the basis of both commercial and military research for liquid body armor.

I'd predict that in the not so distance future, we'll see commercially viable examples of this type of body armor. Until then, I suppose Esther Rosen likely has a lock on the market.

In-canal hearing transceivers:

One of my beta readers turned me onto this little device. For the hearing impaired, hearing aids have come quite a long way from the giant cones our great grandparents may have used to hear better.

Nowadays, the state-of-the-art is a hearing aid that you can barely even see. They're typically custom-fit to the user's ear canal, but the one thing I introduced which was to me interesting scientifically was the concept that the hearing aid could also act as a microphone.

Think about it, we have many blue-tooth headsets today that barely hang off the ear and are able to pick up our voices quite well. So, how would such a thing even work?

The concept is actually simple. A hearing aid is no different than a microphone. It receives sound waves through the air, amplifies them and broadcasts them directly into the ear canal.

Well, conceptually, the same thing could be done, but in reverse. In addition to detecting the sound waves coming across the air, the hearing aid could also detect the vibrations from when a person is speaking, turn that into a digital signal, and then transmit it to an external receiver.

The actual science of this is well understood. The difficulties isn't in any of what I'd stated above, instead, the difficulty lies in the miniaturization of the electronics necessary to act as an efficient radio frequency transmitter. There are non-commercial examples of this already working, so I would wager that in the near future, we may see these types of transceivers being employed in various ways. It's just a matter of time.

Sound cancelling:

While I'm on the topic of sound, it might make sense to talk a bit about the technology employed on the assault of the Gerhard compound.

The scene in question would be this one:

God rest ye merry gentlemen
Let nothing you dismay
Remember Christ our—"
Levi tapped a button on his headgear and the deafening singing almost completely vanished.

The idea that sound travels in waves is well understood. And even the concept that sound can bounce off things or even be aimed has been experienced by most people, especially if you've ever heard an echo.

But when it comes to sound waves being reduced, or cancelled, how does that actually work?

Simply put, using scientific jargon, all one has to do to cancel a sound is to emit a sound wave that is 180 degrees out of phase with the sound you want erased.

To better explain, let me use a jump rope as an analogy. When you wiggle a rope, it makes waves that have peaks and troughs. Any of those peaks or troughs is in effect a sound.

So, sound cancelling technology is really about having a microphone near your ear that detects an incoming sound an instance before your ear receives it. A chip in the headset would be able to analyze those peaks and troughs and emit a sound that is the direct opposite of the wave your ear is about to receive.

What do I mean?

Well, the unwanted sound has a peak of X, followed by a trough of Y. There are many more peaks and troughs, but just use one of each for the example.

The headgear would then emit a sound with a -X in-line with the X, and -Y in-line with the Y. It's like hearing two sounds at once. The headgear would actively be stomping on the incoming sound, so when your ear receives the sound wave, the results are in essence zero and zero. No sound whatsoever. The X and -X cancelled each other out, as did the Y and -Y.

With today's noise-cancelling technology, the chips that analyze and emit these sounds can be tuned to only filter out certain undesired sounds. Whether unwanted conversations coming from the person sitting next to you on the plane, or it's the ominous sound of God Rest Ye Gentle Merry Men.

Resonant inductive coupling (wireless power):

In this novel, Denny introduced Levi to the concept of resonant inductive coupling, also known as wireless power, when he gave Levi a rechargeable belt to wear around his chest. The concept being that it was a battery of sorts that didn't need a wire to power the detection logic that Levi readers have grown accustomed to him wearing.

This might seem somewhat fantastical, but it's a very

real technology, and it was first introduced by Nicola Tesla back in 1894.

Tesla actually demonstrated the wireless powering of a fluorescent light at his lab in New York City, and ultimately filed patent number 593,138 for the technology labeled "Electrical Transformer" which today is the principle used by many of today's electronics for recharging.

I for one have a phone that will consume power wirelessly, and my toothbrush recharges quite happily on base stations which has some induction coils hidden within it.

Suffice it to say that this is well trodden ground, technology-wise. But if you want a really nerdy description, here goes nothing:

Usually wireless power transfer systems use coils to transmit power. These coils don't need to be bulky, but they are present. In the case of the band around Levi's chest, it is acting as a large resonant coil. The coils (both primary and secondary) are designed and energized in a manner that they operate at their resonant frequencies to achieve maximum power transfer. In an inductive power system, the distance and the alignment of two coils play a key role in the power transfer efficiency. With a constant primary current, the output power is proportional to the square of the mutual inductance between two coils. In other words, as the distance between two coils is increased, the output power will decrease significantly.

So, it makes perfect sense for Levi's power source, the band around his chest, to be directly associated with his suit jacket, and the distances between the receiving coil within the suit jacket's liner and the belt are fairly fixed distances. This way, Denny can optimize the power transfer and leverage the technique that Nicola Tesla had come up with over one hundred years ago.

So, in this case, Denny didn't really invent anything. He, coupled with a talented tailor, managed to come up with an efficient system to seamlessly provide power for the suit's most hidden ability.

And since I purposefully didn't go into much of an explanation of how the suit does what it does within the novel, namely detect people staring at Levi, it bears repeating how that actually works.

Levi's suit:

I actually introduced the concept of Levi's rather useful suit in *Perimeter*, but at the time, it was a hat. Let me take a moment to talk a bit about the science behind this.

For those who need a reminder, this suit has a haptic device which gives Levi a light tap through the belt he's wearing around his chest. The tap corresponds to whichever direction the suit has detected someone staring at Levi. In other words, you put this suit jacket on, and when you walk through a crowd, you'll be able to feel if someone is watching you, and from which direction.

It does sound a bit like science fiction, but the technology that would be needed to create such a thing is definitely in our grasp. Sure, some might argue it would be bulky or have some other complaint, but it's definitely possible to construct.

In fact, for me to explain, let me grab a small caption from *Perimeter*, where I think I did a pretty good job of trying to explain things at a layman's level. Note: in Perimeter, I'd build this capability into a hat. The same technology applies to the suit.

Denny unclipped the hat from the belt and showed Levi the film-like electronics encircling the hat's lining. "So, you've seen how at night, when a light shines into an animal's eyes, you see an eerie glow reflecting off of them, right?"

Levi nodded.

"Well, humans don't have that same reflective property, at least not to that extent. For our retina to reflect light, we need something brighter. You've seen what happens when there's a camera flash."

"You mean that red-eye effect?"

"Exactly." Denny pointed at a series of tiny tube-like projections that barely poked through the lining of the mesh cap. "What I have here is something that's a bit nuts, because if you could see the light, your head would probably look like it was a 360-degree flashlight it was so bright."

"What do you mean?"

Denny pressed his lips together. "Okay, so we normally can only see light at certain wavelengths. Let me start simple for a moment. We probably all learned in school about ROY G BIV, the colors of the rainbow starting at red and ending at violet. That corresponds to light at wavelengths of roughly 700 to 350 nanometers. The bigger the wavelength, the closer to red, the shorter, the closer to violet. That's what our human eye can detect. But that's not the limit of the light that exists. For instance, that hat is sending out a bunch of light in every direction at roughly 1550 nanometers. Deep into the infrared spectrum. Each of the tiny lasers in there sucks up a good amount of power, and even though you aren't feeling it, the laser's aim is tilting up and down at about twenty times a second.

"So what you have is basically a hat that's projecting light that nobody can see in all directions. It's strong enough to hit things and bounce off. That's where my electronic filters comes in. I'm heavily filtering what comes back and trying to alert you only if I've detected a signal bouncing back that seems to be following you."

"Does it work from a distance?"

"It should be good out to about a hundred yards. Anything more than that, I'm currently squelching, because the reflection gets dicey."

Levi removed the belt, and Denny put both items back in the case.

"So, let me get this straight," Levi said. "I wear that, and it spits light out that nobody can see in every direction. If someone's looking at me, the light is going to bounce back, and the hat has sensors that will alert me."

So, even though there may not be a commercial product that you can buy that does what his suit does, it wouldn't surprise me in the least if there were such things available for those with certain clandestine needs.

ADDENDUM

1. https://www.nytimes.com/2019/09/14/sunday-review/brett-kavanaugh-deborah-ramirez-yale.html
2. https://www.fbi.gov/services/cjis/ucr/
3. https://ucr.fbi.gov/hate-crime/2017/topic-pages/victims
4. https://ucr.fbi.gov/hate-crime/1996
5. https://ucr.fbi.gov/hate-crime/2000
6. https://ucr.fbi.gov/hate-crime/2001
7. https://ucr.fbi.gov/hate-crime/2002
8. https://ucr.fbi.gov/hate-crime/2017/topic-pages/victims

ABOUT THE AUTHOR

I am an Army brat, a polyglot, and the first person in my family born in the United States. This heavily influenced my youth by instilling in me a love of reading and a burning curiosity about the world and all of the things within it. As an adult, my love of travel and adventure has driven me to explore many unimaginable locations, and these places sometimes creep into the stories I write.

I hope you've found this story entertaining.

- Mike Rothman

You can find my blog at: www.michaelarothman.com

I am also on Facebook at:
www.facebook.com/MichaelARothman
And on Twitter: @MichaelARothman

Made in United States
Cleveland, OH
27 November 2024

11016540R00194